RELIC O

RELIC OF SORROWS

(Fallen Empire, Book 4)

LINDSAY BUROKER

Illustration © 2016 Tom Edwards
TomEdwardsDesign.com

ISBN: 1535569522
ISBN-13: 9781535569521

CHAPTER ONE

The medicine ball slammed into Alisa's chest with enough force that she nearly tumbled to the deck. Nobody would ever accuse her engineer of throwing like a girl. Alisa tossed the ball back, aiming to the side of Mica, so she would have to twist and work different muscles to catch it. Mica did so without so much as a grimace to suggest effort was required.

She tossed it back, flexing her bare arms and glancing toward the walkway above. Yumi sat up there with her legs dangling over the side as she read a book on her netdisc. Two chickens pranced around behind her, having escaped from the makeshift coop in the corner of the cargo hold. Again. Yumi cooed at them, paying more attention to the birds than Mica. Alisa almost made a joke about her engineer's unrequited love, but decided to rein it in since she hadn't had any luck finding love lately, either. Not that she was looking. Recently widowed women weren't supposed to look. It was a rule.

"Yumi, want to join us?" Mica called up, as the ball went back and forth.

"No, thank you," Yumi said. "My breathing exercises provide me with all the workout I require, with no sweating involved."

"Breathing exercises?" Mica arched a skeptical eyebrow.

"A combination of stretching and powerful, forceful breathing that increases your oxygen intake, which boosts circulation, strength, and metabolism. I could show you, if you like."

"Uh." Judging by Mica's wrinkled nose, she thought that sounded like a bunch of mumbo jumbo. It was a testament to her interest in Yumi that she didn't outright say so.

"Can't be any worse than the candlelit séance you let her lead you through a few weeks ago," Alisa said.

Mica frowned at her. "That was a meditation session."

"Oh? Did you call up any ghosts to chat with while you did it?"

"Ha ha."

Mica threw the ball hard enough that catching it almost knocked Alisa off her feet. It *did* pummel her in the chest with a solid thump.

"You're bruising my boobs," Alisa said, hiding a grimace as she positioned the ball to throw it back. Wasn't the idea to give her *muscles* a pummeling?

"Unless you and the cyborg have a date later," Mica said, "I don't see how it matters out here."

Alisa's cheeks warmed, and she looked toward the other side of the empty cargo hold where a barefooted and bare-chested Leonidas was sparring with a fully armored Tommy Beck. They appeared to be too busy to listen in on Alisa and Mica's conversation, but Leonidas had that enhanced cyborg hearing, so who knew?

Neither of them looked in her direction. Leonidas launched a flurry of palm strikes and kicks at Beck, who did his best to block them, but still ended up scrambling backward until his back was against the wall. With Beck in full armor and Leonidas barehanded punching, it had to be like striking solid metal, but no hint of pain ever crossed Leonidas's determined face. He'd explained once that most of his bones had been replaced with nearly indestructible synthetics, but even so, Alisa couldn't imagine punching armor felt good.

Leonidas lowered his arms and stepped back several paces, waving for Beck to come back to the center of their impromptu sparring arena. The very empty sparring arena. Since Alisa and her passengers had missions that consumed their focus, she hadn't taken the time to look for any freight to haul, so the hold held little more than the chicken coop. Unfortunately, a lack of freight meant she hadn't had the funds to fix up the *Star Nomad* with weapons or any of the other upgrades the seventy-year-old freighter desperately needed.

"You barely dented my armor that time, mech," Beck said, thumping a fist to his chest plate as he walked back into their arena. His voice sounded muffled through the faceplate of his helmet. He had dressed in his full kit for this sparring match.

"You know who gets to hammer out those dents, don't you?" Mica muttered to Alisa, throwing the medicine ball again.

"Beck trusts you to do that? You're not an armor smith."

"I have a big hammer. That's all it takes."

"A big hammer, huh? Does Yumi know? Maybe she'd be more interested."

Mica's eyes narrowed as she received the ball. "Watch yourself, Captain, or I'll bruise more than your boobs."

"Your lack of job offers is truly puzzling," Alisa said, referring to her engineer's desire to find more challenging and auspicious work than the old freighter offered.

This time, when the ball came hurtling at her chest, Alisa was ready and absorbed most of the impact. Still, she wouldn't have minded a set of combat armor for herself. Like weapons and parts for her ship, it was on her wish list.

Leonidas sighed as Beck danced around with his gauntleted fists up. "I'm not trying to dent your armor. With the speed and power that suit gives you, you ought to be fast enough to attack me, not just scurry out of the way." He wriggled his fingers in invitation. "Don't be intimidated. You're not when you're fighting other enemies. I've seen you in combat. You're adequate."

"Adequate?" Beck lowered his fists to his hips. "Is that the kind of effusive praise you gave your soldiers when you were a military commander?"

"Only if they deserved it. And didn't use words like effusive."

"I had no idea cyborgs frowned upon vocabulary words."

"We're dumb brutes that like to keep things simple."

Alisa snorted. Leonidas was anything but dumb.

He wriggled his fingers in invitation again.

This time, Beck complied, springing at Leonidas, the servos in his leg armor whirring. A normal man probably wouldn't have been able to dodge out of the way quickly enough to avoid him, but Leonidas seemed to blur whenever he moved. In the split second it took Beck to reach him, he'd dodged to the side and moved forward, so he could attack. Even as Beck landed and tried to spin to meet him, Leonidas struck hard enough to send him flying. Beck landed in a backward roll and came to his feet, but Leonidas was already atop him. The encounter ended with Beck lying on his back like a turtle, raising his hands in surrender.

Leonidas sighed again, backing away so Beck could rise. For the first time, he looked toward Alisa.

"I don't suppose you'd consider taking on another cyborg so I would have a sparring partner," he said.

"If you know any who would like to work for what I'm paying you, I would consider it," Alisa said.

"You're not paying me anything."

"That's because you haven't accepted my job offer." Alisa smiled and raised her eyebrows.

She still hoped that Leonidas would one day tell Alejandro to finish his orb quest on his own, and accept the position of security officer that she had offered him. True, it would be a lowly position for someone who had once been a colonel in command of a battalion of cyborgs, but with the way her ship had found trouble lately, it was sure to keep him busy.

"Maybe you could spar with the Starseer," Mica said. "I hear he has muscles under his robe."

Leonidas shifted his gaze up to the walkway, not toward Yumi but toward someone who had strode out of the corridor overlooking the cargo hold. Abelardus.

He gazed down, his angular face aloof, showing nothing of his thoughts—or whether he had heard Mica's comment. As far as Alisa had heard, Starseers were fully human, with a few quirky gene mutations, and did not have superior hearing, but since they could read minds, maybe Abelardus still knew what everyone had been talking about down here. His eyes locked onto Leonidas's and his lip curled slightly.

"That looks like a challenge acknowledged and accepted to me," Mica said.

"Uhm." Alisa did not think they should encourage "sparring" or any-thing else between Leonidas and Abelardus, both because cyborgs and Starseers had a history of bad blood and because Leonidas and Abelardus had gotten into a fight once before already. She hadn't seen it, but she had heard about it—and that some insults or derogatory comments about *her* had started it. "Actually, I think the sparring arena should close for the day. Beck, what's on today's lunch menu? It's been nice having such good food. Makes it seem like we're on one of those fancy luxury star cruisers instead of on an old freighter."

"I will spar with you, mech," Abelardus said, ignoring Alisa as his eyes remained locked on Leonidas.

Alisa, remembering how many injuries the Starseers on Arkadius had inflicted on Leonidas without ever touching him, shifted uneasily. Their doctor, Alejandro, had spent hours in sickbay with him as soon as they had left the planet, and for the first few days of their journey, Leonidas had been scarce. It had only been in the last couple of days that he had returned to his exercises.

He had to have reservations, but he promptly said, "I accept," his gaze never wavering from the Starseer.

Abelardus lifted his hand, his fingers splayed back toward the corridor behind him. Before Alisa could do more than puzzle over why he was doing that, his black staff flew into sight. It landed in his hand with a smack.

"Anyone else find that creepy?" Mica asked.

"Yes." Alisa looked up at Yumi.

Yumi only sighed wistfully. She had the Starseer genes, but had never manifested any talents, something that disappointed her. It relieved Alisa. It had chilled her to learn that her daughter, thanks to her husband's blood, was developing Starseer abilities. Alisa still wanted to find Jelena and bring her back into her life—and make sure she knew her mother was alive and cared about her very much—but she was no longer certain as to what that life would look like. If Jelena truly could move objects with her mind now, she would need someone to help her develop her talents and teach her the control needed to manage such talent. Alisa imagined a child with the ability to hurl things with her mind being very dangerous if she was untrained. Could Jelena be happy growing up on a freighter with her mother, as Alisa once had? She rubbed her face, not having an answer for that. She only knew that she had to find Jelena before she could figure all of this out.

"Think I'll get out of the way," Beck said and rolled to his feet. He removed his helmet and walked over to join Mica and Alisa in the shadow of the stairs. "You want leftovers, Captain? Or something fresh?"

One of the chickens squawked. It might have been because of Beck's comment or because Abelardus was walking down the stairs, looking imposing in his black robe, his long braids of hair dangling to either side of his bronze face.

Leonidas eyed his staff as he approached, but he did not say anything about it. After all, he had allowed—or perhaps encouraged—Beck to wear his armor to even out the odds. Alisa did not know who would have the advantage in this matchup. Abelardus shouldn't be able to move any more quickly than a normal human being, but he might be able to use his mind powers to keep Leonidas from reaching him.

"Captain?" Beck prompted.

"Leftovers are fine," Alisa said. "Thanks."

Beck trotted up the stairs, either in a hurry to get to his barbecue or in a hurry to get out of the way.

"Should we go up there too?" Mica had stopped tossing the ball, perhaps because Alisa wasn't paying any attention to it anymore, and had it propped against her hip. "Are there likely to be bodies flying everywhere?"

She spoke lightly, but Alisa did not find the idea amusing.

Leonidas looked at her as Abelardus stopped to lean his staff on the railing at the bottom of the stairs while he removed his robe and tied his hair back. Leonidas gave her a single nod. Mica tossed the ball into a crate secured to the wall and trotted up to the walkway. Instead of following after Beck, she sat down beside Yumi where she would have a good view.

Abelardus wore fitted, blue snagor-hide trousers and a sleeveless vest under the robe, one that was tight over his chest, showing off his musculature. He wasn't as brawny as Leonidas, but he had a lean, defined form that would catch many women's eyes. He had a handsome face to go with it, though there was always an arrogant tilt to his chin that Alisa found off-putting. She also found it off-putting that he had used her and Leonidas to buy time for his people to escape an Alliance attack, not caring if they ended up in a brig or dead as a result.

"You're not going to hurl any smoke canisters at me, are you, mech?" Abelardus asked, picking up his staff again.

"Where would I be carrying smoke canisters?" Leonidas flicked a hand at his bare chest and feet. His loose gi trousers did not appear to have pockets.

"How should I know what you keep in your pants?"

"I trust you've seen an anatomy book at least once in your life."

Abelardus smirked and spun his staff as he approached the arena. "I've heard some cyborg anatomy is broken."

Alisa frowned, not understanding the joke—the insult. Leonidas glanced at her, but his expression was closed now, giving away little.

"No smoke grenades or other tricks," Abelardus said, lowering into a fighting crouch, his staff held in both hands before him. Despite his cocky swagger, Alisa thought he looked nervous, with a tense set to his shoulders. He had stopped several feet from Leonidas, leaving himself time to react— or throw a mental attack—before his adversary could strike.

"Fine," Leonidas said. "No trying to give me heart attacks or make my kidneys burst."

Abelardus scoffed, as if it hadn't crossed his mind, but Leonidas's specificness made Alisa suspect he had experienced those things at the hands of a Starseer. She remembered that old man in the library, the pleasure in his eyes as he had tried to hurl Leonidas through that hole in the wall and to the ice a hundred feet below.

"Ready?" Leonidas asked. He was simply standing, his arms loose and relaxed, but Alisa knew he could strike in an instant.

"Ready," Abelardus said.

Leonidas surged into motion, crossing the distance between them faster than an eye could blink. Abelardus had his staff out and started a swing, but it did not matter. It was like swatting at a wrecking ball.

Leonidas bowled into him, and Abelardus went flying. He soared several meters through the air before landing. If that had been Alisa, she would have crashed down butt-first, but Abelardus managed to turn the fall into a roll that put more distance between him and his opponent. He came up facing Leonidas, who gave him a second to recover, but then charged after him.

Abelardus flung his hand out before Leonidas reached him. This time, Leonidas flew backward, as if he'd been the one to encounter the wrecking ball. Even though Abelardus had not physically touched him, Leonidas was hurled across the cargo hold until he struck the bulkhead.

"Shit," Mica mumbled from the walkway above Alisa. "Beck's armor isn't the only thing I'll be hammering dents out of."

Leonidas slid down the wall and landed on his feet. The blow had to have hurt—it would have shattered a normal person's ribs, if not broken his back—but he merely strode back toward Abelardus, his blue eyes intense and determined. Abelardus dropped back into his ready crouch, his staff in his hands. He pointed the tip toward Leonidas, as if it were a rifle instead of a seven-foot-long stick.

The hairs on the back of Alisa's arms rose. She stepped closer to the stairs, as if they might protect her from whatever power Abelardus conjured.

Leonidas dove to the side, as if a bullet were coming out of that staff. Alisa did not see it release anything, but something invisible clipped him on the shoulder, turning his flight into a strange shimmy. Somehow, he got his legs curled under him and turned the dive into an opportunity to spring off the deck and toward Abelardus, who was bringing his staff to bear again. He was not quick enough, and Leonidas reached him first, bowling into him again.

This time, they went down in a tangle of limbs. The staff flew free like a rocket, skidding across the deck to clang off the base of the stairs near Alisa's feet.

She jumped, startled, but she did not take her gaze from the battle. Leonidas had hold of his prey now and was not letting go. They wrestled briefly, Abelardus crying out once in a mixture of fury and pain, before Leonidas came out on top. Abelardus bucked, his movements frantic rather than calculating, as he tried to throw off his foe. But Leonidas pinned him and reached for his throat. Abelardus ceased struggling, and his eyes grew fierce, full of concentration. Before those powerful cyborg fingers wrapped around Abelardus's throat, Leonidas's head jerked back. His eyes bulged and his face contorted in agony, the tendons in his thick neck standing out.

Despite his obvious pain, his fingers inched closer to Abelardus's throat. Then, in a quick burst of movement, they were around Abelardus's neck. Leonidas's expression grew even more pained, and he panted, some invisible force tormenting him. But a very real force tormented Abelardus. Those fingers tightened, cutting off his airway. He grabbed Leonidas's meaty forearms, fingers digging into that muscle, but he could not push them away.

Alisa stepped forward, though she did not know what she could do, only knowing that this had gone beyond a simple sparring match. The two men were locked in tableau, like a statue of ancient warriors grappling before their gods.

Alisa clapped her hands as she approached. "Lunchtime, boys. Who wants lunch?"

Neither man glanced in her direction. Abelardus wheezed as Leonidas's fingers tightened. Abruptly, the force holding Leonidas back, the force *hurting* him, seemed to vanish, as if Abelardus's concentration had slipped.

Leonidas took advantage. He dropped his head like a viper striking, smashing his skull into Abelardus's face. Abelardus's lower body twitched, and he kicked out in pain or frustration, or both. Leonidas was too far up, straddling his torso, for the kick to touch him. He spun Abelardus over, pinning him belly down, face mashed into the hard metal deck.

"Do you yield?" Leonidas demanded, his mouth close to his opponent's ear, his knee grinding into Abelardus's spine.

Abelardus roared, trying to lift his head. Blood streamed from one nostril. Fury stamped his face, but he didn't seem to be able to launch another mental attack from that position. Maybe he was in too much pain to concentrate.

"Do you yield?" Leonidas repeated.

Abelardus clenched his jaw stubbornly, and Alisa worried that he would not say the words—and that Leonidas would not let him go until he did. His face was almost as contorted as Abelardus's, not in pain now, but he almost looked as if he were lost in some other world, that he was locked in mortal combat in his mind rather than simply exercising in her cargo hold.

"Leonidas, Abelardus," she said, stopping beside them and hoping she wasn't being a fool and risking herself by standing so close. "What are your votes for lunch? Leftovers, or shall we have Beck make something fresh?"

For a few seconds, neither man moved, and she thought they would continue to ignore her. Then Leonidas blinked a few times, as if waking from a dream—or a nightmare. He did not let go of Abelardus, but his gaze shifted toward her. He seemed confused, as if he didn't recognize her.

"Let's end it, eh?" she said quietly, holding her hands out beside her in a nonthreatening manner.

Finally, he focused fully on her, and recognition returned to his eyes. He looked down at Abelardus, the braids having fallen from their tie and lying tangled about his head. Blood spattered the deck under his face.

Leonidas released him and stepped away. Abelardus slowly pushed himself into a sitting position, as if the fight had gone out of him, but fury still burned in his eyes when he looked up.

Leonidas opened his mouth, and Alisa thought he would apologize—his expression was slightly chagrined, as if he knew he had taken things too far. Before he could speak, Abelardus's fingers twitched. Once again, an invisible force slammed into Leonidas, the edge of it brushing Alisa. It was like a tornado hitting her, and she stumbled back, barely keeping her feet. Her back struck the stair railing as Leonidas flew across the cargo hold, slamming into another wall.

Abelardus stood up, not sparing a glance for Alisa, and lifted his hand to summon his staff. It flew into his grip. He glowered across the hold at Leonidas. Alisa clenched her fists, irritated by the attack and irritated that she'd almost been knocked on her ass by it. Hells, all she had asked was what he wanted for lunch.

Once again, Leonidas walked away from what must have felt like a ton of bricks being dropped onto his back. He could have charged across the hold, and they could have done it all again, but he only took a few steps before stopping, his eyes locked with Abelardus's.

"Are we done?" he asked.

"Until next time," Abelardus said, his voice cold. He ignored the blood dribbling down his lips and from his chin.

Leonidas inclined his head, as if in respect to a worthy opponent, though Alisa could not tell if the gesture was sincere. "I will look forward to it."

"I bet you will. Asshole." Abelardus grabbed his robe and stalked up the stairs.

Yumi and Mica watched him warily, but he headed back toward the common areas and crew cabins.

"Are you all right?" Leonidas asked Alisa, joining her at the base of the stairs. Had he seen her stumble away as he'd flown across the hold?

"Am *I* all right?" she asked. "You're the one who hit the wall. Twice. You're going to have bruises. If not hernias. Do you want me to walk you to sickbay?"

He snorted, his back straight and his chin high. "That's hardly necessary. He fought fairly."

Fairly. Right.

"If you say so. You cyborgs aren't very good at making friends." Alisa regretted the words as soon as they came out. Abelardus had been the bigger ass in that encounter, at least in her eyes.

"It's not a good idea to make friends with people you might have to kill one day," Leonidas said.

"Oh? Are you planning a disagreeable end for our Starseer passenger?"

"It's just a general comment."

His eyes grew distant, almost haunted, as he gazed toward a wall, and Alisa was tempted to ask if he'd had to do that before, kill someone he considered a friend. She decided she did not want to know, especially since she had started to consider him a friend, and she'd hoped he considered her one too.

A couple of alert beeps came from the ship's speakers.

"So much for lunch," Alisa said, swinging onto the stairs.

"Is that trouble?" Leonidas asked.

"Considering how my luck has been lately? Probably so."

CHAPTER TWO

Alisa passed Alejandro as she jogged through the mess hall and toward NavCom. The comm alert continued to beep softly and insistently. Alejandro followed her, his expression between curious and wary. He was probably worried someone else was after his orb. Alisa wouldn't be surprised, though they were a long way from any planets or stations. She had taken them out of the shipping lanes the day before to head toward the coordinates Alejandro and Leonidas wanted to check. The coordinates that were adding yet another delay to her mission to find her daughter. If she actually knew where Jelena was, she never would have agreed to the detour, but Abelardus was the only one who had a clue, and it wasn't much of a clue.

"Is it the proximity alert?" Alejandro asked.

"No," Alisa said, sliding into the pilot's seat and tapping the comm. "Someone wants to talk to us."

"That doesn't sound too bad."

"We'll find out. I don't know who would be out here in comm range."

Alejandro entered NavCom, and Leonidas also appeared, his big frame filling the hatchway. Alejandro looked at his sweaty bare chest and lifted his eyebrows. Alejandro was, as usual, in a gray monk's robe, the pendant of the Divine Suns Trinity dangling from his neck.

"Workout," Leonidas explained.

Workout. That was an innocuous term for it.

"...in need of assistance," a woman's voice came over the comm. She sounded harried. "To any who hear this message, this is the captain of the passenger transport, the *Peace and Prayer*. We are pilgrims on a journey to visit the holy landmarks, but our engine has failed, and life support will follow. We need help. If you hear this, please respond. We are in need of assistance."

Alisa turned down the volume as the message repeated.

"That a ship you've heard of, Doctor?" she asked, turning toward the sensor panel.

"No." Alejandro gave her a puzzled look, as if to wonder why she would ask.

She waved at his robe and pendant.

"Pilgrims don't report in to me," he said. "I am a lowly acolyte in the order."

She looked to Leonidas, wondering if she would catch an eyebrow twitch or anything that would suggest Alejandro wasn't even that. For a while now, she had suspected he was using the robe as a costume and did not truly have a tie to the religion. Especially since monks were supposed to be peaceful, and he'd proven that he would do just about anything to finish his mission and keep it a secret, even contemplating the murder of nosy pilots.

Leonidas did not react to Alejandro's statement. He nodded at the sensor display. "Can you see the ship? Does the story fit?"

Alisa gave him a sharp look. "Did something make you think it's a trap?"

She hadn't suspected that from the message, but maybe he had heard something in the background to make him suspicious.

"Not necessarily," he said, "but—"

"It wouldn't be the first time pirates have feigned needing help to set up an ambush," Alejandro said.

"True," Alisa said, "but we're on the way to your coordinates that are halfway between nowhere and nowhere. This wouldn't be a logical place to spin your web if you wanted flies to chance into it."

"A valid point," Leonidas said.

Alejandro only screwed up his face into a dubious expression.

"Really, Doctor," Alisa said, "I'd expect you to be the first person to want to go help some pilgrims." Or she would if he was truly a disciple of the Suns Trinity.

"If they are true pilgrims, I am very open to helping them," Alejandro said.

Alisa located a ship at the far edge of the *Nomad's* sensor range. It *did* appear to be a passenger transport, one capable of carrying twenty or thirty people. It was a civilian model, nothing she recognized from the war.

"That part of their story checks out," she said, turning back toward the comm.

The woman's message was playing on a loop, being broadcast out to the maximum range. Alisa wondered if anyone would be at the comm station in that ship.

"*Peace and Prayer*," she said, managing to say the name without making a face, "this is the *Star Nomad*. We've received your message. Are you still in need of assistance?"

Leonidas pulled down the foldout chair behind the pilot's seat and sat at the sensor station, tapping a couple of buttons.

"You're not getting cyborg sweat on my seat, are you?" Alisa asked quietly while waiting for a response to her call.

"I'm trying to see if I can detect the engine failure they reported." He arched his eyebrows at her. "And are you sure it's logical for *you* to mock *my* ability to make friends?"

"You don't think my propensity for cracking jokes and teasing people can win over friends?" She smiled, pleased when he teased her back instead of merely frowning at the inappropriateness of her humor.

"So far, I've mostly seen it get you into trouble."

"Maybe we're a good match then, Leonidas."

Alejandro, who remained standing near the hatchway, frowned at this exchange.

Leonidas looked to the sensor display. "We need to get closer to get a better read on them."

"I know." Alisa disengaged the autopilot and adjusted their course to head in the direction of the passenger ship. Nobody had responded to her hail so she tried again on another channel. "Let me know when you can tell if their engines—and their life support—are working."

She grimaced at the idea of coming upon a ship full of corpses. Even though she hadn't been the one to originally find the *Star Nomad* adrift, with her mother's body inside, she couldn't help but think of that moment and what it must have been like for the freighter captain who had discovered her.

Almost seven years had passed, but Alisa distinctly remembered what it had been like when she had been brought in to make arrangements for the body.

Alisa tapped the internal comm. "Mica, are you in engineering?"

"Where else would I be?" came the prompt answer.

"I thought you might have gone with Beck to help pick out lunch."

"We got a comm message. I assumed that meant trouble."

"It *is* possible for two ships to simply pass each other, chat in a friendly manner for a few minutes, and then head on their separate ways without trouble ever coming into the equation."

"Uh huh. And is that what's happening?"

"No."

A chicken squawked in the corridor outside of NavCom. Alisa turned, intending to tell Alejandro to shut the hatch, but Yumi had come to poke her head inside.

"I was wondering what was happening," she said. "And if you needed a science teacher at the sensor station." She considered the back of Leonidas's head.

"I've got a cyborg there now. And he's leaving a sweaty butt print, so you may not want to sit there after him."

Leonidas ignored her—maybe he was reading something interesting on the sensors—and Alejandro was the one to sigh at her. "We *are* paying passengers, you know."

"I know." It was the only reason Alisa had been able to afford supplies for this next leg of their trip. "Does that mean I'm not supposed to comment on your sweat?"

"One expects a certain amount of decorum from those in customer service positions."

Alisa resisted the urge to make a rude gesture at him. She was the captain, not his servant, and if he didn't like the way she ran her ship, he could get off at the next stop. In fact, she would be thrilled if he did so. It was easier for a dog to shake a tick than it was for her to get rid of him.

"That must be an imperial custom," she said. "In the Alliance, we didn't have a lot of time to spend on decorum."

"Obviously."

"I'm not reading any engine activity," Leonidas said. "It could have been powered down manually."

"Or it could have failed, as she said," Alisa said.

She turned her back to Alejandro, feeling bad for sniping with him when there were people out there who needed help. The *Nomad* had flown close enough to bring the pilgrim ship up on the cameras, so she did so, putting the image on the big view screen.

The transport vessel had an unimaginative oblong body with portholes lining the side and three thrusters bunched at the rear. It was an older ship with scuffs and peeling paint, but there were no signs of battle damage. It had not been attacked. And it still cruised along at a decent speed, its nose pointed forward, so nothing had struck it or derailed it from its path, at least at first glance.

"Science teacher, do you want to plot their course for me?" Alisa waved Yumi to the co-pilot's seat. "See if their current route would take them somewhere interesting."

"Certainly, Captain." Yumi squeezed past Alejandro and Leonidas, but paused to look at the co-pilot's seat before sitting down.

"It should be butt-print free, if that's what you're worried about," Alisa said.

Alejandro sighed again.

Yumi offered a sheepish smile. "I was contemplating if I should find a towel."

"It would be a small miracle if you could," Alejandro said. "The lav is perpetually out."

"The water removers in the sanibox work fine," Alisa said, still studying the other ship. She didn't see any running lights, and again had the concern that they might be too late.

"They pucker my skin," Alejandro said.

"Was it hard being an ER doctor when you're such a delicate doily?"

"No. At the hospital, we had normal water removers, not noisy behemoths from the turn of the century that suck half your skin off as they dry it."

Alisa punched the button to comm the *Peace and Prayer* again, silently pleading for them to answer, not only because she wanted the pilgrims to be alive, but because she wanted a reason to end the chitchat in NavCom.

"They *are* noisy," Yumi said.

Alisa scowled at her. "You got that course plotted yet?"

Yumi slid into the seat and tapped the controls. "Almost."

Leonidas cleared his throat. "The engines are off, as I said, but I am reading life support and minimal power. It looks like they're on the battery backup."

Alisa sat straighter. "Oh, good. But then why isn't anyone answering?"

"Perhaps they find your lack of decorum off-putting," Alejandro muttered.

"Doctor, I think Mica needs your help in engineering."

"I find that unlikely."

"Get out of my navigation cabin, anyway," Alisa said, using her best don't-screw-with-me command tone.

Alejandro looked at Leonidas, as if he expected him to rough Alisa up for being mouthy. Leonidas was looking at the sensors and ignored him.

"I can't tell where they came from," Yumi said, tapping a star map on a computer display. "There's nothing behind them, not in a direct line. They must have changed course since they originally took off."

Alisa nodded. It happened. Sometimes, one ran into unexpected debris—or even the expected debris of an asteroid field—and had to alter course. And navigating the gravitational tangle in the space between the three suns thwarted even experienced pilots' attempts to lay predictable courses.

"They are, however, on a direct heading toward Primus 7," Yumi said.

"A space station full of casinos?" Alisa asked. "Seems an unlikely place to find holy landmarks." She looked at Alejandro, who had retreated into the corridor but had not gone away fully.

"There are medical facilities on Primus 7," Leonidas said. "Perhaps the closest ones to where we are."

"They didn't mention needing a doctor in their message," Alisa said.

"Would you announce your weaknesses when sending out a general distress signal? In a system that's much fuller of pirates and scavengers than it was a year ago?"

Alisa frowned back at him, not wanting to get into another argument about how degenerate the system was now that the empire wasn't in charge. Instead, she asked, "Do you see anything on the sensors that would indicate a medical emergency?"

"Perhaps."

While she waited for him to explain further, Alisa guided the *Nomad* alongside the *Peace and Prayer*, matching their course and speed. She also lined up her airlock port to theirs in case they decided to go over. If the crew was unable to respond because of a medical problem, then she should take people over to help, assuming it wasn't a situation where a quarantine would make sense. She didn't have the facilities or tech for dealing with that, and somehow, she doubted Alejandro would risk himself to go check on people carrying a deadly disease. For a doctor, he definitely had a selfish streak.

"There's nobody chasing them, by chance, is there?" Alisa asked.

"No other ships are in range," Leonidas said.

"There aren't any nearby stations or known pirate hangouts," Yumi said. "As I said, plotting their back-route just shows a bunch of nothingness."

"Nothingness?" Alisa frowned over at her, then back at Alejandro and Leonidas. Leonidas was tapping the sensors, probably trying to figure out if anyone was left alive over there.

Alisa dipped into her pocket for her netdisc. She had the coordinates that Leonidas had provided at the beginning of their journey, coordinates he'd used some Starseer nursery rhyme to come up with, coordinates she had pointed out were in the middle of nowhere. She doubted there would be a link between them and the pilgrim ship's course, but she pulled up the local map, nevertheless.

The gas giant Aldrin and some of its inhabited moons, including Cleon, popped up at the far edge, and distant stars were visible in the background. The three-dimensional holodisplay was easier for looking at objects in space than the flat built-in monitor that Yumi was using.

"Humor me and see if their route went anywhere near that dot there," Alisa told Yumi, swiping her finger to zoom in.

"Why would this ship have visited the coordinates that Leonidas gave you?" Alejandro asked, suspicion in his voice.

What, did he think that Alisa had commed ahead and told some pilgrims to check out his secret spot first?

"It probably hasn't," Alisa said, "but there's nothing else out here, so I'm checking. Maybe someone else likes Starseer nursery rhymes."

It was also possible that Abelardus, even though he hadn't been invited to any of the meetings, had plucked the coordinates out of Alejandro's or Leonidas's thoughts. He could have been the one to comm ahead to someone. Admittedly, Alisa could not imagine him choosing to communicate with pilgrims. Unless there happened to be a Starseer on that ship.

Alisa shook her head. Her mind was dancing without a partner. The odds of there being a relation were—

"That's interesting," Yumi said.

"What is?"

Yumi tapped a few buttons on the console screen, sending information to the netdisc. A dotted line bisected the star map. It went directly through the blue dot that represented the coordinates Leonidas had shared.

"That was their route?" Alejandro asked, stepping back into NavCom.

"If they haven't changed it." Yumi shrugged.

"Shit." Alejandro glared at Leonidas and then glared even harder at Alisa. "Someone leaked the information, and someone else got there first."

"Nobody in here leaked anything," Alisa said. "You're the only one who even *wants* that Staff of Whatzit."

"I assure you, everyone would want it if they knew it still existed."

"Not everybody. The only use I'd have for a big stick is clubbing irritating passengers."

Alejandro looked like he wanted to club *her*. Well, he was welcome to try.

"Abelardus could have gotten the information from us," Leonidas said quietly.

"Why would a passenger ship on a pilgrimage be sent to investigate a Starseer artifact?" Yumi asked, scratching her head.

"Maybe there's a Starseer onboard," Alejandro said, echoing Alisa's thoughts. "The pilgrimage could simply be a ruse." He curled his lip in distaste.

Alisa almost looked at his robe and said he would know all about that, but Leonidas spoke first.

"I only read two people alive on there," he said.

"Two people would be enough to fly a ship like that," Alisa said, "but that message made it sound like there would be more. A bunch of pilgrims."

"If they were there before, they're not there now."

"We should take a look," Alejandro said.

"Because you're worried people are wounded or because you're worried someone over there got your staff?" Alisa asked.

"I hardly think *you* have the right to take the moral high ground with me, Captain."

"I need to keep the hatch to NavCom locked more often," Alisa muttered to Yumi. "Leonidas, is there anything else over there that we need to be concerned about? Engine leaks? Gas leaks?"

He looked over at her. "You do realize I'm using *your* sensor system, right?"

"You're not picking on my ship, are you?" Alisa asked.

"Just pointing out that its scanners are limited."

"Because freighters aren't supposed to scan things. They're supposed to deliver things."

Leonidas stood up, forcing Alejandro to back into the corridor again. "Then you can deliver me to that ship, and I'll go take a look. The sensors in my armor will tell you what you want to know as soon as we open up the hatch to their ship."

"I was hoping to learn that information *before* we opened the hatch and sent people over," Alisa grumbled, as he headed to his cabin to change.

She turned in her chair to see what readings she could get from the old sensor equipment. Unfortunately, Leonidas was right, and there wasn't much. She was surprised he had finessed it into reading life signs.

"Perhaps you could upgrade the ship with more scientific equipment one day," Yumi said, "since you seem to go to a lot of interesting places."

"Right, I'll put it on the list, right after the lav upgrades. We wouldn't want the doctor's fragile skin to have to deal with harsh water removers."

Alejandro opened his mouth, no doubt to comment on her decorum.

Alisa hit the internal comm button and spoke first. "Beck, suit up. We're flying alongside a ship that's in trouble. There might be some people that need to be brought over here for medical attention. Leonidas would be devastated if you didn't join him to help."

Yumi smiled.

"Doctor," Alisa said, bracing herself for an objection, "why don't you get a medical kit ready in case someone over there needs treatment?"

"Very well," he said and walked out.

Alisa turned back to the controls. She would have to line them up even more precisely if they were going to extend their airlock tube and lock on. She hoped one of the two people who were alive over there would be able to answer the door. The idea of forcing their way in made her feel like a pirate, like all those people who had forced their way onto *her* ship. But they might have to do just that. If nobody was in a position to answer the comm over there, chances were they also wouldn't show up when the doorbell rang.

Her comm flashed. Alisa thought it might be the other ship, finally responding, but it was Mica.

"Is this other ship going to need repairs?" she asked.

"Maybe," Alisa said. "They mentioned an engine failure in their distress call, and our sensors do show that it's offline. They appear to be running minimal life support off the battery."

"We don't have any spare parts, certainly nothing that would match the needs of that ship."

"You've got gum and cable ties. Won't that do?"

"Funny."

"We'll worry about it after Leonidas and Beck report." Alisa finished lining up the *Nomad* with the pilgrim ship and stood up. "I'm going down to the cargo hold, Yumi. Will you let me know if anything happens? Such as the other ship suddenly veering away and breaking our tube in the process?" She grimaced at the thought.

"Uhm, is that likely?"

Alisa shrugged. "I hope not."

"Maybe you should stay up here."

"Oh, I have no doubt of that, but I'm too curious not to peek around Leonidas's shoulder as he goes in." She wished *she* could go explore, even though pilots weren't supposed to wander off and explore. Neither were captains.

"I'm sure he'll report whatever he finds," Yumi said, "though I understand being curious."

Alisa started for the hatchway but jumped when Abelardus appeared there.

"We're boarding that ship?" He looked toward the star map floating over Yumi's half of the console. The line through the coordinates remained in the air. If he recognized its significance, it did not surprise him.

"We're checking it out, yes," Alisa said.

"That's not a good idea."

"There are a couple of people still alive over there. At the least, we need to see if they need help."

"It's too late for them," he said quietly.

"What does that mean? What do you know?"

A distant clang echoed up from the cargo hold—the airlock hatch being opened? Alisa glanced at the console. Yes, the tube had been extended and secured. Leonidas and Beck could already be crossing over.

Abelardus turned and strode away.

"Damn it, Abelardus." Alisa leaped to her feet. "What do you know?"

CHAPTER THREE

Alisa dug out her comm unit as she ran after Abelardus. He was heading toward the cargo hold, and he had his staff in hand.

"Leonidas?" she called, speaking into the unit but also yelling. If he was still on the *Nomad*, he would hear her one way or another.

"We're preparing to board the other ship," Leonidas said.

Abelardus strode down the stairs, the tip of his staff clanging on the treads. Alisa ran after him, looking around the hold. Leonidas and Beck were already out of sight. The hatch on their side of the airlock was closed. Abelardus walked straight toward it. Alisa ran around him to get there first. Just as she reached the hatch and glimpsed the back of Beck's helmeted head through the window, Abelardus's hand latched onto her.

"Don't go in there," he said.

"I wasn't planning to." Probably. "Leonidas? Abelardus says going over there would be a bad idea."

Leonidas stood in front of Beck at the far end of the airlock tube. He had reached the other ship's controls and was examining them, but he paused to frown back at her.

"Does he," he said flatly. "He say why?"

Abelardus still gripped Alisa's arm, but he was not looking at her. He bowed his head and closed his eyes.

"Many are dead," he finally said. "The two who live will not survive."

Even though Alisa had seen demonstrations of his power, she shivered as she realized he hadn't been in NavCom when Leonidas had spoken of how many life signs showed up on the sensors. No, Abelardus knew this independently, through the power of his mind.

"Because of a disease?" Alisa asked. "Some virus?"

"If that is the case," Alejandro said, appearing on the walkway with his medical kit in hand, "then that is a reason to go help them, not abandon them."

He wore a determined expression as he came down the stairs and headed toward them. Alisa was surprised he cared about helping and couldn't keep from being suspicious. His true reason for wanting to go over there might be to make sure nobody had found that ancient staff that he sought.

"But not until we check it out," Leonidas's voice came over the comm. "If there's a virus, our suits will protect us."

"Yeah, but we can't let you back over here if there's some horrible disease in the air," Alisa said. "The *Nomad* doesn't have any way to decontaminate you."

"Then we'll have to fly the pilgrim ship to facilities that can deal with a medical emergency."

"You and Beck?"

"You can guide us."

"Oh, sure. Long distance tutoring is a great way to give flying lessons."

"Marchenko," Leonidas said, his tone dry. "Let's see what we're dealing with before panicking."

He tapped at the controls next to the ship's hatch.

"Alisa," she mumbled, watching Abelardus's face for clues that he knew more. Leonidas sounded as calm as ever, but her stomach pitched and heaved with worry.

Abelardus let go of her arm and looked at her. "I apologize."

"For what?" she asked, bewildered. And afraid. He wasn't about to apologize for letting Beck and Leonidas walk to their deaths, was he?

"Knocking you aside earlier when I was attacking the mech."

"Oh." That was the last thing Alisa cared about now.

"I was angry. My control is usually better than that."

"His name is Leonidas."

"What?" Abelardus's brow creased.

"Not mech. Leonidas."

"We're in," came Leonidas's voice over the comm.

Alisa stood on tiptoes to peer through the window. The hatch on the far side of the lock slid open, and Leonidas and Beck stepped into a dim corridor.

"Shit," Leonidas said, halting immediately.

"What?" Alisa blurted, clenching the rim of the window with her fingers.

"It's not a virus." Leonidas turned and pointed at her. "The radiation is off the charts in here. Break the lock and get the *Nomad* to a safe distance while we look around."

"The hull of the *Nomad*—"

"Is meant to protect you from the background radiation in space," he said. "It's like someone dropped a nuke in here. Get away *now*."

"Leonidas," Alejandro said, leaning toward Alisa's comm. "Your suits—"

"Mine will protect me. Trust me, they made sure we could withstand radiation out in the field."

"What about Beck?" Alisa asked. She had no trouble imagining that the empire would have outfitted their cyborgs with the best gear to survive nuclear attacks, but Beck had some off-the-shelf civilian combat armor. He could spacewalk in it, so it had to have some protection built in, but was it rated to last for hours in intense radiation?

Leonidas and Beck looked at each other. Beck's helmet twisted from side to side.

"He's not sure," Leonidas said. "I'm sending him back over, but hurry up and get the ship back to a safe distance."

Beck came jogging through the airlock, a panicked expression on his face. The far hatch clanged shut, and Leonidas disappeared from view.

Alisa bit her lip, afraid for him, but Beck's face made her fear for the rest of them too. He stopped at the hatch, closing the outer one behind him. He looked like he wanted to rip the inner hatch open and run into the ship, but he opened his comm instead.

"Get us away before I come aboard, Captain," Beck said. "And have someone bring my armor case down. It has the means to sanitize and decontaminate. I'll strip off in here and do my best not to make a mess of the ship."

With bleakness filling her, Alisa started to speak, but Leonidas interrupted her.

"Do it," he said, his voice hard.

"I'll do my best to set up a curtain that will keep the contamination to a minimum," Alejandro said, heading for the sickbay.

Alisa cursed and ran for the stairs, bumping Alejandro as she went, barely seeing him. She hated the idea of leaving Leonidas on the pilgrim ship to deal with whatever had caused that problem. It had to have been something to do with the engine. Would Leonidas be able to fix it? Was there a point in trying?

Mica walked out of engineering as Alisa ran along the walkway. "We going somewhere?" she asked.

Alisa only shook her head and continued on to NavCom. Yumi looked at her curiously as she slid into the pilot's seat. Someone had already hit the button to retract the airlock tube into the *Nomad*. Alisa fired up the thrusters and steered them away from the pilgrim ship. An alarm started flashing on the console, warning her about elevated radiation levels. She grunted and turned it off.

"Leonidas," Alisa said as the pilgrim ship grew smaller on her rear camera display, "tie yourself into the ship's comm as soon as you can so you have more range. I don't want to lose contact with you."

"You want me to transmit my camera feed?" He sounded a touch dry, as if he wasn't seriously considering it.

"Hells, yes," she said. "I want to know what's going on over there."

"I found the first body," he said, his voice growing somber.

Mica walked into NavCom in time to hear that. She pulled down the foldout seat behind Alisa. "I see nobody's been sending memos down to engineering again."

"Send your feed, anyway, Leonidas," Alisa said, ignoring her. She wasn't in the mood for humor. "In case there's more going on over there than an engine leak. We should record it for—for—" She rubbed her face, not sure what she wanted, just that someone should know what had happened over there. The Alliance. Or the families of those who had been lost on the ship. Three suns, there were two people still alive over there. Did that mean that they were slowly dying of radiation poisoning? Unless they had sheltered themselves or had combat armor of their own, that was exactly what was happening.

"I will," Leonidas said quietly. "I'm in their navigation cabin."

"Are there bodies?" Alisa said.

"Yes. I believe I see the woman who sent the message. I'm still looking for the two people alive we saw on the sensors. I'm hoping they were shielded somehow, otherwise—"

"I know." She didn't need Alejandro to tell her that it would be too late to save anyone who had been exposed to that much radiation over hours. Maybe days.

She glanced at the star map hovering in front of Yumi. It would have been a day and a half since the pilgrim ship traveled through those coordinates. Of course, their engine failure could have happened at any point in their journey. The coordinates should not have anything to do with it.

"Except, why don't I believe that?" Alisa muttered.

"Captain?" Yumi asked.

"Just talking to myself. Ignore me."

"Transmitting my helmet feed now," Leonidas said.

Alisa leaned toward Yumi to access the controls on the far half of the console. She sent the feed to her netdisc, so they could see it on the holodisplay. The view of an unfamiliar corridor came up, the panels along the side seeming to move as Leonidas strode forward.

Alejandro walked into NavCom, took Alisa's wrist, and clipped a dosimeter onto her finger. She pointedly did not look at the readout, instead focusing on Leonidas's camera feed.

"I'm heading to engineering," Leonidas said.

"Right, make sure you really test your armor by going where the radiation will be the worst," Alisa said.

He did not answer.

"I'm sorry," Alisa said. "That was inappropriate humor, if you weren't sure."

"Yes, I've learned to identify it."

Alejandro moved the finger clip to Mica and then to Yumi as Leonidas passed several doors, moving toward the back of the pilgrim ship. His head turning to look at plaques. The long, narrow vessel only seemed to have one corridor.

"Ouch, Doctor," Mica blurted, spinning in her seat. "What are you stabbing people with?"

Alisa glanced back in time to see Alejandro retracting an injector.

"A bit of a cocktail. Some potassium iodide for your thyroid, and a drug that will bind with radioactive plutonium, americium, and curium in your body and help you piss it out."

"Is it just me or do all of your cocktails make people piss?" Alisa asked, though her blood had gone cold. Even though she'd seen the warning alarm flashing on the console, she hadn't realized there had been that much exposure for those on the *Nomad.*

"It's one of the ways the body clears toxins. I can make you sweat, too, but I know you have an aversion to butt prints." He leaned forward and touched the injector to her neck.

By all that was blessed and holy, he was going straight for the veins, wasn't he? Alisa almost batted the injector away, but fear of what might happen if she wasn't treated stilled her hand. She swallowed, staring into his eyes and remembering that he had been willing to have her killed not that many weeks earlier. The injector hissed, and a soft, quick jab delivered the substance.

"Take some vitamins later," Alejandro said as he withdrew the injector. "Our levels are borderline, and I've given you a minimum dose, but you'll lose your zinc, magnesium, and manganese too."

"Damn, those are my favorite minerals."

"Will there be any side effects?" Mica asked.

"You'll probably throw up. But that was going to happen regardless." Alejandro withdrew the injector from Alisa's neck, thumbed a new dosage into the slot, and leaned toward Yumi.

Alisa almost commented on the lack of sterilization going on between patients, but she was too relieved that Mica and Yumi were getting the exact same thing. He had no reason to kill *them.*

"Did we take on that much radiation?" Mica asked.

"Beck showed me his helmet sensor stats."

Alisa took that for a *yes.* "Is he all right?"

"He received minimal exposure. His armor protected him."

Alisa should have listened to Abelardus.

"Their reactor must be leaking like a waterfall," Mica said.

With that thought, Alisa turned back to the console. They had traveled far enough for the *Peace and Prayer* to disappear from her cameras, so she slowed the *Nomad* to a stop. She did not want to be too far away if Leonidas needed help.

His camera feed showed him entering the double doors to engineering. Alisa expected to see a ruptured reactor front and center, but nothing appeared out of place initially, not from what she could see. Admittedly, that wasn't much. The illumination was dim, emergency lighting only. Leonidas did not have a flashlight on, and she remembered that his night vision was better than normal. She made out a few flashing buttons and the outline of equipment, but not much more.

Leonidas stepped over a body on the floor and stopped before a control panel.

Mica stood up and leaned closer to peer at the display. "The engine doesn't look like it's turned on."

"No," Leonidas said, the view shifting as he moved his head from left to right. "It's not." He turned back toward the housing for the engine itself. "My sensors are telling me this isn't the source of the radiation. It was stronger back in the middle of the ship."

A screech sounded somewhere near Leonidas, and Alisa nearly jumped out of her seat.

He spun, and blazer fire brightened the dim engineering room. His bolts slammed into the chest of a wild-eyed man with missing clumps of hair, a man leaping toward him from atop something. A knife was clenched in his hand. The video lurched as Leonidas leaped away to avoid him. The man tumbled to the deck, clutching at his chest.

"The eye of the gods," the man screeched, his eyes gleaming with insanity. "The eye of a god opens."

He groaned and looked down. There was no blood, the blazer blasts cauterizing as they struck, but Alisa doubted he would survive the attack. He wore simple clothing, no armor.

"We went to see," the man moaned, pain leaking into his voice now. "The true ones. We were called. The eye opens. To see the eye open. You are not believers. You aren't welcome. Intruders. We went to see...to see...dark, finally it's dark." The man slumped onto his side, his head clunking against the deck. Those insane eyes remained open even in death.

Leonidas sighed. "I didn't mean to kill him."

"It was a mercy that you did," Alejandro said. "I couldn't have done anything for him, not at that stage."

"That was more than radiation poisoning, wasn't it?" Leonidas asked, the video shifting as he returned to scanning engineering, the tip of his rifle just visible in front of him.

"What do you mean?"

"I don't recall insanity being on the list of symptoms from radiation exposure."

Alejandro hesitated. "Delirium is. Plus, he's seen all of his crewmates die, and he knew his own death was coming. That's enough to drive a man crazy."

"Perhaps." Leonidas looked at the body crumpled on the deck.

Alisa shuddered at those haunted, frozen eyes.

Leonidas knelt down, and a soft twang sounded. He looked at his arm, revealing one of the razor knives that could be extended from his armor.

"What are you doing?" Alisa asked as he poked the dead man's wrist with his blade, then dabbed his gauntleted finger in it. Her lips curled in disbelief as Leonidas wiped a dab of blood onto his armored forearm.

"Taking a blood sample."

"That's a weird way to do it."

"I don't have needles and slides." Leonidas rose to his feet. "This man lived significantly longer than the rest of the crew. I want to know why."

"Maybe his craziness saved him," Alisa said.

Yumi and Alejandro frowned at her. She lifted an apologetic hand.

Yumi opened her mouth, but paused, looking past Alisa's shoulder. A retching sound came from behind the pilot's seat. Mica's face was pale.

"Mica?" Alejandro asked, reaching for her shoulder.

She bent between her knees and threw up. Alejandro grimaced and withdrew his hand.

"To think, I was worried about sweat," Alisa muttered. "Alejandro, I think your side effects have started."

"Yes, or the effects of the exposure itself. I admit to feeling queasy myself."

"Why don't you and your new patients go to sickbay and relax?" Alisa turned back toward Leonidas's feed and drummed her fingers on her thighs, wishing she could do something besides sit and watch. "There's nothing to be done here."

"I feel fine," Yumi said, "but I'll help."

She stood and offered Mica a hand. Alejandro led the women away.

Alisa thought about cleaning up the mess, but figured she would be adding to it before long. So far, she did not feel nauseated, but she had no doubt it would catch up with her.

On the display, Leonidas had left engineering and was opening the doors leading to the crew cabins. More than one person had died lying on his or her bunk, some in pairs, some alone with nobody to tend to them. Alisa blinked away tears, distressed by the idea of people dying alone, distressed by this entire situation. Maybe it wasn't humane, but she wished the *Nomad* hadn't been close enough to pick up that comm message and had flown past. Then she would have nothing worse than cyborg-Starseer relations to worry about.

As if summoned by her thoughts, Abelardus walked into NavCom. He stepped over the mess and sat in the co-pilot's seat.

"You come to throw up at my feet too?" Alisa asked.

"Doubtful." He dropped his chin onto his fist and watched the video play as Leonidas continued to check cabins. He did not appear sick, nor was there any vomit clinging to his black robe.

"Because you're a Starseer and therefore special?"

"Quite special."

"And so modest," Alisa said. "I suppose you'd be too special to clean up the mess on the floor if I asked you to."

"Infinitely so, yes."

"I hear something," Leonidas said over the comm. The camera paused as he listened at a doorway.

"The last survivor?" Alisa guessed.

"Perhaps so." Leonidas shouldered his rifle. "I'll try to subdue this one."

Alisa remembered Alejandro's words, that it would be too late to help those people and that shooting was a greater mercy than keeping them alive. Still, if there was someone there who could explain what had happened, surely Leonidas had to try questioning the last person.

"The door is locked," Leonidas said. "The others weren't."

"Maybe you should knock," Alisa said.

Abelardus and Leonidas snorted at the same time.

Leonidas did, however, raise his gauntleted fist to knock.

Something like a muffled yowl came through the comm. Alisa could not tell if it was a cry of pain or of madness.

"Her mind is not right," Abelardus said, his eyes closed.

"Whose?" Alisa asked. "The person on the other side of the door?"

"Yes."

"Well, she's had a bad week," Alisa said.

Abelardus frowned at her.

"Sorry," she said.

She seemed to be saying that a lot. She didn't feel like explaining that she was deeply disturbed by all of this, and that if she actually admitted it out loud, she would end up breaking down in tears. She couldn't do that. She was the captain, and this was her ship. Captains didn't break down.

The camera view shifted to a close-up of the door. It took Alisa a moment to realize Leonidas was trying to force it open. A faint beeping sound came over the comm.

"That ship's not trying to self-destruct on you, is it?" Alisa asked. She was still worried about Leonidas being over there, suit or not, especially since people here were throwing up after what had to be a minuscule exposure in comparison to over there.

"No, that's my suit," Leonidas said, then grunted as he put effort into opening the door.

"*It's* not self-destructing, I hope."

"It's informing me that I'm close to dangerously high levels of radiation."

The door slid open before Alisa could respond. Unlike all of the other rooms on the ship, this one was brightly lit with a yellowish glow that reminded her uneasily of Alejandro's orb. Leonidas stepped into the doorway and scanned the room, a simple sleeping cabin with a bed and desk. Clothes and blankets were strewn about, along with cups, silverware, and old-looking pieces of equipment—she spotted something that looked like a spacesuit helmet from another era. Leonidas did not focus on it long enough for her to get a better look. The camera turned toward someone squatting in the corner, a bald woman. She was hugging something to her chest.

"You can't have it," the woman cried. "She's ours. She's ours."

Alisa did not see the attack, only the way the camera blurred as Leonidas dodged to the side. A gun fired, a bullet clanging off a wall.

The focus returned to the woman. She gripped a weapon that looked like an even older version of Alisa's Etcher. Was that a revolver? With a handful of bullets instead of a clip? It looked like something out of the Old West back on Earth.

The woman fired again. This time, Leonidas did not dodge. The bullet pinged off his chest plate. He simply stood there, taking it.

"Zoom," he murmured, and the camera closed onto the item that the woman held to her chest. It was responsible for the bright light, which made it hard to pick out features, but it appeared to be a plaque. "This room is the source of the radiation," Leonidas said.

"How can that be?" Yumi asked.

Alisa hadn't noticed her return, but she stood in the hatchway.

"Last one," the woman cried. "The last one shall not be for a heathen. The saint, she awaits me."

She turned the muzzle of the gun toward herself and thrust the tip right into her mouth. Leonidas surged forward, but then halted. Maybe he could have made it in time, but he decided to let the woman end her own pain. The old gun fired, the last bullet blowing out her brains.

Alisa winced and looked away, wishing Leonidas and his camera had too.

Abelardus dropped his face into his hand.

"Dearest gods and suns," Yumi whispered.

Leonidas walked forward and looked down. The view shifted from the woman's face to what she cradled in her arms. The gun had fallen from her lifeless grip, but the plaque remained hugged to her bosom. He bent and tugged it free. Words seemed to be etched in it, but the light hurt Alisa's eyes and made it impossible to read.

"Light filter, on," Leonidas said. "Reduce intensity by fifty percent."

The fierceness of the glow dimmed, and Alisa could read the plaque.

"Alcyone Station?" Abelardus read, sounding stunned. Or maybe awed.

"That's a place?" Alisa had never heard of it.

"It's supposed to be her final resting place."

"And the location of that staff?"

"I…actually don't know. That's not mentioned in any of the histories. According to official records, all of the Staffs of Lore were destroyed, deemed too strong, too galaxy-changing. All except one." Abelardus's eyes were locked to the plaque as he spoke. Leonidas was turning it over now, one of his gloved fingers brushing a charred corner that appeared to have been damaged by a blazer or similar weapon. Or perhaps an explosion had ripped it from whatever wall or bulkhead to which it had been mounted. "But the Toriphant, the orb, as you call it, and other clues promise to lead to Alcyone's staff, the last remaining Staff of Lore."

"Guess it would be handy if it were on her station," Alisa said.

Abelardus frowned at her. "You do not regard those who lived and died and shaped the past with enough reverence."

"Yeah, I'm told I don't regard much with enough reverence. Leonidas, what do you want to do now? Are you done exploring?"

"My suit is warning me of the intense radiation in here and that I should back away for my own health," he said.

"It's good to get health tips from your equipment."

"Can you bring any of those items with you?" Abelardus asked. "They look old. Perhaps they're artifacts from the station."

"They're the source of the radiation," Leonidas said, setting down the plaque. "Unless you want what happened here to happen on the *Star Nomad*, I plan to leave them."

"How can a *plaque* be radioactive?" Alisa asked, looking at the rest of the items on the floor as Leonidas walked out, the silverware and cups, the helmet. Were *all* of those things radioactive?

"Induced radioactivity," Yumi said. "When lighter elements such as aluminum are bombarded with alpha particles, there will be a continuous emission of radioactive radiations, even after the alpha source is removed."

"All right," Alisa said, "I guess I've heard of that happening in nuclear reactors, but to this degree? That the radiation could kill everyone in that ship within days?"

"Apparently."

"And why would they have picked up radioactive souvenirs? That doesn't seem bright."

"That I couldn't tell you," Yumi said, "except that it's possible they had no idea that what they were picking up was radioactive. That ship did not appear to be equipped for scientific testing."

"Yumi, that plaque was *glowing*. Who needs a test to see that?" Alisa thrust her hand toward the video, even though Leonidas had now moved out of the woman's cabin and was back in the ship's navigation cabin.

"Yes, that's interesting. Radioactive elements don't glow, at least not in a way that creates light that's visible to the human eye. Some substances, however, will emit visible light if they're suitably stimulated by the ionizing radiation from a radioactive material."

Abelardus's forehead wrinkled. Alisa wished she could pretend she had a better understanding, but she was just a pilot. If Mica weren't busy throwing up in sickbay, she would fetch her for this conversation.

"Who would do that?" Alisa asked. "Or do you think that it could have happened naturally?"

Naturally. As if glowing plaques were natural.

"They may have been running some tests on the items they picked up, trying to figure out why everyone was getting sick," Yumi suggested.

"I would have just punted everything out the nearest airlock," Alisa said.

Abelardus made a choking noise. "Those could be invaluable Starseer artifacts."

"Artifacts glowing with radiation. Besides, what do you care? I thought Alcyone betrayed your people and you were holding a grudge."

"She did, but that doesn't mean we wouldn't be interested in recovering artifacts from that time period."

Alisa waved her hand in dismissal. They could talk more about this later, when they had recovered Leonidas and gotten far, far away from that ship.

"Leonidas, are you ready to be picked up soon?" Alisa asked, tapping her controls. She was surprised he wasn't already at the airlock, eager to escape. "What are you doing in navigation again?"

"Changing the distress call to warn ships away," he said, his own fingers dancing over the controls, "and seeing if I can change its course, so it won't make it to Primus 7. If your ship had weapons, I would suggest blowing it up."

Alisa shuddered at the idea of blowing up the final resting place of those people, but she agreed that it would be better not to make Primus 7 deal with the problem. "Couldn't you toss the artifacts out into space?" she suggested. "Then the ship might at least be recoverable."

Abelardus made that choking noise again.

"Or could we decontaminate them somehow?" Alisa asked.

"No," Yumi said, "not when the materials themselves are radioactive. If particles had just fallen onto them, such as onto Beck's armor, it would be one thing, but not this."

"I'm leaving them," Leonidas said. "And I could use a pickup."

"Heading your way," Alisa said.

"Should we risk getting that close again?" Yumi asked. "We've all already had some exposure, and as you admitted, this ship isn't set up for decontamination. When Leonidas comes aboard, we'll get another dose."

"He can take off his armor and stick it in his case in the airlock, the same as Beck did."

"Someone still has to open the hatch and hand him the case."

"We're not *not* picking him up," Alisa said.

"Put the case in the airlock before I arrive," Leonidas said dryly. "To further minimize exposure, I can push off the outside of the ship, and you can pick me up out in space."

Alisa was surprised he trusted her that much to suggest such an action. That would take a lot of faith, and she shivered as she imagined herself in that situation.

"Would that make a difference?" Alisa asked Yumi.

"It might help. Getting an airlock with a radiation scrubber would be even better."

"I'll put it on my shopping list."

Yumi smiled faintly. "Before or after the sanibox upgrade?"

All Alisa said was, "Get ready, Leonidas. We're coming to get you."

CHAPTER FOUR

Alisa carefully guided the *Nomad* toward the red suit of combat armor drifting through space at the velocity with which he had jumped from the *Peace and Prayer*. She placed her freighter in his path, assuming he could find something to grab. Then he could magnetize his boots and lock onto the hull.

Once again, she marveled at the trust Leonidas displayed by jumping into the middle of nothing and waiting for her to pick him up. What if she had never come? He would have floated in space until his oxygen ran out. Could she have done the same thing if she had been in his position, with him here at the helm?

Yes, she decided. She wasn't sure when it had happened, but she had also come to trust him that much. Even so, taking that leap of faith would have terrified her.

"I suppose you would be irritated with me if I took over control of the ship and arranged for him to miss," Abelardus said, his expression wry as he looked over at her.

Yumi had gone to see if Alejandro needed help in sickbay, leaving Alisa alone in NavCom with Abelardus. Alisa now wished she hadn't. The fact that he could make a joke about such a thing made her want nothing more than to dump him on the nearest planet or space station.

"Irritated?" Alisa asked. "I'd do my best to choke you with your pendant."

"I've been choked enough for one day. I'll pass." He sniffed and looked at the control panel. "Besides, I don't know if I could fly this ancient piece of takka."

Alisa clenched her teeth. "You know what's a big bowl of steaming takka?" She turned toward him, pointing a finger at his nose.

The comm flashed.

"Captain?" Alejandro asked.

"Hold that thought." Alisa lowered her finger. She should probably thank Alejandro for the distraction. Getting in an argument with someone who could hurl a two-hundred-odd-pound cyborg across the cargo hold could not be good for her health. "What is it, Doctor?"

"Beck is experiencing side effects, but I'm treating him. He's decontaminated his suit. Mica and I verified that his case is equipped to do so. I'm prepared to do my best to get Leonidas aboard without further contaminating the ship." Alejandro sounded tired, maybe queasy.

"Thank you," she said. "How's Mica doing?"

"I hate everyone and everything," Mica wheezed in the background.

"It sounds like she's her normal self," Alisa said.

Alejandro grunted. "She's been sick. I'm monitoring her. How are *you* doing?"

"Me? I'm fine so far." Alisa did not hear the clunk of Leonidas touching down, but one of her monitors caught him landing on the hull of the *Nomad*.

"Are you?" Alejandro asked. "Hm."

Abelardus looked over at Alisa thoughtfully.

"Leonidas is making his way to the airlock now," Alisa told Alejandro. "He'll be ready for your attention soon."

"Understood." The comm light winked out.

Abelardus was still looking at her.

"I know I'm fascinating, but what?" Alisa asked, returning his look frankly, but not holding it for long. It still bothered her that he could read minds. She started laying in their course, though she was less certain than ever that she wanted to visit the source of Leonidas's coordinates.

"Starseer blood?" Abelardus asked.

"Who?"

"You."

"Me?" This time, the look she gave him was incredulous. "No. What are you talking about? Why would you even think that?" Alisa did not have

Starseer genes. Her daughter was the one with the special blood, and that had come courtesy of Jonah.

Abelardus's thoughtful expression had not faded, and she found herself scowling at it.

"You can read my mind and tell that's the truth," she said.

"I see that you *believe* it's the truth. Have you ever been tested?"

"Of course. I had a medical exam before I went to flight school and another before they let me into the Alliance army."

"They don't sequence DNA for an army physical," he said. "Were you born in an imperial hospital?"

"No." Her scowl deepened. This was silly. Why would he think she had Starseers for ancestors? He could see that she had no special powers. If she had them, she would have used them to strangle him with his pendant when he had suggested leaving Leonidas behind.

He threw his head back and laughed.

"Asteroid kisser, you're in my head, aren't you?" she asked.

"Naturally." He smirked at her.

"Why are you asking all this? Because I'm not down in sickbay throwing up?"

"All Kirian descendants have a higher tolerance for radiation than the average human. When the original colonists were contemplating the planet for a place to land and establish their civilization, they underestimated how much radiation was getting through the weak atmosphere and overestimated how quickly they could get domes up to shelter the population. It didn't help that one of the colony ships carrying much of the engineering and terraforming equipment was destroyed during the descent. Our ancestors were exposed to a great deal of background radiation. A lot of them ended up dying young. Others survived and had children, and our scientists tinkered with their genomes to make them and their descendants more resilient to the cosmic rays."

"Right. I've heard that story, that it was some of those mutating genes that caused that...*that*." Alisa waved at his face, indicating his arrogance as much as his power.

He snorted. "Lady Naidoo was right. You say whatever's on your mind most of the time, don't you?"

"It's part of my charm. And I'm not a Starseer."

"No, but you could have the genes without knowing it, especially if you weren't born in an imperial hospital." He tilted his head. "Where were you born?"

"On board this ship, actually." Alisa thought about saying it had been in his cabin, and that her mother had gotten amniotic fluid all over his bunk, but she presumed her mother had given birth in sickbay, or perhaps in her own cabin. "According to her, she had just reached a space station—she was piloting while having contractions—and meant to have me in a proper medical facility, but I was a demanding and ornery baby and came early."

"Ornery. Imagine."

"But my mother was born on Perun, in the capital city," Alisa said, ignoring his teasing—or maybe those were insults. She did not feel that they knew each other well enough for anything that could be considered teasing. "She would have been tested in an imperial hospital when she was born."

"And your father?"

"Er."

He raised his eyebrows.

It was silly, but Alisa had never known her father, so he never figured into her thoughts or equations for anything. "I don't know. Mom said he was a fling on a border world."

"A fling that she decided to turn into a child?" Abelardus raised his eyebrows.

She scowled at him, but she understood what he was implying. Birth control implants had been required in the empire, and a man and woman—or other suitable cohabitation couple—had been required to ask permission from the government before having the implant removed and proceeding to have up to, but no more than, three children. Accidental pregnancies had been rare, especially on core planets. Even out on the border worlds, popu-lations had been controlled and monitored. Only gypsies and pirates who kept to the skies and stayed off the grid had flown under the empire's radar.

"From what my mother told me, she wanted a child and wasn't going to let the empire tell her that she couldn't have one just because she wasn't partnered with anyone." Alisa waved her hand, trying to dismiss the conver-sation. She had no wish to discuss her origins or her family background with some strange Starseer. She'd already said more than she was wont to do and wondered if he might have been tinkering with her mind.

That faint smirk touched his lips again.

"Not me," he said. "Maybe you're just in a chatty mood. Maybe you want to know the truth about your heritage."

"No, I don't." The *Nomad* was back on course, so Alisa pushed herself to her feet. "I'm going to check on Leonidas. Don't touch my controls."

Abelardus lifted his hands in innocence.

"Alisa?" he said as she stepped through the hatchway.

"What?" She did not look back. She was tempted to tell him to call her *Captain* instead of using her first name.

"I only meant to tease you, not insult you."

Once again, the knowledge that he had been in her mind, reading her thoughts, chilled her.

"Stay out of my head."

———

Alisa found Leonidas in sickbay with Alejandro. Mica and Beck must have been sent to their cabins to rest.

"How are you doing?" Alisa asked Leonidas as she walked in. He wore trousers and one of his T-shirts, one that fit him like a second skin. His crimson armor case hovered in the corner of sickbay, humming softly.

"I'm fine," he said, nodding to her. "The doctor is examining some blood."

"Did he give you a shot to make you pee?"

"No. Is that desirable?"

Alejandro was bent over his microscope, but he frowned over at them. "Leonidas had his combat armor on the whole time, including when we were flying up to the contaminated ship. His only exposure came when he removed his suit, and you've never seen a soldier strip so quickly and slam the pieces into his armor case. I checked him, and his radiation levels were minimal."

"That armor is handy," Alisa said. "I do need to get some."

Leonidas regarded her, his eyes growing gentle. "Have you been sick too?" he asked quietly.

"No," she said, then added, "Not yet."

She did not want anyone else to notice that she, Yumi, and Abelardus were in the same group of people unaffected by the exposure, to start thinking that her father might have been some staff-twirling robe-wearer. She did not want to think about it herself, either, and yet…a part of her couldn't help but wonder. From everything she had heard, it was far too late for her to develop any talents if she *did* have the Starseer genes, but maybe it would make things less odd between her and Jelena when they were finally reunited. Would Jelena be delighted by developing powers, or would she worry about being thought a freak? Alisa was not sure how she would have reacted at that age. But if they all had the unique genes, she could say, "Look, we're the same. You, me, and Dad, all the same blood. Nobody's odd here." Or maybe they could all be odd together.

"It's Starseer blood," Alejandro said, and Alisa flinched.

Leonidas nodded. "The woman probably had it too. I wish I'd had an opportunity to question one of them as to what happened, but I doubt I would have gotten anything understandable out of them."

"The madness was unfortunate," Alejandro said. "Especially since it affected both of them. As I said, delirium can be a side effect of radiation poisoning, but I thought they acted oddly, even given the circumstances."

It took Alisa a moment to wrench her thoughts away from herself and to focus on what they were talking about. Not her blood, but the blood sample Leonidas had brought back on his armor.

"Emotional traumas, perhaps?" Leonidas said. "I've seen men snap in battle and spout nonsense."

"Seeing everyone on their ship dying around them and knowing they would follow could not have been easy," Alejandro said, though he did not sound convinced.

"Could the artifacts themselves have held some power beyond the radiation?" Alisa asked. "Like the doctor's orb?"

"Who would infuse a plaque with Starseer power?" Leonidas asked.

"Well, if it was *Alcyone's* station, maybe she did it. Or maybe there was something else on the deck in that cabin. You looked like you were stepping over a lot of clutter."

"Yes. And bodies." He sighed.

Alisa wondered if he, too, wished they hadn't heard that distress call and diverted. What good had come of all this? The only thing she could think of was that they had dealt with it out here in the middle of nowhere and that the ship hadn't floated up to Primus 7 where more people might have been affected by the radiation. Of course, whatever sensors Primus 7 and its ships had might have been able to detect the radiation long before sending people to board. She hoped that no one on the *Nomad* would suffer long-term health effects from this side trip.

"You've put the ship back on course toward Leonidas's coordinates?" Alejandro asked, turning away from the microscope. The way he asked it made it sound like he expected the answer to be yes, and that he would be disappointed if he heard anything else.

"I have," Alisa said. "But are we sure we want to continue on?"

"Of course. What do you mean?"

Leonidas leaned his hip against the exam table and crossed his arms over his chest, but he did not say anything. He merely watched the conversation.

"You saw the star map," Alisa said. "Do you think it's a coincidence that the pilgrim ship came from the exact spot in space that we're on our way to search?"

"Of course it's not a coincidence." Alejandro brushed past her, and she thought he would stalk out of sickbay, but all he did was look up and down the corridor, then pull the hatch shut. "Those damned Starseers know where we're going, and I'll bet my left testicle that Abelardus sent word ahead so people could investigate the coordinates before we got there, people with Starseer blood." He pointed toward his microscope. "It's not as if this rust bucket is the fastest thing in the galaxy. Many other ships could have reached it by now. That's why we can't delay any further."

"First off," Alisa said coolly, taking exception to the rust bucket comment, "closing the hatch isn't going to keep Abelardus from knowing what we're in here talking about. And second, who in all of the suns' fiery hells do you think wants one of your testicles?"

Leonidas snorted.

Alejandro glared. "I see you're going to take this conversation seriously."

"This is your mission, not mine. *My* mission is being delayed *again* because of you and your orb. You tell me what about that is supposed to make me serious."

"The dead people we just left in our wake," Leonidas said grimly.

Alisa flinched, immediately feeling childish. Alejandro rubbed her the wrong way and made her want to lash out. But Leonidas made her feel... she didn't know what exactly. Ashamed that she wasn't a better person. She doubted that was his intent, but it still stung. Jonah had never made her feel ashamed.

She turned toward the hatch, blinking at the unexpected emotion that welled within her.

"She's impossible to deal with," Alejandro said and stalked back to his microscope.

"No, she's not." Leonidas walked over and put a hand on her shoulder, frowning at her, in concern not condemnation. "Thank you for picking me up," he said. "Not everybody comes back for irradiated cyborgs."

"Your *suit* was irradiated, not your cyborg parts," Alejandro muttered, his back to them.

"I'll thank the three suns for that." He lowered his hand.

Alisa wished he hadn't. She felt the urge to lean against him, whether he had shamed her or not. Alejandro turned back toward them, so she leaned her shoulder against the bulkhead instead.

"We will need to be careful approaching the coordinates," Alejandro said, having apparently decided he could have serious conversations with her after all. "Those contaminated artifacts came from somewhere."

"It'll be interesting to discover somewhere in the middle of nowhere," Alisa said.

Alejandro made a disgusted noise and headed for the hatch. "I'm going to lie down. Let me know if anyone needs medical assistance."

He opened the hatch and stalked out.

Leonidas smiled faintly at Alisa. "You really do vex him."

"Good, he vexes the hells out of me. I know he—" Alisa caught herself from saying that Alejandro wouldn't mind if she were dead. That had come out in a confidential conversation between Leonidas and Alejandro, one she had eavesdropped on. "I know he never forgets that I'm Alliance and that I don't want what he wants."

"No," Leonidas said softly, his eyes growing hooded.

"You do sometimes, I think."

"I don't forget it. I suppose I just hope that you'll come around to my way of thinking someday and realize the Alliance doesn't care about you any more than the empire did. Now that you've been getting in their way, they probably care even less."

She swallowed, annoyed that there was some truth in his words. "I'm only in their way because you two thugs sucked me into your orbit," she grumbled.

"Thugs?"

"Thugs." She reached out and squeezed his biceps. "Surely, it's not the first time you've been classified as such."

He arched an eyebrow, and she withdrew her hand, regretting the joke. Every now and then, he deigned to banter with her, but it didn't seem to be his natural reaction. She had probably offended him again.

"Many times," Leonidas said, "but I was puzzled as to your classification of a scrawny man in a robe as such."

"I've seen his bare shins under that robe. Those leg hairs are definitely thugly."

He snorted.

She smiled, relieved that she hadn't offended him. "That almost sounded like a laugh, Leonidas. I'll get it out of you one day."

"Perhaps." He did return the smile, though his smiles were never huge and toothy. They were always a subtle stretching of the lips, and there always seemed to be a sadness in them, one he could never fully shake.

Someone tugged the hatch open further, and Alisa expected Alejandro to walk in, returning for something he had forgotten. But Abelardus stepped in.

He eyed Leonidas. "Such a shame that you made it back on board. I tried to suggest to our captain that she leave you behind, but she was oddly unamenable."

Leonidas stared back at him, all of the humor gone from his face, the smile only a memory. Alisa rolled her eyes.

Abelardus's gaze shifted to Alisa. "I saw you were in here and figured you were checking your blood."

"And that I'd need your help?" she asked, aware of Leonidas looking curiously in her direction.

"I'm curious as to the answer."

"I'm not."

He smirked. "Yes, you are."

"Didn't we talk about my feelings in regard to you being in my head?"

"My apologies. It's a bad habit, I know." Abelardus looked back to Leonidas. "Why don't you take a walk, mech? You must be tired after your adventures."

"I'm rarely tired."

"No? Not even when you sleep so poorly?" Abelardus smirked again.

Alisa wanted to punch him in the mouth. No, she wanted *Leonidas* to punch him in the mouth. That would hurt him a lot more.

"You're monitoring my sleep?" Leonidas asked. "I didn't know I was such a fascination for you."

"Know thy enemy."

"Why don't you both go get some rest?" Alisa said. "And leave me alone so I can hunt up some painkillers. For some reason, I'm getting a headache."

"Well, I doubt it's from the radiation," Abelardus said.

"I doubt it is, too," Leonidas muttered and walked out.

Alisa watched him go. She wouldn't have minded if he had stayed. She just did not want the two of them sniping at each other. She made a shooing motion, hoping Abelardus would follow. A moment alone sounded quite appealing. Her thoughts were a tangle, and she needed time to consider them. And perhaps time to see if she could figure out how to work Alejandro's DNA sequencer. She *was* curious, damn it. She didn't want to be, but she was.

"I helped the Alliance, you know," Abelardus said, drawing her attention back to him. "My brother didn't. We argued a lot. He supported the empire and was even working for them in the end. I don't know if it's true, but according to him, he tutored the emperor's older son. Before the kid died. I'm not sure if the younger boy has had any training. I never cared. Honestly, I didn't care about the Alliance either in the beginning, but I came around to the idea of the empire's vise grip on the system being lessened."

"Why are you telling me this?" Alisa asked, wanting to shove him out the hatchway after Leonidas, but making herself pause. This was new information. She didn't care who he'd fought for, but if his brother was the same

Durant that had taken her daughter, wouldn't it be useful to know more about him? If Durant was an imperial loyalist, what did he have in mind for Jelena?

Abelardus tilted his head. "I thought it might matter to you."

"I'd like to hear more about Durant."

His mouth twisted. "I was hoping you'd rather know more about *me*."

Er, why?

"Not unless you kidnapped my daughter."

"I wouldn't do such a thing. Look, I know you think I'm a jerk because I don't like your cyborg friend, but I find it puzzling that you *call* him a friend. He's everything the empire stands for. I bet he enjoyed enforcing their laws and squashing dissenters under his big booted feet."

"I think you're a jerk because you messed with my mind and convinced me to fly up to that Alliance warship and sacrifice ourselves to them, all to buy time for your people."

"I thought the mech might be sacrificed, but I doubted they would do anything to you. I have no quarrel with you, Captain."

"That ship's commander jabbed me in the throat with a blazer and seemed perfectly happy to sacrifice me."

Abelardus stared into her eyes, and the hairs on the back of her neck rose. She stepped back, certain he was sifting through her thoughts.

"He was bluffing," Abelardus said. "The Alliance commander. He wouldn't have hurt you, but he could tell that the mech had feelings for you—" he sneered, "—and that he would give up rather than see you sacrificed."

"You weren't there. You didn't read his thoughts. You can't be sure. I'm not even sure."

"I'm sure." Abelardus shrugged. "Even if I wasn't, you should know that Lady Naidoo's first response to learning that your ship had a beacon on it and that you'd led those warships to us was to want to blow you, your crew, and your ship off our dock. She figured that would take care of the beacon. Those of us with saner minds talked her out of it. Yumi Moon's mother, for one. And I argued against it too. It's one thing to protect our turf from invaders but another to kill in cold blood."

"I don't know why I should believe you."

"Because we're the same." He surprised her by grinning and thumping her on the arm with his fist. "Go test your blood and find out."

She grunted. "Why would that matter? I can't do anything that you can do. Sylvia—my sister-in-law—said lots of people have Starseer genes, but that it's rare for them to manifest."

"Lots? Not lots. They're dominant genes and do get passed on easily enough, but our people were almost annihilated after the Order Wars. Nearly extinct. A few centuries hasn't made a huge difference, and we don't generally get along that well with outsiders—I can't imagine why." He quirked his eyebrows. "So, we're not out there breeding with normal humans like glow worms on a rampage." He touched her arm again. "Check your blood. It'll be fun."

"Uh." Alisa didn't know what to say. Playful Abelardus was more alarming than asshole Abelardus. "You know what would be fun? If you could get in touch with your brother and ask him if he's been kidnapping little girls lately. I would appreciate that."

"Yes, I suppose you would. I sent a message as soon as we left Arkadius, but he didn't respond. I'll try again."

"Good. Thank you."

"Test your blood," he repeated, then bowed and walked out, his robe sweeping over the bottom of the hatchway.

"Weirdo," she muttered.

Alisa pulled the hatch shut and leaned against it. She closed her eyes, relieved to be alone. She had not been lying about that headache, and she could feel sweat breaking out on her forehead. Was that from stress? Radiation? Or were the side effects of Alejandro's potions starting?

A painkiller and a nap were what she needed.

And yet...she found her eyes opening, her gaze turning toward Alejandro's tools. She could work a microscope, but she didn't know how to use the DNA sequencer. Would it be difficult to figure out? Should she try? What would it truly change if she had some gene mutations? Who didn't?

Her legs felt numb as she walked around the table to the counter. The DNA sequencer sat next to the microscope, the blood sample from the pilgrim ship still in it. She peered at the small display on the compact device. It showed several double helixes that meant absolutely nothing to her—she couldn't even tell if they were actual images taken from cells or pictorial representations—but the columns of text on the other side of the display were somewhat more illuminating. The familiar ATCG letters were lined up in various combinations on the left, and in most instances, matching combinations lay in the columns to the right. But in several spots, the combinations on the right were highlighted, and letters had been inserted, deleted, or shifted.

"All right, so these are the genes of a crazy person who's somewhat resistant to radiation," Alisa murmured.

She dug her netdisc out of her pocket and took a picture. Next, she poked around on the machine until she found where Alejandro had inserted a sample on a small tray. She slid the tray out and started toward the sink but realized he might want to look at it again. Instead, she hunted through the paraphernalia strewn across the counter until she found an eyedropper and another tray. She didn't see anything she could use to prick her own skin and settled for pulling out her multitool. The laser knife would simply cauterize, but there were a couple of small physical blades tucked into the tool. She washed the small knife and her finger in the sink and also found some sanitizer to use. Since she did not truly know what she was doing, she hoped she could take a sample without contaminating it with all manner of outside bacteria. With her luck, she would end up sequencing the DNA of some microbe that hung out under fingernails.

Once she pricked herself and dropped a sample into a fresh tray, she paused. This probably wouldn't work without Alejandro's help, which she did not want to ask for, but what if it did? Did she truly want to find out that she had the same mutant genes as Abelardus and all those asteroid kissers in that temple who had looked down their noses at regular humans and cyborgs?

No, these were the same mutant genes that *Jelena* had, she told herself. Her daughter. And Jonah had possessed them. Yumi had them too. Perfectly normal people. Besides, as she had told Abelardus, it wasn't as if it would change anything about her. It was too late for her to manifest any weird talents. All it would mean was that if she had more children, she could pass the genes along, and *they* could manifest weird talents.

"Lucky them," she said and shoved the tray into the machine.

It beeped indignantly, and she thought she had done something wrong, but it locked down on the tray, and she could not pull it back out again. The display on the screen changed. Red, green, yellow, and blue squiggles scrolled past on an axis with the letters they represented underneath.

Alisa shifted from foot to foot, waiting impatiently, and reminded herself that this had taken years when they had first started doing it back on Old Earth. Since she hadn't tinkered with the settings, she had no idea if the machine was doing all of her DNA or only looking for Starseer mutations. She was on the verge of going to find something to eat when it beeped, and the word *complete* flashed on the screen. A readout similar to the one that had been on it before filled the screen. Mutations were highlighted. She brought up the holodisplay on her netdisc, the picture she had taken floating in the air. The mutations were the same.

For a long minute, Alisa merely stared at the displays, the reality slowly sinking in.

"Congratulations, Alisa," she finally said. "You're a freak."

She snorted at herself.

"What's new? Nothing."

She removed the tray, washed away her blood, put everything back where she had found it, and walked out of sickbay.

CHAPTER FIVE

Mica was sitting in the co-pilot's seat in NavCom when Alisa woke from her nap and walked in to check on their flight. It hadn't been a particularly restful nap, thanks to several trips to the lav. She might have Starseer blood, but apparently, that could not save her from the side effects of Alejandro's potions.

Fortunately, Mica did not look as pale as she had before. The mess on the deck had been cleaned up.

"Anything interesting happening up here?" Alisa waved at the view screen as she slid into her seat.

"Just looking at the stars and wondering if my hair is going to fall out."

"Would you miss it much?" Alisa looked at Mica's short, tousled locks. "It's not like you brush it or spend any time primping it."

Mica gave her a sour look. "I still like to *have* some. Gives my partners something to grab onto in bed."

Alisa grimaced. "Mine just gets in the way in bed. Someone's usually lying on it or accidentally trapping it under a hand or arm." Maybe short hair would be easier.

"Someone? Nobody specific?"

"Jonah."

"I thought you might have experimented with others."

"Well, *before* him I did."

"And since?"

"Of course not. It wouldn't be—it hasn't been long enough." Alisa looked toward the stars and pointedly did not think about Leonidas. "I still miss him a lot."

"Ah."

Alisa tried to decide if there was skepticism in that short noise. Her words were not untrue, but she had been so busy since she got out of the hospital that she hadn't thought of him as much as she should have. She wished there had been more time to spend with Sylvia, time to go out to the farm to see the rest of Jonah's family, and time to truly say goodbye. After she found Jelena, perhaps they could do those things. Or hold a memorial of their own.

That thought made her reach for the comm controls. She wanted to know if Abelardus had sent messages to his brother, or if he was lying, telling her what she wanted to hear. After all, why would he care about Jelena? He was here for the orb and the staff, the same as the rest of the galaxy.

Mica looked at her hand, and Alisa hesitated. She usually reserved eavesdropping and snooping for when she was alone. Oh well. Mica knew she wasn't a paragon of virtue.

She pulled up a list of all the outgoing comm messages from the last week, the headers of everything everyone had sent since the ship left Arkadius. Most people encrypted their communications, or had mail services that did it automatically, but she could see the side of the videos and messages that had been recorded here, before they were encrypted and sent, since they had to be boosted through the *Nomad's* transmitter. She wouldn't necessarily get the other side of the message, but they hadn't had real-time communication since they had moved away from the core worlds, so any recent messages would be one-way, regardless. Besides, all she needed to see was one side of Abelardus's message to know if he had commed his brother.

"You're reading people's mail?" Mica asked as Alisa skimmed through the accounts.

"Not everyone's."

Alisa glanced at the hatch to make sure nobody had a nose pressed to the window, then selected the messages on Abelardus's account.

"Good, because mine is private. I don't want people knowing about the smutty romances I order."

"Do engineers watch romances that don't involve tools and machinery?"

"Who says mine don't?"

Alisa waved her fingers in a semblance of a salute. "I wasn't looking at your vid collection or opening your messages, though I did notice a lot of mail going out to engineering firms and exploratory mining operations. Résumés?"

"Résumés. I need to get out of here before I get irradiated."

"I'm wounded that you're so determined to leave. Once we get rid of our artifact hunters, life would be normal again. Just me helping Jelena with her schooling while cargo sits in the hold as we carry it from moon to planet to station."

"Will that schooling involve teaching her how to hurl cyborgs against the wall?"

Alisa grimaced. "I hope not. But she probably will need to learn about her new talents. Maybe I can hire her a Starseer tutor. An innocuous one."

"Is there such a thing?"

"Yumi's sister seemed decent. Maybe she would like to have adventures in space for a while and teach Jelena the fine art of not being an ass."

"Adventures? See, I knew you had more planned than simple cargo hauling."

"Don't you think you would be bored at a job that didn't have at least some adventure?" Alisa ignored several messages that Abelardus had sent to Lady Naidoo, though she might watch them later. It *would* be good to know if Abelardus or the other Starseers had been alerting people to the coordinates they were heading out to explore. "After all, your time in the army couldn't have been that sedate. I know we had excitement on the *Silver Striker.*"

"The fighter pilots had excitement. The engineers sat inside the heavily shielded warship and waited for the wrecked remnants of that excitement to come in for repairs."

"Hm."

Alisa spotted the name Durant Shepherd in one of Abelardus's earlier messages, and her heart seemed to thud harder in her chest. She glanced at the hatch again as she pulled it up. She did not know why she bothered to check it. Abelardus would find out later that she had been spying. The next time he surfed through her thoughts, he would pluck out the information. She wouldn't feel bad about it either. He spied on her thoughts, so she could spy on his mail. It was only fair.

Abelardus's face appeared on the small monitor nestled into the console. Alisa did not tie in her netdisc to get a holodisplay this time. This would be harder for someone looking through the window behind them to see.

"I wonder what kinds of vids he orders," Mica said.

"If it's romances involving tools and engines, would you fall in love?"

"I might fall into his bed. He's pretty."

"I thought muscular men weren't your type."

"I can make an exception if they're pretty. Look at those cheekbones. And that perfect skin. And all that hair. Plenty to grab onto." Mica offered a wicked grin.

"Uh huh." Alisa imagined sex with *two* people with long hair and wagered it would involve even more hair getting caught under body parts. "You're going to make Yumi jealous if you drool openly on him."

"Sadly, I keep seeing Yumi chatting with Beck. I think he's winning her over with his cooking."

"Maybe you should show some interest in her hobbies."

"I tried meditating with her. It was boring."

"What about the chickens? Do you like animals? Birds?"

"Absolutely. They taste excellent."

"Maybe the mushrooms and whatever else she's growing in her cabin. Have you gone in to take a look?" Alisa hit play on the message, interrupting the conversation.

"Durant," Abelardus said—the recording date was seven days earlier, the day they had taken off from Arkadius. "Have you been kidnapping little girls? Naidoo is concerned for your soul, and the mother wants her kid back. Let me know what you're doing out there and if you're still on Cleon. Your last message was cryptic. Mom's worried about you. Out."

Alisa dropped her chin to her fist. She had almost expected to find that Abelardus either hadn't commed his brother or hadn't inquired about Jelena. That he had actually done what he'd said he had done left her feeling nonplussed. Maybe because she preferred thinking of him as a jerk and being irritated with him. This did not necessarily make him less of a jerk, but it left her less irritated with him.

"He has a mother, huh?" Mica asked. "I suppose that's usually how it works, but with some people, it's hard to imagine them having parents.

Like your cyborg. You kind of just imagine that he was always this killing machine, and that's how it was."

Since Alisa now knew Leonidas's story and how he had signed up for the cyborg program to help his mother, she had no trouble imagining him as a young man or even a boy, before he had become a "killing machine." She kept the thought to herself. If Leonidas wanted other people to know about his past, he could tell them.

"There aren't any return messages," Alisa said, disappointed.

She might not have been able to listen to them, but it would have been nice to know that Durant was in communication with Abelardus. He—and Jelena—would seem closer then, more attainable. The implication that Durant was missing and that his family did not know why worried her.

Another message flashed into existence at the top of her queue. According to the time stamp, it had just been sent. She did not hesitate to open it.

"Durant," Abelardus said, his face appearing on the monitor again, "talk to me. Are you getting my messages? Are you in trouble, or just ignoring me? Look, we need to talk. I won't judge you for backing the imperials and not giving up on them, even when they've been smashed. There's some interesting stuff going on. People are hunting for the Staff of Lore, and it looks like someone might actually find it this time. I'll give you more details if you give *me* some details on what you're up to. Why'd you take that girl on Perun? I'm on the ship with the mother—did I mention that? I just found out she has Starseer genes. I suppose that stands to reason, if the girl's got them, but she thought they only came from the father. The girl might have a lot of potential with two parents of Kirian descent—you know how rare it is for offspring to come out of those unions. But maybe you already knew that, eh? When you picked that girl? What are your plans? The mother could be a part of them. That would be the right thing to do. Though you might have to brainwash her into going along with whatever your plans are, especially if they have to do with the empire. Damn it, Durant, I don't know what you're up to, but you're missing out by not answering my messages."

Abelardus signed off, his face disappearing and the display returning to a list of messages. Alisa sat back in her chair, digesting the information— and shivering inside at the idea of some Starseer wanting to brainwash her.

She already knew they could do that in the short term, such as to suggest that flying up to visit an enemy ship was a good idea, but could they make brainwashing stick long-term? Did she want to know?

"I think he likes you," Mica said.

"What?" Alisa had forgotten she was there.

"Usually, when men talk about doing the right thing for a woman, they mean doing the thing that's going to allow them to jump into her bed."

Alisa turned off the display, leaving the other messages for later snooping. "You seem to have sex on your mind a lot."

"It's been months since I got any. What can I say? I'm horny."

Months. It had been more than a year since Alisa had been home on leave and seen Jonah in the flesh. If she had known that would be the last time she ever saw him…She rubbed her eyes, thinking of the last night they had spent together. She wished she had realized how special it was and enjoyed it more, appreciated him more. She wished she had *told* him how much she appreciated him.

"Did you see the miscreants on Dustor?" Mica went on. "Half of them didn't have teeth, and none of them had money. Since I've been on this rusty boat, you haven't put in to any stations for long enough for us to have some personal time. Clearly, I need to redouble my efforts with my options here. Chickens? Really? You think that's the way to a woman's heart?"

"That or the herbs and mushrooms," Alisa said, only half listening. "Just don't let yourself get too involved in scheming your campaign. I need your mind working if any emergencies come up."

"My mind always works."

A beep came from the comm, and Alisa winced. She expected that to be Abelardus demanding to know why she was listening to his messages. But it wasn't. The signal was coming from outside the ship.

She leaned forward and tapped the button to play the message as she also hunted for the source.

"…This has been an automated warning message. You will not receive additional warnings. Ignore at your own peril. Closed area identified via an attached data file. Repeat. This is an Alliance Transmit Buoy delivering a message authorized by First Governor Ingvar Vestergaard of the Tri-Sun Alliance. This area has been quarantined due to a medical emergency. All ships must reroute to avoid the affected area. The quarantine will be strictly enforced, and any vessels breaching the closed area may be disabled or destroyed in order to ensure the safety and wellness of the rest of the system. I repeat, all ships must reroute. Failure to do so could result in extreme measures. This has been an automated warning message. You—"

Alisa stopped it before it could repeat. She grabbed the data file that had arrived with the verbal warning and opened it on the screen.

"That's ominous," Mica said.

"Yeah. Especially since Leonidas's coordinates are in the middle of the closed area." Alisa pointed at the star map that had been sent.

"How much do you want to bet that the ship full of radiation has something to do with all this?"

"I certainly wouldn't bet against that possibility."

Alisa leaned back in her seat again, considering their options. Over on the sensor display, she could now see the buoy that had sent the message. It was almost dead ahead. The Alliance had likely sprinkled buoys all over the perimeter of their closed-off area. Their quarantined area. An interesting word choice. To Alisa's mind, it implied a virus or bacterial emergency rather than a radiation leak, but she supposed she could see the word being used for both.

"I vote for obeying the warning and not going in," Mica said. "Just in case you're taking votes and listening to pragmatism today."

"I'd like to. There's nothing for me at those coordinates. I—"

A thunk sounded as someone knocked on the hatch to NavCom. Alisa turned, wishing she had locked it. Abelardus's long, thin braids were visible through the window.

Alisa draped her arm over the back of the chair and waited expectantly. She wasn't surprised he had shown up, but she did not know if he had somehow sensed the buoy warning coming in or if he had been sifting through her thoughts and knew she had been reading his comm messages.

Abelardus walked in, considered her briefly, then gazed at the view screen. The forward camera feed was displaying on it, but nothing except stars was visible out there yet. He would have to look at the sensor display to eyeball the buoy.

"Got lonely by yourself in your cabin, huh?" Alisa asked.

"Incredibly so," he said. "The ship received a message."

"I believe the correct term is *warning*. In about a half hour, I'll have to turn us onto a new course, or we'll be violating a quarantine that the Alliance set up. The coordinates you all are eager to explore are inside of the quarantined area. I figure we can go to Cleon Moon and look for your brother first, and then come back here in a week or two. Maybe the quarantine will have been lifted."

It sounded perfectly reasonable to her, but she was not surprised that Abelardus started shaking his head before she finished speaking.

"We can't delay," Abelardus said.

"Who's talking about delays?" came Alejandro's voice from the corridor.

Alisa sighed toward Mica. "I can understand how a Starseer would know when we've received a message or something interesting is going on, but how does a simple doctor always know to show up at the right time?" Or maybe it was the wrong time.

"Maybe his orb tells him," Mica said.

"They do have a close relationship."

"They probably watch romance vids together."

"Ew."

Abelardus stepped aside to let Alejandro walk in, a scowl on his face. "What delay?"

Leonidas came into view behind him, stopping in the corridor since there wasn't room for anyone else to squeeze into NavCom. As it was, Alisa felt claustrophobic. She also felt that large, powerful men were about to force her into making a foolish choice.

"Your coordinates are quarantined," Alisa said tersely, not wanting to explain everything again.

"By whom?" Alejandro asked.

"The Alliance." Abelardus smirked at him, as if pleased by the development. That was odd. He had claimed to be an Alliance supporter, but wouldn't he still object to the military getting their hands on the special staff first? Surely, he would prefer that it return to Starseer hands. Alisa had assumed that was why Lady Naidoo had sent him along. Maybe he was just pleased to see Alejandro's plans thwarted. He certainly seemed to take pleasure in tormenting Leonidas.

"How would the Alliance have learned about the coordinates that we figured out?" Alejandro asked, his voice hard. His gaze landed on Alisa.

Hells, she wasn't the one smirking at him. "Why do you always look at me? Why do you think I care about your orb quest? I have my own mission, and it has nothing to do with artifact hunts."

"You would be pleased to see us fail," Alejandro said, "and for the staff to fall into the hands of the Alliance."

"Based on what I've heard, I don't think that staff should be in any-body's hands."

"That's not your decision to make, *freighter* captain."

Alisa gave him the twisted fingers. She refused to be cowed or dismissed, as if being a retired doctor was so much more important than running cargo. People *needed* cargo. They didn't need retired bullies.

Leonidas eased closer, his broad form filling the hatchway. He stood right behind Alejandro and must have bumped him, because Alejandro looked back. Abelardus noticed Leonidas, and his smirk turned into a lip curl.

"I'm not taking us into a quarantined area," Alisa said. "Here, listen to the message, especially the part about ships being disabled or destroyed if they're found in the zone."

She played it for them, standing with her arms crossed, leaning against the console as she did so.

"That's a huge amount of space," Alejandro said at the end. "The Alliance doesn't have ships to patrol anything a tenth of that size. The odds of them finding us and destroying anything are minuscule."

"They have sensors and might even have set up a sensor grid in there with their buoys," Alisa said. "Besides, they wouldn't need to patrol the whole area. If they know about the coordinates, they could have their ships waiting right there."

"Why are you sure they know about the coordinates?" Alejandro growled. "What do you know?"

"I don't *know* anything. But clearly people are aware of them. That pilgrim ship went right through them. Maybe you should argue with our newest passenger instead of with me," Alisa said, waving at Abelardus. "He's the one who could telepathically broadcast the coordinates to the entire system."

"My range isn't quite that large," Abelardus said.

Alejandro studied him, but he did not start an argument. Instead, he asked, "Can you see inside her mind? See if she's telling the truth?"

Alisa clenched a fist. The last thing she needed was for those two to become allies and start working together.

"Of course," Abelardus said brightly. "I like spending time in her head. She's feisty."

"I may vomit again," Mica grumbled.

Leonidas glared at Abelardus.

Alisa also felt like throwing up. Perhaps on Abelardus's boots. Feisty. Please.

He grinned over at her.

"Is she telling the *truth*?" Alejandro asked again. Apparently, her feistiness did not interest him.

"She hasn't been in contact with anyone from the Alliance since the battle above our temple," Abelardus said, sounding certain.

It was the truth, but his certainty and the prompt way he answered disturbed Alisa. Had he searched through her thoughts that quickly? Or had he been monitoring them since they left? That would be creepy, for more reasons than one. She wanted to get rid of him as quickly as possible and almost regretted that the quarantine might delay things.

Or you could just get used to having me around, Abelardus spoke into her mind. *I'm not that bad. I'm handy. I can get things off high shelves for you, if not with my hands, then with my mind.*

Get out of my head.

"Then who blabbed?" Leonidas asked, speaking for the first time. "Neither the doctor nor I told the coordinates to anyone outside of this ship. In fact, Alisa is the only one I gave them to. Isn't it odd that you know all about them, Abelardus?"

"You call her Alisa?" Abelardus asked.

Leonidas hesitated. "She asked me to."

May I call you Alisa? Abelardus asked into her mind, as if he hadn't done it already. Maybe he knew that he didn't have permission and that it irritated her.

No.

Why couldn't he take a hint and keep out of her thoughts? He was so damned brazen about his intrusion, too, giving no hint that he considered forcing his way into a person's mind rude—or criminal.

A strange, wistful expression crossed his face.

"Answer the question, Abelardus." Leonidas nudged Alejandro aside so that he could ease into the cabin, even though there wasn't room for it. He stood very close to Abelardus, who merely looked back at him, showing no sign of intimidation.

Alisa hoped they did not end up in a physical—or mental—fight. She did not want bodies flung into her consoles, where equipment might be broken. Nor did she want *people* broken.

"You think I'm going to let the empire have the Staff of Lore, mech? Are you truly that stupid? Both of you?" Abelardus looked back and forth from Leonidas to Alejandro.

Both men looked like they wanted to strangle him. Leonidas's fingers twitched, as if he was seriously considering it.

"What are the odds of me making it out of here to use the lav without getting smashed?" Mica asked Alisa.

"I don't know, but while they're posturing at each other, I'm changing our course," Alisa said. "I have no intention of getting destroyed by an Alliance ship because we crossed into their quarantined area."

She shifted toward the controls, though she left her head turned enough to keep Alejandro and Abelardus in her peripheral vision. It made her back itch to have them behind her.

Abelardus reached for her shoulder. "Do not—"

Leonidas lunged and caught his wrist before he touched her.

"*Don't* bother her," he growled.

"I'm not *bothering* her," Abelardus said. The hells he wasn't. "But we *are* going to those coordinates."

Leonidas's response was silence. Or maybe he and Abelardus were communicating mentally. Both men glared at each other, their faces less than a foot apart, intense concentration in their eyes. Was Abelardus launching some mental attack? Was Leonidas applying pressure to Abelardus's wrist? Alisa had no doubt he could break bones with his grip, if not grind them to a powder. And she was starting to feel extremely nervous about having the two men so close to her, the tension between them palpable in the air. Maybe she and Mica should *both* sneak out to use the lav.

Instead, Alisa deliberately and determinedly punched in a new course. She would not be cowed, not on her own ship.

"Leonidas," Alejandro said quietly, "you're grabbing the wrong person's wrist. We have to investigate those coordinates immediately, before any more ships get there. Before the Alliance gets there. From all my research, I was led to believe the orb would be crucial in acquiring the staff, but if there's a way to circumvent it…we can't let the Alliance try. This is too important. It's not just my mission and his dying request; it's our *only* chance to regain what we had. Without it, we don't have the resources, and it could be generations before we're able to rebuild and reestablish ourselves."

Neither Leonidas nor Abelardus was looking at him. Maybe neither man even heard him. They seemed to be locked in a silent battle.

Abelardus was the one to finally break. He gasped and dropped to his knees, turning his body and grabbing at the hand locked around his wrist. Leonidas released him and pushed him away from the pilot's seat, from *Alisa*. He put his back to her, but he stood close enough that she could almost feel the heat from his body. He glared at Abelardus, and he also glared at Alejandro.

Alisa had wanted him as a bodyguard, as an employee, but this was not how she had imagined it. She wasn't even positive that was what he was doing. Was he guarding her so nobody could force her to change course? Or had he just not wanted Abelardus touching her?

Her hands shook slightly as she finished laying in the new course, one that would skirt the quarantined area and take them toward Cleon Moon.

"Leonidas…" Alejandro said, watching him and also watching Alisa work. "We have to get there as soon as possible."

Abelardus pushed himself to his feet, massaging his wrist as he stood shoulder to shoulder with Alejandro. "I agree. What those people on that ship found, it's the tip of the iceberg. I don't know how it's possible, but the staff may very well be waiting for us."

Leonidas shrugged. "Convince her then. With words," he added, his voice hard as he glared at Abelardus.

Alisa exchanged a bleak look with Mica. She did not want to be *convinced*, with words or anything else. While she appreciated Leonidas stepping in and keeping Abelardus from forcing her to change course, she could not allow herself to forget that he was not on her side, not in this.

"I have better range than this primitive freighter's sensors," Abelardus said, tapping the side of his head. "I can warn her if there are ships in our path or heading in our direction, and Captain Marchenko could fly us out of their range before they sense us. If they somehow got close, I could get into the heads of their bridge crew, whoever's monitoring sensors, and make him believe he doesn't see us."

"What if there's a lot more radiation up ahead?" Mica asked. "We don't have the equipment for dealing with it."

Technically, the *Nomad* could warn them if the radiation levels were dangerously high outside—Alisa had seen that alert when dealing with the pilgrim ship—but she didn't see the point of going into the quarantine zone at all if they wouldn't be able to get close.

"We'll at least know what we're dealing with," Abelardus said. "And *who* we're dealing with. Plus, if there are Alliance ships in there, already properly equipped, we can take what we need from them."

"Oh yes, stealing from the Alliance," Alisa said. "You're really sweet-talking me into helping you now."

"I'm saying that we can find a way to handle any obstacles we cross," Abelardus said. "There's no reason to turn away."

Then why could Alisa think of a dozen reasons without trying?

You have a fecund mind, Abelardus announced into her head.

She sighed. Why wouldn't he leave her alone?

"Alisa," Leonidas said, turning enough that he could look down at her.

She studied the controls and avoided meeting his eyes, a premonition making her stomach flutter with nerves. The others might not convince her, not with words, but if Leonidas asked, it would be different. It would be much harder to say no.

She took a deep breath to brace herself. She *had* to say no. This was a foolish mission, one that could keep her from ever finding Jelena, from even living through to the end of the week.

"Help us with this," he said quietly, his words for her and not the others, "and I'll accept your job offer when we're done. I'll work for you, and I'll do my best to help you find her." He looked like he wanted to say more, but he glanced toward the others and shut his mouth.

It did not matter. It was enough.

Alisa closed her eyes.

All along, she had been eager to have Alejandro and his orb leave her ship, but she had deeply regretted the idea of Leonidas walking away with him, of her never seeing him again. If he hired on, he wouldn't leave, no matter what Alejandro planned for the remnants of the empire. And even if Alejandro somehow got this staff, could he manage to do anything else without Leonidas's help? Already, Leonidas had saved his life several times. If Leonidas was here, he wouldn't be helping rebuild the empire. And more than that, he would be with her, on her ship. How much safer would she and Jelena be out in the freight lanes with an elite cyborg soldier to protect them? A thousand times safer. And more than that...she wanted him here for non-practical reasons. Because she liked him. Because she could see *more* than liking him, if he ever indicated that he was interested in that.

He touched the side of her head, fingers brushing along her hair. It was the lightest touch, but it raised gooseflesh all over her body.

"Damn it, Leonidas." She thumped a fist down on her console, and he pulled his hand back.

A hurt expression flashed through his eyes. She wanted to kiss him, to let him know she was frustrated with the situation, not with him, or at least mostly not with him. But she was well aware of Abelardus and Alejandro staring at them.

All she did was drop her hands onto the controls and reprogram the course again.

"Doctor, give our Starseer guest some caffeine pills," Alisa said. "He doesn't get to sleep until we're out of this quarantine zone. I want to know *well* in advance if any ships are coming our way."

"I can do that," Alejandro said, the relief clear in his voice as he walked out of NavCom.

"I don't need drugs to stay awake," Abelardus said. "I'm an evolved human being."

"Take your evolved ass to your cabin. I don't want to see you unless it's to warn me about trouble."

"As you wish." Abelardus offered that bow again, then strode out.

"I'm sorry, Alisa," Leonidas said softly when the two men were gone.

"For manipulating me or for being on the doctor's side?" She tried not to sound bitter.

A big part of her knew she should change the course back to Cleon as soon as they all left NavCom. But she also knew she would not do it.

"Yes," he said, touched her shoulder lightly, then walked out.

"You better be telling the truth about coming to work for me, Leonidas," Alisa called after him. She lowered her voice to add, "And we better not both be irradiated before it can happen."

"I am," he called back.

"Sure he is. He'll probably only work for me for two weeks before sending his résumé out all over the rest of the system." Alisa looked over at Mica, expecting a comment about résumés.

Mica had her head in her hand and looked utterly dejected.

"You think we're in trouble, you say?" Alisa asked.

"I knew we were in trouble as soon as he touched your hair." Mica lifted her head, her face aggrieved. "Damn it, Captain. Can't you ever make the choice that's more likely to preserve your own ass? And the asses of your crew? Do you really think we're going to survive this? If the radiation doesn't kill us, the Alliance will."

Mica pushed herself to her feet and stalked out of NavCom.

"Optimistic as always," Alisa murmured, staring at the view screen ahead.

She reached up and touched the stuffed spider hanging over the co-pilot's seat, feeling the need for luck. She prayed that Mica would be proven wrong, but a queasy feeling settled in her stomach as the warning buoy came into view and the *Star Nomad* sailed past it.

CHAPTER SIX

Alisa knew she should get some sleep, especially given the challenges that may lie ahead, but she found herself heading to the mess hall instead of to the lav to sani her teeth. Too many thoughts were spinning through her mind, and she doubted she would do anything but stare at the ceiling if she went to her bunk now.

She was not the only one awake. Leonidas's hatch stood ajar, light slashing out into the night-dimmed corridor. She stopped a few paces away. It almost seemed like an invitation, but did she want to take it? She missed having someone to lean against, to sit with on the sofa or in bed while reading or watching a vid. It had been so long since she had that normalcy in her life.

But if she went in to see Leonidas, they would only end up talking about this suicidal mission. And she wasn't that happy with him right now. He had finally agreed to what she'd wanted for weeks, but he'd done it to manipulate her. He had been open about it, not trying to be sly, but it was what it was.

"I don't understand," a voice said from inside the cabin, not Leonidas's.

It was Alejandro, and Alisa's lip curled of its own accord.

"Even if we find the staff there," Alejandro went on, "which seems like wishful thinking, that's only the beginning of things, not the end. You can't simply go off to be a bodyguard on some insignificant freighter. We have to find the boy after that, and teach him, make him worthy of his destiny, of the millions—billions—who will follow him. Just because he has the staff—"

"Doctor," Leonidas said, sounding weary, "that's your quest, not mine."

"You're an imperial officer!"

"I *was* an imperial officer. It's been eight months since anyone deposited money in my account."

"I don't believe for a second that you wore that uniform because of the money. You risked your life every day for the empire, for the *emperor*. And you told me you risked your life for the boy too."

"Yes, I did, and I don't regret it," Leonidas said, his voice becoming clearer, as if he had turned toward the hatch.

Did he know Alisa was standing out there? Had he heard her walking through the corridor? She wouldn't be surprised. Maybe she should continue past, pretend she hadn't heard anything, but the hatch was open enough that he would see her go by if he was facing it. And besides, they could have closed it if they wanted a private conversation. This time, the eavesdropping wasn't her fault.

"But my twenty years came up last year, Doctor."

"So, I'd been thinking about retiring. It was the war that kept me from seriously contemplating it then, but now…"

The war? Leonidas had admitted to Alisa before that he didn't know what he would do with himself if he retired. That fighting was all he knew. No, that wasn't entirely true. Back on Arkadius, he had been about to admit that there was something else he would consider doing, but they had been interrupted before he could tell her what it was. They hadn't had many moments alone since then, many moments when he might have resumed that conversation.

"Now, your services are needed even more," Alejandro said.

Alejandro made a disgusted huff. "Is this really about retirement? Wouldn't you be bored plodding through the system in a freighter?"

"I haven't been so far," Leonidas said dryly.

"Are you sure this isn't just about you wanting to run around the galaxy, rutting with abandon?"

"You know that's not what I want," Leonidas said, the lightness gone from his voice.

"If you just want kids, there are other ways. There are—"

A hatch opened behind Alisa. She jumped and spun, torn between hustling back to her cabin and continuing down the corridor. Was Leonidas still turned toward the hatchway?

Yumi stepped out carrying a lit candle in a holder. "Greetings, Captain," she said cheerfully.

Alisa grimaced. Well, if the two men hadn't known she was skulking in the corridor before, they would now.

"Yumi," Alisa said, "it took you long enough. I thought we were getting a snack."

"Uhm?" Yumi gave her a quizzical look.

Before she could say more, Alisa took her arm and guided her past Leonidas's hatchway without looking in.

"I didn't realize you were waiting for me, Captain," Yumi said as they continued toward the mess.

Alisa's grimaced deepened, since she was sure Leonidas and his enhanced ears would hear the words.

"Did Mica tell you that I'm going to perform a group prayer and meditation session in the mess hall?" Yumi went on. "You are, of course, welcome to join us."

"It does seem like it would be a good time to pray," Alisa said as they walked into the mess.

The lights were on, and a couple of plates sat on the table. Beck stood with his head in the refrigerator, humming to himself as he inspected his options. He wore baggy plaid trousers and fuzzy slippers that almost matched the shag carpet in the rec room. Oddly, he also wore gloves. Alisa hadn't seen him bother with such sanitary methods when preparing food before.

"Oh, Tommy," Yumi said, "are you also going to join in the group prayer and meditation session? You'll find it a relaxing way to unwind before bed."

Beck turned, a miso jar in hand. "Er?"

Yumi set her candle on the table. "Just let me go check on my chickens. I've been worried about them due to the radiation exposure. I convinced the doctor to modify his cocktail for them."

"I bet that was fun," Beck said.

"He grumbled about not being a vet, but he did supply me with something."

As Yumi continued through the mess hall and toward the cargo hold, Alisa slid into the table, hoping Beck would share whatever he was making if she looked hungry enough.

"Are you shedding?" Beck asked.

"Pardon?" Alisa asked.

He held up his gloved hand. "It's like I have a sunburn that's peeling. I'm not sure whether to blame the radiation or Doc's medicine."

"The radiation, I think." Alisa hadn't experienced any skin issues. Only the side effects from Alejandro's "cocktail." If she had known about her special blood before, she would have passed on that treatment.

"Hope the chickens aren't shedding," Beck said. "Or de-feathering. They're homely enough as they are. They'd look funny without feathers."

"They're not so homely that you object to eating their eggs." Alisa frowned. "We may want to pass on that for a while."

"Seems smart." Beck pulled out some sliced meat and a knife, which he flipped and caught a few times without cutting himself. "Something on your mind, Captain?"

Everything.

"Why do you ask?" Alisa resisted the urge to glance back toward Leonidas's cabin.

"You don't usually show up for Yumi's meditation sessions."

"Do you?"

"Me and Mica do sometimes, though I prefer it when it's just me and Yumi." He gave her a wink, though his expression soon turned sour. "Last night, the Starseer showed up too. That was intolerable."

"Is he not a skilled meditator?"

"That's all he wanted to do. He got cranky with me when I asked Yumi questions. He said people aren't supposed to talk when they meditate."

Maybe Alisa would tell Abelardus she was meditating the next time he spoke into her head.

"But since we haven't started yet, you can talk if you want to," Beck offered. "I'm making a sandwich. Want one?"

"Yes, please. Do I look like I need to talk?"

"Well, maybe. I heard what happened in NavCom. Wish you'd called me up there when they were all trying to bully you into changing course. I was working out and didn't know anything was going on."

"I don't think anyone else would have fit in NavCom."

"If you don't want to go on this diversion, just let me know." He waved his knife, then sighted down it, as if it were a gun. "We'll lock you in NavCom, and I'll stand outside the hatch and deal with anyone who tries to come force you to go where you don't want to go."

"You'll deal with Leonidas and Abelardus?"

"Absolutely. They both eat my food, you know. I can do dire things to them, if not with poison, then with some undercooked meat. How're they going to make you change course when they're doubled over in the lav for hours with crippling—"

"Thank you," Alisa said, flinging up a hand to stop the imagery. "I'll keep your offer in mind. Though I do think Leonidas's enhanced taste buds might warn him when he's in danger of…being crippled."

"What about the Starseer?"

"I'm not sure. I'd settle for being able to keep him out of my head. I wish I knew some Starseer tricks myself for that."

Alisa remembered Yumi mentioning some drugs she had that supposedly made it hard for a Starseer to see a person's thoughts. Should she ask for some of those? She could see a time coming when it would be useful to keep Abelardus from rummaging in her mind. Too bad she had some busted genes but not actual Starseer skills. It would have been helpful to have the mental powers to block him from intruding.

"Then you'd be one of those freaks," Beck said with distaste, spreading miso on slices of bread.

Alisa winced. Of course, he had no idea that she had recently been put into the freak category. And he knew little of Jelena, certainly not that she had developed Starseer powers. Alisa could not blame him for talking that way. After all, he still called Leonidas a mech. Beck did not have the smoothest tongue.

"Would it matter if I was?" she asked, not sure why the words slipped out.

"Guess that would depend on if you were wearing one of those robes and hurling people around the room with your mind."

"Right, I doubt I would do that." She forced a smile, but this conversation had given her new matters to worry about.

Would other people's perceptions of her change if they knew? Would *Leonidas's*? He hated Starseers, and given the way Abelardus treated him, and the way the people in the temple had treated him, how could he not? Further, one had been responsible for unleashing those bears on the research station, thus killing the one man he'd hoped would help him. If he found out about her blood, would he think less of her? And what about Jelena? Since he had agreed to work on the freighter, once Alisa found her, he was sure to notice Jelena floating dishes around the mess hall with her mind.

She had imagined the two of them meeting before, even told Leonidas that Jelena would probably like him because she adored the cartoon character Andromeda Android, but she hadn't considered his loathing for Starseers. And what did Jelena think of cyborgs? Was Durant even now indoctrinating her to think like a Starseer? To share their prejudices?

"You don't look so good, Captain," Beck said, pushing a sandwich on a plate toward her. "Probably that radiation. Why don't you get some rest?"

"I believe I will." She picked up the plate. "Thank you."

"We'll find your girl, Captain. Don't you worry."

She had started toward the crew cabins, but she paused to look back at him. "I…Did I tell you about that?" She couldn't remember now who she had shared the details of her mission with, but she thought she had been keeping it private from most people.

He shrugged. "Things get around. I just wanted to let you know that I'm your man if you need help. And kids love me."

"Because of your boyish personality?"

"Nah, because I can make yummy sweets."

"On the grill?"

"Sure. Just need to get some fresh ingredients, and I can do amazing things. Maple-cinnamon bacon on a stick. Grilled peaches with a sweet bourbon glaze. Give me a pot, and I can even melt chocolate and grill up some bananas for dipping."

"Chocolate?" Alisa was suddenly disappointed that all she had to take back to her cabin was a sandwich. "It won't just be kids that love you, Beck. Hells, I might even marry you for some bananas dipped in chocolate."

He saluted her with his knife.

Alisa grinned, turned toward the corridor, and almost crashed into a muscular chest. Her plate *did* bump into it, and her sandwich teetered, threatening to pitch to the deck. Leonidas caught it before it slid off and stepped back. He raised a single eyebrow. Alisa hoped he hadn't heard the part where Beck had threatened to serve him undercooked meat. She also hoped he wasn't angry that she had inadvertently heard some of his conversation with Alejandro.

"Sorry," she said. "I wasn't looking."

"My fault," he said, stepping aside. He did not appear to be angry. "I wasn't ready for sleep," he offered.

"I wasn't, either. I was afraid I'd have bad dreams after everything."

"Yes." His eyes grew sad as he gazed down at her, and she wondered if he regretted that bit of manipulation he had plied on her. Or did he even realize he had done it? Men could be oblivious at times. Even Jonah, who'd had a poet's soul, hadn't always been cognizant of his social blunders.

Something in his expression tugged at her heart, though, and she almost asked him if he wanted to join her in her cabin to watch a vid. What did he enjoy for entertainment? War stories? That seemed too gruesome for bedtime relaxing. Maybe they could find something light and comedic.

"You want a sandwich, mech?" Beck asked. "Or to taste the chutney I'm working on? You and your enhanced tongue?"

"An enhanced tongue?" Mica asked, coming into the mess hall from the opposite side. She must have been working late in engineering. Alisa hoped there weren't any problems brewing down there. "Sounds like a handy thing to have." Though her visage remained as dour as it had been earlier, she did manage a bit of a leer in Alisa's direction.

Alisa blushed, waved goodnight to them all, and headed toward the cabins. She regretted not asking Leonidas to come with her, but felt shy with so many witnesses. Besides, her earlier thoughts still percolated in her mind, her concern that Leonidas would find it distasteful when he found out about Jelena's talents.

She headed toward her cabin, but paused before going in, her gaze drawn to the next one up the corridor and on the opposite side. The hatch lay in shadows, the night-dimmed lighting even dimmer at the end of the corridor. Her mother's cabin. It had been locked when Alisa had recovered the *Nomad* from the junk cave, and she had left it that way. Besides, the junkyard owner had probably removed and sold all of her personal belongings. He'd left items such as the stuffed spider hanging in NavCom, but nothing of value remained.

Still, for the first time since retrieving the *Nomad*, Alisa found herself curious about the contents. More specifically, for the first time in more than twenty years, she found herself curious about her *father*. Would there be anything left in there that might identify him? Her mother had always implied that she'd barely known his name and that she hadn't kept in touch over the years. Was that the truth? Or had there been a reason she hadn't told her only daughter more details? Alisa had never found the circumstances of her birth that mysterious as a girl, but Abelardus's words returned to her mind, the way he had pointed out that accidental pregnancies weren't that common and that her mother might have tampered with her implant to make it happen. Had she? And if so, why? Wanting a child was understandable, but wanting some random stranger on a space station to be the father? That did seem odd.

Alisa grasped the latch, even though she knew it wouldn't open and she would have to press her hand to the palm reader on the computer override. But the latch turned. She stopped and stared at it, shocked. The hatch was unlocked? Why?

She remembered checking that hatch when she first took over *Nomad*, before Mica had gotten it repaired enough to lift off from the junk cave. It had definitely been locked then. She was the only one programmed into the computer system to be able to override the locks on the passenger and crew cabins. And she knew she hadn't opened it.

She finished turning the latch and pushed inward. It was dark inside, and the cabin smelled dusty and disused. As it should. She walked inside, and the integrated lights flickered a few times before coming on. The cabin, the *captain's* cabin, was a little larger than hers, but there was still only one room, and it only took her a couple of steps to stand in the middle. She set her plate down on the bed and looked around slowly, trying to detect if someone had been in there recently.

The floor was bare—her mother had stripped out the orange carpet that had been in there during Alisa's youth—and the fur rugs that had replaced it had been taken. Items of value, apparently. A fold-down desk identical to Alisa's was tucked into the wall, making the space seem large. A couple of blankets lay on the mattress, and a pillow slumped at one end. A few tattered and yellowed books hunkered on shelves built into the wall, a glass protector in place to keep them from flying out during a rough landing—or an attack. Alisa remembered that a jewelry box and some keepsakes had also been on those shelves in her youth. They were gone now.

Though she did not expect to find a diary or anything that helpful, she walked over and lifted the glass protector. It did not fit well, and dust had made its way inside. Alisa froze, staring at it. The dust on the shelves had been disturbed. Recently. It looked like someone had reached in and patted around with their fingers.

"What the—?" she muttered, looking toward the corridor and then toward the old books.

She pulled them out and flipped through them. A bookmark fell out, but nothing more interesting. No notes to old lovers. Alisa lowered the glass and opened the rusted metal doors of a built-in armoire. Several dusty garments hung inside, including a baggy blue sweater with a large slouchy neckline. Unanticipated emotion thickened Alisa's throat as she looked at it, remembering how often her mother had worn it, the way she'd often said, "We're a long ways from anywhere, so we can't waste energy on heat. Go put on a sweater if you're cold."

She touched the sleeve, running her hand down it, blinking away tears and an intense sense of loneliness that came over her. Her ship was full of people, but they were people she'd only known a short time. She missed her family, missed having people that she shared history and memories with, that she loved. Jonah, Jelena, Mom. Everyone. She regretted that her mother had barely gotten to know her granddaughter before the accident had taken her life.

Her chin dropped to her chest. Even with tears blurring her vision, she spotted dust on the bottom of the armoire, dust that had been disturbed.

Alisa pushed aside her feelings, using the new mystery to avoid dealing with the disappointment that her life had become.

Had Leonidas searched this cabin, and perhaps all of them, when he had first come aboard the *Nomad*, intending to fix it up and claim it for his own mission?

She crouched to look more closely. As with the shelves, the disturbed dust was recent. There hadn't been time for it to fill back in. It looked like someone had been in here within the last few days, not a month or two earlier.

Mica could have figured out a way to override the locks if she'd been determined, but why would she care about Alisa's mother's cabin? Leonidas could have forced his way into a locked hatch, but that would have left a broken mechanism behind. And again, why would he have snooped? No, there was only one person who came to mind, one person who hadn't been on the ship for long but who was oddly interested in Alisa, at least in her blood.

Had Abelardus used his mental powers to unlock the hatch? She could imagine him being able to do it. She was not sure why he would want to, but she could come up with a couple of guesses. Maybe he wanted to find out more about her—and her mother—to give the information to his brother. Would Durant find it useful to know Jelena's lineage for the training or whatever he had in mind for her? Or maybe Abelardus was simply curious for his own reasons. Because he liked feisty women.

Alisa shuddered inside, not wanting any of the Starseer's interest turned her way. Even if she had liked him, she wouldn't have found it flattering that his interest had only started up after he'd learned she had the right kind of genes.

"Genes that came from where?" she murmured, remembering her original reason for coming in here.

She resumed her search, patting down the pockets of the garments in the armoire. She found an old ticket stub to a gypsy show and a few hairpins, but nothing more substantial. The vault set into the wall behind the desk had been found, forced open, and—judging by the dust—cleaned out long ago. Alisa was on the verge of leaving when her gaze fell across the mattress again. The sheets were still on it, tucked around the corners, so she doubted anyone had disturbed it. She knelt and lifted it, peering into the shadows. Dust tickled her nose, and she sneezed. Another book lay near the head of the bed, and she tugged it out.

It had a yellow hardback cover with the title, *Planets and Moons*, embossed on the front in elegant script. Alisa recognized the book, remembering her mother reading it numerous times. It was supposed to be a modern retelling of *Romeo and Juliet*. Alisa had never read it, preferring adventures to romances, happy endings to tragedies.

She flipped it open to the title page and spotted a dedication. *To my exciting and wonderful Oksana. I wish our planets and moons could have aligned. Stanislav.*

"I didn't think to look under the bed," Abelardus said from the hatchway.

Alisa whirled, almost dropping the book. Abelardus leaned casually against the jamb, watching her. How long had he been there?

"You *were* here," she said, surprised he was openly admitting it. Didn't he know that you weren't supposed to confess to spying and eavesdropping on people?

"You already figured that out," he said, pushing away from the hatchway and walking inside.

Alisa itched to back up, not wanting to be anywhere close to him, but she stood her ground and glared defiantly at him. "Why were you snooping? What could possibly be in here that has anything to do with you?"

"You didn't know who your father was," he said, stopping in front of her. "I assumed the odds were better that your mother did." He offered that smirk that might be what passed for amusement from him, but it always looked smug and supercilious more than anything else.

"Why do you *care?*"

"I was curious as to your heritage, or more specifically, your daughter's heritage. At this point, I don't know if Durant is roaming the system, collecting children with Starseer abilities, or if he only took your daughter. If the latter, then there must be a reason she was singled out."

"Yeah, her father was dead and her mother was too far away to do a damned thing about it." Alisa's voice tightened as she spoke, and the last few words came out squeaky. Damn it, she was on the verge of tears again. She would not show her frustrations—her weaknesses—in front of this man.

"I'm sure he must have had a reason." Abelardus lifted a hand toward her shoulder.

She lurched away from him, the backs of her knees bumping against the bunk. What was he doing? Trying to comfort her? He was the *last* person she wanted comfort from. It also disturbed her to realize he could thwart the locks on the cabins whenever he wanted.

"A reason?" she demanded. "Such as that he's a criminal who doesn't care who he hurts?"

"That's not the reason I would have come up with, but it could be." He lowered his hand and smiled. "May I see the book?"

Her first instinct was to refuse, but it would be better if he was looking at the book than trying to touch or comfort *her*. She thrust it toward him.

"Stanislav, huh?" Abelardus asked, perusing the dedication and then flipping through the rest of the pages. "I'll have to look in our databases to see if anyone interesting comes up."

"Even if my father had Starseer genes, that doesn't mean he had any talent, right? Or that he would have had anything to do with your people. Lots of people in the system have those genes, and it doesn't mean anything. Except, apparently, that you get to live long enough to see all of your crewmates die if your ship is exposed to radiation." She thought of those poor crazy people that she had seen through Leonidas's camera.

"It doesn't necessarily mean anything," he agreed. "It's an indicator of potential, nothing more. But Durant's interest—"

"Is surely based on my *husband's* abilities. Also, I have no way of knowing that this Stanislav was my father. That book could have been given to my mother at any time during her life, maybe even after I was born. She never got married, but she wasn't a chaste hermit."

"Hm." Abelardus looked at the dedication again. "She was apparently exciting and wonderful." He grinned at her. "And feisty I bet, like her daughter."

Alisa snatched the book from his hands. "Go away. Aren't you supposed to be looking for ships? That's the deal, remember?"

He lifted his hands. "Yes, you're right. And—" He glanced toward the open hatchway.

Alisa did not see or hear anyone coming, but he lowered his voice.

"Look, I'm sorry. I know I can be cocky, and I don't bother to hide it. A lot of people are falsely modest, and it's annoying. Don't you find it to be so? I know I have a tendency to say whatever comes to mind, but don't you find that refreshing? I thought—I mean, you're sort of the same way, so I guess I thought—or I keep hoping—that you'll understand me. Or at least not hate me. I'm not trying to make your life harder. Or uncomfortable."

His words seemed honest, and Alisa did not know what to say. She didn't like him, and she didn't want to soften her stance toward him or give him any indication that she wanted him around.

"Here." He offered his hand. "Let's make a deal. I'll stay out of your head, as you've requested, and your mother's cabin, and you…"

"Yes?" She narrowed her eyes, not anticipating that he would offer her anything she would find acceptable or appealing.

"Promise not to murder my brother when we find him." He smiled. "At least until after I've spoken to him and had a chance to find out what he's up to."

Alisa kept squinting at him, feeling nothing but suspicion. She wasn't a cold-blooded killer and hadn't been planning to murder anyone—though maybe she would strangle this Durant a little—and the request seemed to come out of nowhere. They hadn't been talking about his brother.

But Abelardus stood there with his hand out, his eyes earnest. And the suns knew she would like it if he would stay out of her head…

Hoping she wouldn't regret it, she shifted the book so she could clasp his hand. He bowed his head and laid his other hand atop hers.

She was trying to decide if this was some Starseer custom or if he was simply being overly dramatic when movement in the corridor drew her eye. Leonidas looked in at them, a sandwich held in his hand. He looked at their clasped hands, blinked, and backed away.

Alisa frowned and pulled her hand away from Abelardus's, wondering how that had looked from the outside. She hoped Leonidas didn't think she was in here intentionally having private moments with Abelardus. Not that Leonidas had indicated that he wanted to have private moments with *her*. But she didn't want anyone misconstruing anything. Especially when Leonidas and Abelardus had so much animosity toward each other.

Abelardus let her go and lifted his head. His face was hard to read.

Alisa grabbed her plate off the mattress. "I need to get some sleep," she said, taking it and the book with her. "Lock the door when you leave, please. I gather that's something you can do without trouble."

She walked out, hoping she might catch Leonidas in the corridor and explain the situation. But he was gone.

CHAPTER SEVEN

A knock woke Alisa from a confusing jumble of dreams that involved her mother, a mysterious figure who might have been her father, and Leonidas. Thankfully, Abelardus hadn't been a part of them. The last thing she wanted was for him to appear in her dreams as well as on her ship.

With that thought fresh in her mind, she opened the hatch. Abelardus stood there, in nothing but trousers, his long braids dangling down his bare chest and back.

"What?" she asked casually, though she was fighting not to blush, uncomfortable at knowing he may have been reading her thoughts just then. He had said he wouldn't do that anymore, but who knew how he interpreted that deal? Maybe he believed it would be enough if he didn't speak into her mind.

"There's a ship that will come into range of your sensors soon," he said. "I don't think it'll be an issue for us, but I knew you'd want to be alerted."

"Yes, thank you. I'll head to NavCom shortly." She was in thin pajamas and wanted to change into something more substantial before roaming around the ship. She shut the hatch, hoping Abelardus would not linger. It was too early in the morning to deal with him.

Alisa dressed and slipped out into the corridor, the lights still dimmed for night. She had only slept a few hours.

"What's new?" she muttered and headed toward NavCom.

A thump came from Leonidas's cabin as she drew even with it, and she paused. More nightmares for him? She wondered if he would appreciate being woken from them. From Abelardus's warning, it did not sound like she would need Beck and Leonidas to leap into combat armor to defend the ship, but maybe she should use the possibility as an excuse to rouse him.

Or maybe she should let him get his sleep.

She started past, but another thump came from within. She bit her lip and knocked softly. If he didn't wake easily, she could leave him be.

But it was only a few seconds before the hatch opened, and a shirtless Leonidas looked out, his hair mussed and his eyes haunted, the shadows deep behind him. She wondered if anything in the waking world disturbed him as much as his dreams did.

"Sorry to bother you," Alisa said, knowing he wouldn't want to admit to his nightmares, "but we're coming up on another ship. It's probably nothing, but I'd feel safer if you were awake."

"I'll come up as soon as I dress," he said, and closed the hatch.

Alisa trotted into NavCom, relieved when nobody except the stuffed spider dangling from the ceiling awaited her. Maybe Abelardus had gone back to bed or back into his cabin to dress. The men on her ship certainly liked to sleep with their shirts off. Maybe they hoped one of the women would be overwhelmed by their muscular masculinity and jump into bed with them. Well, Abelardus might think that. She doubted Leonidas did. It might even be dangerous for someone to fall asleep next to him. What would happen if he rolled around in his dreams and thunked his bed partner with an elbow, an elbow that could, with his strength, knock a hole in a wall—or a person?

She slid into her seat. Nothing showed up on the cameras yet, but the sensors displayed not one but two ships. Nerves jangled in her stomach, and her first thought was that Abelardus had underestimated the potential trouble that lay ahead. And *ahead* was the right word. Both craft were in the *Nomad's* path. Not directly, but they would pass to the starboard side, close enough for the other ships to detect.

She tapped the console. Should she change her route to make a circle around them? Or was it too late? Had they already detected her? It wasn't as if the *Nomad's* sensors had the greatest range of any ship out there.

Leonidas slipped into NavCom. He bent to study the sensors with her.

"I can't tell yet if they're Alliance ships," Alisa said, "but they're close enough to each other to be having a heavy make-out session."

His eyebrows twitched. She expected him to ignore the silly half of the comment, but he asked, "How close would they be if it was a light make-out session?"

"Nose to nose. Right now, they're sidled up to each other, maybe with an airlock tube attached."

"They're not moving," he observed.

"No, it doesn't look like it. Maybe it's a rescue."

"Or a forced boarding."

Alisa imagined an Alliance ship taking on prisoners after disabling a nosy craft that had meandered into the quarantined area. She turned toward the controls. "I'm going to give them a wide berth, hope they're too busy with each other to notice us."

"A good idea." Leonidas sat down in the co-pilot's seat, his head brushing the spider.

As Alisa adjusted their course, a soft beep came from the sensors. A *third* ship had come into range. This one was moving, sailing along in the direction she had been about to head.

"There are a lot of ships out here for a quarantine zone," she grumbled and pulled her fingers back. The comm flashed, and she groaned. "So much for not being noticed."

One of the ships from the pairing wanted to talk.

"What do you think?" Alisa looked toward Leonidas. "Should we pretend we're all sleeping and ignore them or see what they want?"

"Are they transmitting a message?"

"Not yet."

Alisa checked the sensors again. Since they had flown closer, she could now read a few more details.

"I don't think those are warships." She sent out a ping, which the ships should automatically respond to with Alliance IDs—if they were Alliance craft. Nothing came back. "Or Alliance ships."

"That looks like a salvage tug," Leonidas said, pointing to the larger one of the pair.

"The empire has some of those in the fleet." Alisa distinctly remembered the one they had boarded near Perun's moon.

"I doubt the empire has ships this far out anymore. The other ship looks like a freighter."

Yes, a larger, newer version of the *Nomad*.

The comm flashed. The salvage tug again.

Alisa answered it. Now she was curious about what those two ships were doing out here.

"This is Captain Marchenko of the—" she started to respond.

She was interrupted.

"This is our find," a man said. "Back the hells off, or we'll blow you out of space."

"Such tough words when addressing a freighter with no weapons," Alisa said. "Do you chat up Alliance warships with that mouth? Because there's one flying around not far behind me."

Leonidas arched his eyebrows.

Alisa muted the comm. "I like to start my morning off by making jerks wet themselves if I can."

"Just stay out of our weapons' range, freighter captain, or we'll—"

She un-muted the comm. "Blow us out of space. I got it. Thanks for the tip." Alisa closed the channel. She adjusted her course slightly, to make sure the *Nomad* would not pass into the tug's weapons' range, but since that third ship lurked at the periphery of her sensor range, she did not veer far.

"Have you ever considered using more tact when addressing ships with far more firepower than yours?" Leonidas asked.

"I thought that *was* tactful. I didn't insult his mother, his intelligence, *or* mock his penis size."

"If I'm taking a job here, I'll expect you to take my advice in security matters."

"What would that advice be?"

"That we outfit this ship with weapons and find you some combat armor. Perhaps revoke your comm privileges."

"Maybe we can dress you up in your pretty red armor, put a couple of blazers in your hands, and have you record the automated response message. That might keep people from harassing the *Nomad*, especially if you're wearing your grumpy expression." She pointed to his face. "Yes, just like that."

Abelardus walked up to the hatchway, put his hands on the jamb, and frowned at Leonidas before meeting Alisa's eyes. "Any trouble?"

"Nothing I can't handle," Alisa said.

"Or exacerbate," Leonidas murmured.

"Sh," she said, smiling at him.

Abelardus's frown deepened, but all he did was push away from the jamb and disappear back down the corridor.

"Leonidas, are you a Starseer repellent?" Alisa leaned over and swatted him on the shoulder. "We need to spend more time together."

"Hm." At least he did not glower at her for presuming to swat him.

The pair of ships had come into camera range, so Alisa tapped the controls to bring them up on the view screen. They had correctly identified the salvage tug, but it lacked any markings to suggest imperial or Alliance ownership. The freighter looked like a civilian ship. Scorch marks charred large parts of the hull, and one of its thrusters had been blown off. She doubted it could even fly. Had it wandered into the quarantined area and been attacked by an Alliance patrol ship? Then been left to fend for itself? Perhaps the tug had been flying along the border of the quarantined area, looking for opportunities for salvage. Or maybe it had been the one to attack the freighter.

Either way, the tug did not move away from its prize to chase the *Nomad*. Her route ought to make it clear that she would fly past without bothering them.

"Why did you join the Alliance, Alisa?" Leonidas asked softly, looking over at her.

Her first instinct was to bristle and keep her past to herself, especially since he might be looking for a way to tell her the error of her ways, but he did not appear nosy or calculating. He had put on the T-shirt he wore under his combat armor, but he only had socks on his feet, and his hair was still tousled. He looked approachable, even friendly. Had he ever asked her about her past? She didn't think so. She hated to rebuff his interest. But she hesitated. He was loyal to the empire. Would he understand?

She bit her lip and gazed at the view screen. "It's a long story."

"I'm not leaving until we're positive that tug won't come after us."

"All right." Alisa leaned back further, pulling her knees into her chest, and resting her feet on the edge of the console. "I think I've told you that I grew up on this ship, flying around the system from place to place with my mother, picking up and delivering cargo."

Leonidas nodded.

"She made sure I kept up with schoolwork and could pass all the usual tests, but she'd always assumed that I would stay with her, share her career, keep to the stars. I enjoyed flying, but I wasn't enamored with piloting the *Nomad* around. I dreamed of going to flight school and expanding my horizons." She smiled. "That's what I used to tell my mom. I really just wanted to fly fast and shoot things."

"I can imagine."

"When I was old enough, I applied to a number of universities. Perun Capital had a mathematics and gravities undergrad degree and also a good post-grad flight school. The government recruited top graduates for the fleet."

Leonidas glanced at her in surprise. "You were thinking of joining the fleet then?"

"Where else would I get paid to fly fast and shoot things? But don't get too excited. I was also considering becoming a bounty hunter."

He snorted.

"Anyway, I went to the university there, and the classes were interesting and fun, but it was even more exciting for me because I was an only child and hadn't had many other kids around to play with when I was growing up. All of a sudden, I was surrounded by people and interesting things to do. I signed up for the forceball team, debate club, martial arts, and even a volunteer dog-walking association. I made friends, including a girl named Tamra, who became my roommate—and a close friend. We were almost like sisters. I'd never had a sister and was delighted. We weren't very similar people— she was very pretty, very likable, hardly ever abrasive and sarcastic." Alisa grinned, though she was getting to the part of the story that was painful to share, even after so many years. "She thought I'd had a terribly exotic life and always asked me about the places I'd been. She was very smart, studying to be a doctor. A good person." Her grin faded. "Around third year, some of the students in the clubs I belonged to were getting into politics and staging protests against the tyrannical oppression of the empire." She looked at Leonidas, who was listening to her but did not comment on this. "I wasn't that much of an activist, but I ended up getting involved in a peripheral way. The empire hadn't offended me personally at that point, but I did remember how hard it was for my mother to make enough to pay her taxes and pay all the tolls along the shipping lanes. I also remembered a couple of times when she had been bullied by some of the officials working in those places, harassed because she was a single woman without a burly man around to protect her. She was as mouthy as I am and could generally take care of herself, but I know there were some moments she wished I hadn't witnessed."

"Bureaucratic asses can be found in any government," Leonidas said.

"I'm sure, but the empire always seemed to have more than its fair share. But that's not what turned me into an Alliance sympathizer." She closed her eyes, remembering the campus, the idealistic young students organizing protests, certain they would change the system for the better. "There was a big protest planned that spring. We wanted free speech, something that people have fought for all throughout history and that has often been considered an unalienable human right. Something that the empire seemed to fear. I don't have to tell you that there were fines for disparaging the emperor and the government, and that people who did it repeatedly sometimes disappeared or were brainwashed and came back... different." She remembered a favorite professor, a grumpy white-haired chemist who'd said whatever came to mind, heedless of the consequences. She liked people like that.

This time, Leonidas did not argue with her. He had to have seen such things himself. Maybe as one of the empire's soldiers, he'd even gone in to grab people. Probably not, though. Alisa imagined cyborgs being reserved for trickier situations. How hard was it for an armed soldier to stalk into someone's classroom and take him away? Oh, usually, it had been campus security that had done the removals, but sometimes, if someone was believed to be dangerous, the soldiers had come.

"Tamra told me not to go to the protest," Alisa said, "that I was only a year from graduating and that I'd never get into the fleet to fly if I had a record as a dissident. She was right. I told you she was smart, didn't I? Much smarter than I. But I had friends who were going, and I wanted to support them. Also, we were all going out to drink afterward. That's what passes for priorities in school, you understand."

"I remember," he said quietly, his tone somber. Maybe he could tell what was coming.

The *Nomad* was passing the salvage tug and the wreck, and the camera zoomed in on movement. Several people were out in spacesuits, hunting for items to collect. A giant hole had been blown in the hull of the wreck's belly.

Alisa stared bleakly at it, still worried the same fate could befall the *Nomad* in the quarantine zone.

Leonidas looked over at her, so she made herself pick up the story again. She always dreaded telling this part.

"So, I went to the protest. The turnout was huge, students with signs, face paint, wild clothes, hover bots screaming our message. We took over the entire campus and walked out into the streets, created traffic jams. Spy boxes floated thick in the air above us, recording our movements, but we thought we were invincible since there were so many of us. They'd never be able to arrest us all, and the news cameras were recording. We thought we were getting our message out." Alisa shifted in her seat, eyeing her feet. "Tamra ran up out of nowhere and found me. She grabbed my arm and said that I had to get out of there, that she'd been watching the news and that the fleet was being sent in to stop everything.

"I didn't truly think we were in any danger—I figured, at most, they might gas us—but I let her lead me out of the middle of it. I didn't truly want *protester* on my record, not since I was still thinking of becoming an officer and flying for the fleet then. Well, just as we got to the edge of the crowd, chaos came down on us. Drones, soldiers in shuttles and choppers, people rappelling out of the skies, as if we were enemy hordes raping and pillaging our way through the city. More troops ran in from the sides, humans, robots, armored vehicles."

Alisa paused to take a deep breath. This had happened more than ten years ago, but for some reason, these memories were much clearer than many others from back then. She recalled the scared shouts, the cries of pain, and even the smell of the horrible smoke the soldiers had launched into the crowd.

"People broke up quickly when that happened," she said, "and everyone was trying to get away. Tamra and I ran smack into a tank. Someone shouted that we had a weapon. We didn't. I think I had my backpack. That's it. I pulled on Tamra's arm to get her out of the way, but we were jammed in, couldn't run. Soldiers fired into the crowd. I kept pulling on her. I couldn't figure out why she wouldn't move." Alisa touched her chest, remembering the blood, the scorch marks, the terrified and betrayed expression on her friend's face.

Alisa cleared her throat, figuring she didn't need to spell it out for Leonidas. "She wasn't even a protester. She was a good student who never bucked authority. She only came because she was worried about me." She blinked a few times, looking toward the sensors so Leonidas would not see the moisture in her eyes. "That was the day I went from disliking some of the empire's policies but being willing to live with them to actively wanting to overthrow the government."

"A lamentable situation," he said.

She gave him a dark look. What an understatement.

"As I recall," Leonidas said slowly, "the government—and the emperor—considered that a horrible debacle. The soldiers were supposed to break it up, nothing more, but tensions were high. There had been recent terrorist attacks on Arkadius and Haywire Station. The rebellion was already growing back then."

"Know all about it, do you?" Alisa turned back toward him, not able to keep the bitterness out of her voice. Hundreds of students had been killed that day, and the emperor had considered it a horrible debacle? Gee. Everyone there had been unarmed, protesting only for the right to speak their minds. "You weren't there, were you?"

She did not remember any red combat armor—her nightmare encounters with soldiers wearing *that* had come later, after she had been flying for the Alliance.

"No, I was on a ship orbiting Arkadius. We were hunting for the bombers who tried to blow away the floating gardens in the capital."

"I would have signed up for the Alliance that day, if things had been more organized then and I'd known how. But like you said, they were just some crazy rebels back then, attacking whatever they could get close to. I've heard that what they started calling the Perun Arcade Massacre was one of the catalysts that unified people."

"Yes."

"I finished school—it was amazing and horrifying that things just went on. There was a memorial, but that was it, at least on the surface. I went to flight school, as I'd planned, but there was no way I would join the fleet after that. They even tried to get me. I didn't have the highest test scores in my class, but I was good in the cockpit. I told them to balls off. They didn't try to recruit me again. I did some tourism stuff right out of school, but I'd met and married my husband by then. We talked about having a family, so I went for the stable delivery gig. It was as boring as watching a moon spin. But it was responsible. Adult. I never forgot Tamra and the others that died that day. When someone approached me about joining what was becoming a respectable rebel force…it didn't take much convincing. It didn't hurt that I still wanted my chance to fly, to *really* fly. It was selfish, leaving Jonah and Jelena, but I thought I could make a difference too."

She checked the sensors. They had moved out of camera range of the wreck. Interestingly, the other ship she had detected, the one that had kept her from veering off to the side as far as she would have liked, had altered its path and was cutting toward the salvage tug now.

"I understand why you joined the Cyborg Corps, Leonidas," she said, having heard his story about needing money for his mother's illness, "but why did you stay? After events like that—and it's not like that's the only atrocity that occurred—didn't you ever question what you were doing? How could you remain loyal to the empire?"

"It was less about being loyal to a government and more about being loyal to a person. Governments are always problematic. The bigger and more bloated they get, the more opportunity there is for corruption, and the empire was no exception. When I met Markus—the emperor—I was probably about the age you were when you lost your friend. He chatted very candidly to my platoon in the Cyborg Corps—I was just a corporal then—and thanked us for being there and for enduring the surgery to be able to better serve. He was only a few years older than I was and had only recently lost his father to assassins. He had the responsibility of running an empire spanning more than fifty planets and moons on his shoulders. I saw him now and then over the years, more frequently when I was commanding the Corps, and he was always straight and honest with us. When things went wrong, he tried to fix them, but the throne is—was—an illusion. An illusion of power. In the early days of the empire, it was real, especially when some of those emperors had Starseer powers, but the corporations have been running things for decades, if not centuries. Markus met resistance at every turn when he tried to make real changes. Many of the men around him had been placed there by his father's regime, and they were puppets with strings, owned by money. I know one of his regrets in the end was that he sometimes let them pull his strings, too, that he gave up ground in exchange for small victories. When his sons showed Starseer powers, first the eldest and then the youngest, he hoped that might be what would allow his family to finally turn things around, to have real power that could fight back against financial power."

Leonidas waved his hand. "I know, this isn't the story you asked for, but the answer to your question is that sometimes all options are unpalatable, all you can do is choose the lesser of two evils and try to be the voice of reason within a system that isn't always reasonable. If there's nobody left on the inside that cares, then the fall into atrocity is swift and horrible. To *not* support Markus would have been unthinkable."

"The Alliance isn't—wasn't—an unpalatable option," Alisa said sturdily, even as she felt surprised that Leonidas had been close enough to the emperor to speak of him by first name.

"Yes, it is. Your revolution destroyed the infrastructure of the entire system, and if you think those same corporations don't have their hooks in your new government, think again. In the meantime, your Alliance is just as happy to threaten people as the empire was." He waved toward the sensors. "Who do you think destroyed that ship? And for what? Because it wandered into a quarantined area? It's not like what's inside of here is a matter of interplanetary security."

"Are you sure about that?" Alisa asked, thinking of the staff that Abelardus had described. And then there was that radiation. What if more affected ships flew out of the quarantined area? What if the pilgrim ship had reached Primus 7?

Before Leonidas answered, the comm light flashed.

Another check of the sensors showed that the new ship had made good time and had already joined the other two. Alisa did not know if they were allies or competitors and didn't much care, so long as they were occupied with each other and continued to ignore her.

"Yes?" she asked, answering the comm. It came from the salvage tug, the same as before. She braced herself for some dire ultimatum.

"We need help," the voice said—it was the same person who had threatened to blow up the *Nomad* earlier.

"Really."

"We'll split half our salvage with you. Just get this other ship off us."

Alisa frowned over at Leonidas. "Does he realize we don't have weapons?"

"Perhaps not."

"Please, to anyone who can hear this," the voice shouted. "Send help. We—" The message broke off as an explosion sounded in the background. Someone screamed. A woman.

Alisa looked at her sensor display. "The new ship is firing on them," she said, stating the obvious.

"Do you want to do anything about it?" Leonidas asked.

"Like what? It would take us twenty minutes to get back over there, and we don't have anything to throw at them. You wouldn't be able to board if their shields were up, and I'm sure they are."

Leonidas spread his hand, palm up. "I don't know what we could do, but sometimes, you come up with interesting schemes."

"Schemes. Please. The only scheme I want to enact right now is the one where we wake up Mica so she can try to get us more power from the engines."

"Very well."

She scowled at him. He hadn't said anything condemning, but why did she have the sense that he wanted her to try to help? What was she supposed to do?

Alisa made a disgusted noise and tapped on the comm controls, trying to target the newcomer. "Hello, there! This is Captain Marchenko, and I just thought I'd warn you that Alliance warships have been spotted in the area. This might not be a good time for blowing up other ships in a dramatic and noticeable way."

The other ship did not answer. A few seconds passed, and the salvage tug disappeared from her sensors, leaving only a smattering of wreckage where it had been.

"Sorry," Alisa told Leonidas. "It's hard for me to come up with brilliant and sophisticated schemes before breakfast."

"Would you like me to bring you something?"

She looked over at him, half-expecting that to be sarcasm, though she wasn't sure why. But he appeared earnest in his offer. Huh. Who ever would have thought an imperial colonel would offer to fetch her breakfast?

A beep came from the sensor display. Alisa turned toward it, and her shoulders slumped.

"Forget breakfast," she said. "I think I need you to bring all of the weaponry you can muster."

The newcomer had left the wreckage and was zooming straight toward the *Nomad.*

CHAPTER EIGHT

After Leonidas left NavCom to put his armor on, Alisa commed Mica's cabin. She feared she would need brilliance from her engineer more than she needed an armed cyborg. The ship chasing them had obliterated the tug, not boarded it. And Leonidas couldn't do anything unless they ended up engaged in hand-to-hand combat with a boarding party.

"The ship better be on fire," came a groggy snarl.

"I need you up, Mica. We're being pursued."

"Not by a lustful cyborg, I suppose."

"A ship that just blew up another ship is closing the distance quickly," Alisa said.

"Fine, I'm on my way to engineering."

Alisa put the rear camera display on the view screen. It hadn't taken long for the new ship to come within visual range. A few more minutes, and it would be within firing range too. It was sophisticated and modern, with a bluish-gray, aerodynamic hull designed to hit mach speeds in a planet's atmosphere. Clearly, it had no trouble finding speed in space, either. She recognized some of the weapons attached to the hull, such as e-cannons and torpedo launchers, but there were others she could not name. The ship looked like some prototype that had come out of a secret engineering facility.

She hailed them. "Greetings, speedy ship. This is the captain of the *Star Nomad*. I see you're headed my way. We have sandwiches and coffee if you'd like to join us for breakfast. I wouldn't be surprised if my security chief could finagle a way to make waffles on his grill too. He's quite the talented chef."

She didn't expect an answer. Judging by the design, that looked like the kind of ship that would be full of arrogant jerks who did not feel compelled to respond to messages—or accept breakfast invitations.

"Greetings, *Star Nomad*," a polite voice came back to her. She could not tell if it belonged to a man or a woman. "This is Captain Echo of the *Explorer*. Breakfast is unnecessary. We have scanned you, and we believe you have a Starseer artifact aboard."

They had scanned her interior from that distance? *And* been able to pick up the orb's power signature? That was definitely a state-of-the-art ship.

"Did you?" Alisa asked. "How interesting."

"We are collecting Starseer artifacts and are prepared to offer you ten thousand tindarks for yours."

That wasn't the follow-up she had expected, especially after watching the *Explorer*—that name seemed wholly inapt for what that ship could do— blow away that tug.

"Oh? What did you offer the tug for its artifacts?" Alisa had no idea if the salvage ship had gathered any artifacts, but buying time seemed like a good idea. The *Nomad* was about six hours from Leonidas's coordinates. There *might* be an Alliance ship there, one that wanted to enforce its quarantine. If she made it there, maybe she could convince them that the *Explorer* was more of a threat than her innocuous freighter.

"The tug was unwilling to negotiate with us," Captain Echo—what kind of name was that?—said. "We were forced to pursue more ruthless methods of acquiring artifacts. My employer has assured me that these methods are acceptable and not illegal out here beyond the Alliance's sphere of influence."

"He sounds like a nice fellow."

"My employer is female."

"Even nicer. Who do you work for?"

"Does the identity of my employer factor into your willingness to sell the artifact?" Echo asked.

"It might." Alisa muted the comm. "Leonidas?" she called down the corridor. "Do you want to get Alejandro? Or Abelardus? Or whoever is holding the orb now?"

"Neither will sell it," he said, striding into view, all of his armor on except for his helmet.

"We can at least pretend to negotiate. Buy time."

"Buy time until what? Do you expect to find allies out here?"

"I expect to find Alliance ships enforcing their quarantine," Alisa said. "Whether they're allies or not is up for debate, but this Captain Echo may hesitate to blow us up in front of their noses."

Leonidas grunted and headed for the passenger cabins.

"Please inform me if you are considering my offer, Captain," Echo said.

Alisa un-muted the comm. "I've called for the owners of the artifact. I'm just flying this ship. You'll have to negotiate with them."

"Very well. You have ten minutes."

So generous. "You sure you don't want to come aboard for waffles?" Alisa asked.

"I do not require sustenance."

The clues clicked together, and Alisa realized what she was dealing with. An android.

She slumped back in her seat. With all their ahridium frameworks and gold circuitry, androids cost a fortune to build, but whoever owned that ship clearly had money to spend. As a pilot, an android would have faster reflexes than she had, and as a combatant, if it had been programmed to be one, it would have even greater strength and speed than Leonidas. She also doubted Abelardus would be able to tinker with its mind, or computer banks, or whatever androids technically had.

Leonidas returned with Alejandro and Abelardus. Alisa also glimpsed Beck in the corridor behind them.

"That's not the ship I warned you about," Abelardus said, eyeing the *Explorer* on the camera. It had settled in behind the *Nomad's* wing, well within firing range.

"It blew *up* the ship you warned me about," Alisa said. "Doctor, someone wants to buy your orb."

"It's not for sale," Alejandro promptly said.

"*I'm* the one who's holding it now," Abelardus said.

"Does that change the truth of my statement?" Alejandro asked.

"No."

"Then you two have the job of convincing that captain over there that he doesn't want it," Alisa said.

Abelardus gave her a suspicious look, but he turned and gazed at the back corner of NavCom. Maybe he was gazing through the bulkheads and in the direction of the ship. It did not take long for him to turn back around and frown.

"The captain isn't human."

"So I've gathered," Alisa said.

"Neither is his—its—crew."

"How large is the crew?" Leonidas asked.

"It's hard for me to tell—they're androids and don't register as typical life for me—but I believe there are three total. Maybe four."

"Put on your armor, Beck." Leonidas brushed past him. "I'm getting more weapons."

"And here I thought someone mentioned breakfast and waffles," Beck muttered, turning to follow Leonidas.

"Captain?" Echo asked, comming again. "Have you decided yet if you wish to accept my fair offer?"

"We're discussing what the orb is worth and if your offer is, indeed, fair," she said.

"It's under current market value, but my employer has only authorized certain amounts of payment for the artifacts we seek. I must also point out that I am authorized to use force, if necessary, to acquire the object in question. I've analyzed the capabilities of your ship. You have few alternatives, so I advise you to take my offer."

"Uh huh. And what *is* the current market value of a glowing yellow orb?"

Alejandro's lips flattened, and he reached for the comm to turn it off. Alisa blocked his hand. They should keep the android talking as long as they could, especially if the alternative was being fired upon.

"It's impossible to know what it would bring at auction," Captain Echo said, "but we estimate its value at one hundred and eighty-five thousand tindarks."

A hefty sum. Almost as much as the Alliance was willing to pay for Leonidas and information on Prince Thorian's whereabouts.

"And you're only offering us ten thousand?" Alisa asked. "Seems stingy."

"As I've explained, it's a fair offer, especially considering the alternative is to have your ship destroyed so I can pluck the artifact from your wreckage. My mission is to acquire all Starseer artifacts and return them to my employer. I will not be thwarted in this matter. I am an excellent captain."

Alisa watched Abelardus as the android spoke. His eyes were closed to slits. She hoped he was figuring out a way to sabotage that other ship. His Starseer brethren had used their minds to bring down some of the Alliance ships that had attacked their temple.

"I'm sure you are," Alisa replied. "And just out of curiosity, how much is the staff worth?"

Alejandro glared at her. "Stop giving away intel," he whispered.

"Oh, I think Captain Echo already knows about it," she said, not bothering to mute the comm. "Why else would he be out here? Why are *all* of these ships out here?"

"Because someone blabbed."

"Someone, yes." She looked at Abelardus. She ought to search through the rest of his video messages when she had time.

"I've only spoken to Lady Naidoo," he murmured.

"You do not have the staff in your possession," Captain Echo said. "I have scanned your ship thoroughly."

"But we could help you get it if we received a sufficient cut. I have a Starseer about, surely an asset that you don't claim."

"My employer has received all the information from her Starseer acquaintances that is necessary for this artifact hunt. Also, to answer your question, I estimate the value of the Staff of Lore at approximately 75.3 million tindarks on the black market."

Alisa let out a low whistle. "Not bad. What would you offer us if we got it for you?"

Alejandro scowled at her. Abelardus smiled faintly. At least someone knew she was scheming for time and hoping an opportunity to escape the *Explorer* came their way.

"Your help is not required, Captain," Echo said, his voice flat with no hint of emotion. Of course, that was always the case with androids, and it did not give Alisa a way to tell if he was intrigued or if he was simply shutting them down without considering the offer.

"Not at all?" Alisa asked. "Would you pay me for my Starseer? He could be an excellent guide for you."

Abelardus's smile faded, and he frowned at her. "Trying to get rid of me, Alisa?"

That would be a perk.

"Just trying to save my ship," she said.

"I have no need for a guide, and human frailties would be a burden as we get closer to the coordinates."

Alisa muted the comm. "It sounds like he expects more radiation."

"Something that wouldn't affect an android." Alejandro made a fist. "We can't let some money-snatching treasure hunter get there first."

Alisa was more concerned with getting there at all.

"Your time is up, Captain," Echo said. "Will you accept the offer of payment? Or will I be forced to employ less pleasant methods of acquiring the artifact?"

The defense controls beeped, informing her that several weapons were locking onto the *Nomad*. Her fingers twitched toward the button to raise the shields, but she hesitated. Raising them would be even more of an answer than speaking.

"Of course we're going to accept the payment," Alisa said, "but you can tell your employer that it's an unfair offer, and I hope she sleeps poorly at night, knowing she has androids roaming the system, threatening to blow up people's ships."

"Excellent," Echo said, "prepare to be boarded. If the artifact is not waiting as soon as we open the hatch, offensive measures will be engaged."

"We wouldn't want that."

As Alisa closed the comm, Alejandro said, "I don't care for your ruse. Assuming it *is* a ruse."

"Of course it's a ruse. If I'd just said no, our wreckage would already be strewn throughout space, just like with that other ship. This way, Abelardus, Leonidas, and Beck get to fight an android, while I...try to think of something else clever."

"*Else?*" Alejandro sneered, apparently not thinking she had thought of anything clever yet. She couldn't argue. "This isn't going to be like fighting pirates. Even Leonidas might not be a match for an android. And you said there are three of them?" he added, looking toward Abelardus.

"I believe so. Three androids and a great deal of other mobile machinery. Some of it may also be autonomous."

"Wonderful."

CHAPTER NINE

"This won't go well," Mica said.

"You're starting in with the pessimism already? They haven't even attached to our airlock yet." Alisa stood in the hatchway to engineering while Mica assembled rust bangs, corrosive explosives that could eat through combat armor along with most metal-based alloys. They *might* have some effect on an android, or so Alisa thought. Mica was dubious. Androids had synthetic skin over their frameworks, and it was much more similar to human flesh than to the casing of some machine.

"It's never too early to be pessimistic."

"Captain, should I move my chickens?" Yumi asked, coming to stand behind Alisa. She kneaded her dress in her hands as she looked back and forth from Alisa to the coop in the corner of the cargo hold.

"Androids are always logical," Alisa said. "I doubt they would have a reason to intentionally shoot chickens."

"I was thinking more of Beck and Leonidas." Yumi nodded to where the two men were suited up in their combat armor, checking weapons as they waited near the airlock hatch. "And unintentionality."

"Unintentionality?" Mica asked as she soldered the top onto a canister. "Is that a word?"

"It's like unpredictability," Yumi said, "except with a higher chance of death being the result."

"She sounds so confident when she makes things up," Alisa said. "You almost believe her."

"That's because she's a teacher," Mica said. "We trust teachers not to lead us astray. Unless unintentionality is involved."

"How can you two be so calm?" Yumi seemed to realize she was kneading her dress because she switched to smoothing it. The gesture appeared just as nervous. "I feel the need to engage in a breathing exercise. As soon as I move my chickens."

"I'll help you put them in your cabin, if you want." For good or ill, Alisa was useless at the moment. The *Explorer* had locked onto them with a grab beam, so she couldn't pilot them anywhere. "Maybe you can find something to calm your nerves in there."

"I don't think this is the time for mind-altering substances."

"No? I was hoping you might have something that would affect an android. In case the rust bangs don't work."

Yumi shook her head and jogged to the chicken coop.

A clang came from the hull outside of the airlock. The *Explorer* must be attaching to the *Nomad* with its tube.

Alisa followed Yumi, wondering why the captain did not simply spacewalk over. It wasn't as if androids needed air or warmth to operate.

"You two ready?" Alisa asked Beck and Leonidas, though it was clear that they were. As the captain, she felt that she should be doing captainly things, which meant being redundant by pestering people who knew their jobs already.

"Yes, ma'am," Beck said, slapping the side of an assault rifle.

"You should wait in NavCom with the hatch locked," Leonidas told Alisa. "You'll only be in danger down here."

Alisa resisted the urge to stick out her tongue at him. He was right, and she knew it. Besides, she could watch what was going on from up there—there were a couple of cameras in the cargo hold that she could use for observation.

"I will as soon as we move the chickens." Alisa waved to Yumi, who was trotting toward the stairs with two tucked in her arms. "You two be careful, please. That orb isn't worth dying over."

"Dr. Dominguez would disagree," Leonidas said.

"He's not down here. I think he's hiding in one of the stalls in the lav with his orb."

"He's in his cabin." Another clank came from the hull, and Leonidas touched her shoulder. "Go."

He used his command voice, and even though she was the captain, Alisa found herself obeying. Probably because it was the wisest course of action. As soon as the android realized they had no intention of giving up the orb, a firefight would erupt down here.

Alisa jogged over and pushed aside the netting on the coop so she could reach inside. The chickens did not cooperate, scurrying from her grasp. She supposed Yumi would not be amused if she suggested they let the chickens go to peck at the boots of the androids.

"Captain?" Mica said.

Alisa lunged for a chicken and missed. She inadvertently made a hole in the fencing, and another one darted out, scuttling across the deck.

"Yes?" Alisa asked, glad Yumi was on her way back down.

"Here." Mica tossed her a hand tractor, then delivered her freshly made batch of rust bangs to Beck and Leonidas, who hooked them onto the utility belts of their armor.

"Thanks." Alisa flicked on the tool and turned the hover technology onto several chickens squawking from a corner of the pen. Working like the grab beam that held the *Nomad*, it caught and restrained five of the birds, and she was able to lift them as one.

She strode for the stairs, carefully carrying her load ahead of her. Abelardus stood at the bottom, his staff in hand, and he raised an eyebrow.

"I could have done that for you if you'd asked," he said.

"I wasn't sure if there was a rule against using legendary Starseer mind powers for something as prosaic as moving chickens." She headed up the stairs, grimacing when he followed her. Shouldn't he be readying himself for battle?

"Not really. I've used them to pick the raisins off oatmeal raisin cookies before."

"Because your fingers weren't working?"

"Because my hands were dirty. And raisins are disgusting. I can't believe the first colonists brought the seeds over from Old Earth." Abelardus made himself useful by picking up the escaped chicken from the deck and floating it along after them. Yumi gathered the last two in her arms.

"Technically, they brought grape seeds with them," Alisa said. "It was a plucky colonist who decided he wanted to shrivel up the first batch of fruit grown in our new system into raisins."

"What a savage."

Alisa glanced toward Leonidas and Beck before leaving the walkway. Leonidas was watching her—or perhaps Abelardus. She gave him a firm nod, hoping he truly would be careful. An android would not be an easy opponent, and who knew how many were coming?

Another clang sounded, and Leonidas turned toward the hatch again. Beck already had his rifle pointed at it. Alisa wished she had some nice crates stacked in the hold that they could take cover behind.

Leaving the fighting to them, she dumped the chickens in Yumi's cabin, only taking a second to gawk at the other ones strutting about on her bunk and on the various planters, mushroom logs, and grow lights strewn artfully about the space. Yumi caught up with them and secured the chickens.

A *thud-clunk* came from the cargo hold. Alisa hurried into NavCom. Alejandro was already in there, sitting in the co-pilot's seat with the internal camera feeds up on the view screen. The orb box sat on the console in front of him.

"Thought you'd be under a table somewhere," Alisa said.

"I've hidden beneath this console before. It's sufficient."

"Glad to hear it." Alisa reached to close the hatch, but Abelardus and Yumi slipped inside first.

"You're not going to help Leonidas and Beck?" Alisa asked Abelardus while waving Yumi to the seat at the sensor station.

"It's easier for me to manipulate matter when I'm not in mortal danger. Besides, the mech might accidentally shoot me instead of an android."

"He wouldn't do that."

"He'd like to get rid of me."

"He still wouldn't shoot you."

"I've seen inside his mind when he's fighting someone. You haven't. He's unpredictable. Trust me—don't ever piss him off."

"I've fought alongside him. He's never unpredictable. Maybe you just irritate him in a special way."

Abelardus snorted. "Of that I have no doubt." Then he grinned. What a loon.

"They're coming in," Alejandro said.

Alisa slid into her seat to watch, wishing she could do something helpful. She checked on the grab beam. If it, for some reason, failed or became disengaged, she would happily veer them away from the *Explorer* and break their airlock tube while androids were tramping through it.

Abelardus locked the hatch door behind them. Alisa heard it but did not take her gaze from the view screen. The camera was up above the walkway, facing the cargo hatch, but the airlock hatch was also in view to one side. As Alejandro had said, it had swung open. No one had come out yet. Leonidas and Beck were not in view. She checked another camera. They were under the walkway, using the metal stairs for cover, their weapons aimed at the open hatchway.

Leonidas fired before Alisa could see anything. An instant later, something rolled out, spewing smoke. Beck opened fire. Alisa bit her lip, wishing the camera had a better angle on the inside of the airlock.

"Got it," Abelardus said.

She barely heard him, and it did not register that he was doing something until the canister lifted into the air and floated back into the airlock.

"Thanks," Alisa said.

"It won't matter. There's nobody human inside of that airlock tube. There's…not an android either. I'm fairly certain."

"Then what—"

Several drones streaked through the smoke, the miniature craft reminding Alisa of the quad-winged Strikers she had flown for the Alliance. Blazer fire erupted from under their noses as no fewer than ten of them weaved and dove through the cargo hold. They zeroed in on Beck and Leonidas immediately. They fired back, neither man appearing alarmed. Their shots were calm and accurate, Beck using his assault rifle and Leonidas wielding a pair of blazer rifles. The men struck the drones numerous times, but the speedy craft were surprisingly well armored. One took five hits before it burst into smoke and flames and went down. It skidded across the deck, banging off a bulkhead before stopping under the walkway. Beck and Leonidas paid it no attention, merely concentrating on the others.

Several more drones shot into the cargo hold, and clangs reverberated through the entire ship as something much larger came through the tube.

"I don't think the android captain believed you ever meant to sell the orb," Alejandro said, resting a possessive hand on the box.

"Androids can beat human chess masters," Yumi said. "I'm sure it weighed the odds and came properly prepared."

"So, you're saying we're unlikely to beat it with logic?" Alisa eyed the orb box, wondering if she would have to implement a plan driven by desperation rather than rationality.

One of the drones ran into a bulkhead, then pitched to the deck and lay still.

"That was me," Abelardus said. "I think I've got them figured out now. I'll work on the others."

Several more exploded under Leonidas's and Beck's fire, but another squadron of them zipped into the cargo hold. A miniature tank with armored treads and a hulking, armored body rolled in after them. It looked like it had been specifically designed to fit through an airlock tube. Two artillery guns protruded from the front of it, and the barrels swung to point at the stairs.

"Shit," Alisa said. "That's going to wreck our people. *And* my cargo hold." Three suns, they could end up with a hole in the side of the ship if that thing started firing rounds. "Abelardus, you figure out how to stop that thing, and I'll have Beck make you something special."

"I'd rather have something special from you."

"I can't cook."

"A kiss would do."

She shot him an incredulous look. "Just concentrate on helping them."

He smiled cockily at her. Loon.

Alisa opened the comm to engineering. "Mica, are you staying out of trouble down there?"

"I have heavy things piled in front of the hatch, and I'm hiding in the closet. It sounds like a war zone out there."

"It is," Alisa said grimly. "Stand by."

The two artillery guns fired at the same time, energy rounds blasting toward the stairs. Beck flung himself one way, rolling and firing at the tank as he did so. Leonidas sprang away as the rounds hit, the stairs exploding in warped metal, shrapnel, and smoke.

He raced across the cargo hold faster than the tank could readjust its aim. Its guns rotated toward him, but he leaped into the air too quickly for them. They fired after he was already landing atop the tank. He'd shouldered his rifles while in midair, and as soon as he touched, he bashed downward with his fists, cyborg power combining with the power of the armor to let him crush through what had to be a strong alloy. He grabbed one of the gun barrels and yanked it so hard that the metal bent with a squeal that Alisa heard all the way in NavCom.

He jammed a grenade into a crevice in the tank, ripped open one of Mica's rust bangs and left it in another crevice, then sprang free. With its one remaining gun barrel, the tank spun, trying to target him. The grenade exploded first.

The boom shook the entire ship, and alarms flashed on the control panel. Alisa gripped the console with both hands, helpless to do anything. Smoke filled the cargo hold, and she could barely tell what was happening. The drones continued to zip about, firing energy bolts that lit up the gray haze.

"I guess Leonidas gets the kiss," Yumi said, pointing to the hulking body of the tank. Its treads had been blown apart, and it had stopped moving.

Abelardus growled.

"More trouble coming," Alejandro said.

An armored humanoid figure had appeared in the smoke at the airlock entrance. It carried weapons and an energy shield, the front crackling with white light and power.

"I bet that's the captain," Alisa said. "Or one of his men. Androids. Whatever they have."

The figure leaped straight toward Leonidas.

Something slammed into the hatch to NavCom, and Alisa jumped from her seat. A red blazer bolt splashed against the thick glass of the window. A drone hovered in the corridor on the other side.

"Duck," Alisa said, having no idea how much damage that window could take. Not much, she was sure. A prolonged blast would melt the glass easily.

Alejandro flung himself under the console, with the orb box. Yumi took deep noisy breaths. Alisa grabbed her Etcher, wishing she had thought to ask to borrow a more powerful weapon from Leonidas. Abelardus turned toward the hatch, his eyes narrowing to slits as he waved his staff.

The drone fired again, this time maintaining the blast. Glass snapped and melted. The energy beam burned through, slamming into the bulkhead below the view screen.

Alisa slammed down on the comm button. "Mica, I need you to get out of the closet. I need a…" She groped for something that would help with this new development.

"I'm rather comfortable in here, right now," Mica replied, the booms of whatever was going on in the cargo hold nearly drowning out her words.

The beam halted abruptly, leaving a scorched divot in the bulkhead and a giant hole in the hatch window.

"Hah," Abelardus said, a clunk sounding as the drone fell out of view.

Two more drones flew through the corridor toward them. Abelardus cursed.

"Mica," Alisa said, careful to keep her head below the level of the window, "can you open the cargo hatch so everyone not locked behind a door will fly out? The way Beck and the others did when we had a squadron of soldiers in here?"

"They won't fly anywhere with the grab beam holding us," Mica said, "or I would have already done it. The ship might as well be in a tub of gelatin right now."

The two drones outside fired at the hatch, this time aiming for the handle and locking mechanism instead of the glass. They wanted in.

Abelardus waved his staff, and one of the two dropped out of sight.

"Can you do that all day, or do you get tired?" Alisa asked.

"I have excellent stamina."

"That doesn't answer my question."

"Depends on how many drones they send," Abelardus said.

That didn't answer her question either. Another one zipped up the corridor, joining the one remaining. The stench of burning metal wafted into NavCom, and the hatch itself was starting to glow red around the handle.

What would those drones do when they got in? Kill them? Or did they simply want the orb?

Remembering the armored android, Alisa looked toward the view screen to check on Leonidas. She could see Beck near the stairs, firing at something else trying to come out of the airlock. Neither Leonidas nor the android was in view. Several ominous bangs reverberated through the ship, and she could imagine them hurling each other into bulkheads.

With little else she could do, Alisa tried comming the other ship again. "Captain Echo, are you there?"

She had no idea whether he had come personally to collect his orb or sent another android to do it.

"I am here," came the now-familiar emotionless voice. "Do you wish to surrender?"

Alisa licked her lips. Was that an option?

"No," Alejandro snarled.

How could a man wedged under a console be so vehemently unyielding? Maybe she should shove him out the hatch to deal with some of those drones himself.

"Is the offer of ten thousand tindarks still on the table?" Alisa asked.

"Not at this juncture, but I am willing to spare the lives of your crew and withdraw my forces."

"Magnanimous."

"Yes," Echo said, no hint that he grasped the sarcasm in her voice. Maybe he grasped it and just did not care.

More clangs echoed up from the cargo hold. Alisa wished she could see how Leonidas was doing. Dozens of drones hovered in the air around Beck, all shooting at him. He was trying to use the warped support for the stairs—all that remained of the structure—for cover to lessen the number of hits he took, but his armor was already scorched and melted in places.

Alisa shook her head. This wasn't worth it.

"Those two won't be bothering us again," Abelardus said, jerking his staff toward the smoking hatch. For the moment, the corridor was clear of enemies.

But how many more could the android captain send? Money had not been an obstacle when outfitting that ship.

"Anyone in here have a blazer?" Alisa asked.

"Captain?" Echo asked.

"I do," Yumi said, lifting a compact hand pistol up. "Tommy gave it to me."

Alisa bent down and grabbed the box out of Alejandro's hands before he could react. His head clunked on the bottom of the console as he tried to snatch it back. She held her other hand out to Yumi.

"What are you doing?" Alejandro clambered to his feet and reached for her.

Alisa did not have Leonidas there to protect her this time, but she reacted without hesitation, grabbing the blazer and pressing the barrel against his chest.

"Back off, Doctor."

He froze, his eyes bulging as he gaped at her. Then he clenched his jaw.

"Captain?" Echo asked. "Are you prepared to hand over the orb? My automatons have severely damaged your cargo facility."

"I've got the orb right here, Captain," Alisa said and tapped the button to transmit a video feed as well as her voice. Juggling the box, the blazer, and manipulating the controls was not easy, not with Alejandro looming next to her, looking like he would attack if she took the blazer from his chest. It was going to be hard to do a good bluff with him standing there, ready to take advantage. "Abelardus, would you mind pulling the doctor back?"

Abelardus hesitated, looking between Alejandro and her. She doubted he cared much about Alejandro, but he probably knew what was in her mind, knew that even she wasn't sure if she intended to bluff—or go through with the threat.

Ultimately, he lifted his hand and nodded to her. "He won't attack you."

Anger burned in Alejandro's eyes, but his expression—his entire body—was frozen.

Another boom came from the cargo hold.

Alisa gritted her teeth and flipped the orb box open. Its yellowish glow poured out, making her squint. Her arm hair stood on end. The temptation to stare at the orb came to her, nearly overwhelming in its intensity. If not for the clamor of weapons fire in the ship behind her, she might have struggled to resist, but she ground her clenched teeth and jerked her gaze away.

"Can you see me, Captain Echo?" Alisa asked.

"I see you." For the first time, the android's face came through on the flat display embedded in the console. He had short, neatly combed white hair, silver eyes, and a bland and forgettable face that was slightly more male than female.

"If you don't call your automatons back and let go of my ship, I'm going to destroy this artifact." Alisa tossed the box aside and pressed the barrel of the blazer to the surface of the orb. A jolt of energy ran up her arm, electrical shocks coursing through her nerves. She moved the muzzle back a half inch, but did not let any sign of the pain show on her face. If the android had been programmed to decipher human expressions, she did not want him believing that she was uncomfortable—or bluffing.

Off to her side, Alejandro continued to look enraged, but he did not move. *Could* not move.

"Starseer artifacts are not easily destroyed," Echo said.

"Are you sure?" Alisa said. She had no idea if a blazer pistol would break the orb, but the android couldn't be that positive, could he? "Do you want to risk it?"

"A blazer can damage a Starseer artifact," Abelardus said, stepping closer so the android could see him behind Alisa's shoulder. "Perhaps not a staff of power," he added, "but this orb is a key, not a weapon."

"Yes, I require its use as a key." Captain Echo gazed at them, his face impossible to read.

"If you don't remove your robots from my ship and let us go, nobody's going to get to use it as a key," Alisa said.

"You are the Starseer?" Echo said, meeting Abelardus's eyes.

"Yes."

"You may be useful in recovering more artifacts. It would be challenging to keep you alive, but I have suits that could be altered for human protection."

"Good to know, but I'm not going with you. Any artifacts that get recovered will be going back to my people."

Alejandro growled deep in his throat. It was the only protest he could manage.

"I will take you prisoner if possible," Echo said, "and spare your life."

"Didn't you hear me, Captain?" Alisa said, waving the blazer. "If you want this artifact, you're going to spare all of our lives. And my ship."

An alarm blared. It was not a small alarm on the control console this time. The noise came through all the speakers on the entire ship. "Hull breach," the computer announced. "The hull has been breached."

Alisa wanted to comm Mica to see if there was anything she could do, but she dared not interrupt this conversation with the android. Besides, Mica would know what to do on her own. *If* anything could be done. Alisa had no doubt that breach had occurred in the cargo hold, and Mica would be suicidal to run out there amid the drones and whatever else was going on.

"You have minimal time, Captain," Echo said. "I suggest you deliver the artifact to my automatons now. You may still be able to repair your ship after we depart."

Alisa's grip tightened on the blazer pistol. The android did not sound worried that she would blow up the orb. Alejandro seemed to believe it far more than Echo did.

"Marchenko," Leonidas said over the internal comm, the blaring of the alarm coming over the channel even more loudly than it was sounding in NavCom.

Alisa muted Echo and answered Leonidas. "That's *Alisa*, and what? Are you all right?"

She could still see Beck on the camera, shooting at drones. A few more of them had crashed to the floor, but he remained under siege, with more blast marks dotting his armor since the last time she had checked. And she still couldn't see Leonidas.

"The android intruder is dismantled," Leonidas announced, even as he strode into view of the camera. He smashed the butt of his rifle into one of the drones attacking Beck, and it flew across the cargo hold to slam into a wall. It crumpled and dropped to the deck, more affected by his raw power than by blazer bolts.

"Uh, good," Alisa said, half-stunned. She had thought the men were losing down there. Echo certainly had not done anything to indicate he expected anything other than victory.

Another voice sounded on the comm. "Captain," Mica said, "I can't get to that breach to see how big it is and if I can patch it, not with a war being fought in the cargo hold."

"Working on it," Alisa replied. "Leonidas, if you could disable the grab beam on that other ship—"

"There are still robots within *this* ship," Leonidas said, smashing another drone into a wall. "We should finish them off first, to ensure—"

"Abelardus will handle them. We need that other ship to let us go. And it would be even better to have that android captain out of commission."

"Understood," Leonidas said. "Beck, come."

"Come?" Beck asked, ducking as one drone fired at his head and two more sailed straight toward him.

Leonidas grabbed one of the drones out of the air, his hands moving too fast to track. He gripped the device from either side and crushed it in his grip. Beck fired at another one, a barrage of blazer bolts, and it flew into the support post over his head. It bounced off his shoulder and crashed to the deck.

Leonidas destroyed one more drone, and he and Beck jogged toward the airlock. The still-smoking tank blocked the way. Leonidas heaved it to the side. Alisa watched her men disappear into the airlock tube.

On the monitor, Echo had stopped looking at Alisa and Abelardus. Something on his own panels seemed to have demanded his attention.

Figuring she had better distract him if she could, Alisa toggled the mute. "All right, Captain," she said. "We're ready to surrender. You win."

The android lifted his silvery gaze toward her. "Humans are very duplicitous," he said, then stood up, having the look of a man—or an android—who had business to attend.

The channel closed down.

Alisa grimaced. Abelardus had said there were at least three androids on that ship. Even if Leonidas had managed to come out on top when battling one, that meant he had two more to deal with and whatever other assault robots and drones remained on the *Explorer*.

"Here, Doctor," Alisa said, shoving the orb at him. "Stay here with Yumi, and keep the hatch shut."

Abelardus must have released Alejandro from his mental grip because he grabbed the orb and returned it to its box.

"Where are you going, Captain?" Yumi asked over the continuing blares of the alarm.

"Abelardus and I have a date." Alisa eyed her broken hatch window and the smoky corridor beyond it.

"Oh, will there be kissing, after all?" Yumi asked.

Abelardus quirked an eyebrow.

"Yeah, I'm going to watch him give the kiss of death to any drones left on my ship. We've got to clear the cargo hold so Mica can fix our breach. If Leonidas and Beck manage to get rid of that grab beam, we need to be ready to fly. Mind if I keep this?" She waved the blazer pistol.

"It's all yours, Captain."

She touched the hatch, not surprised to find it still hot. She pulled down her sleeve, grabbed the latch, and tried to tug it open. It did not budge. She cursed. How was she supposed to save her ship when she was locked in NavCom?

"Look out," Abelardus said, pulling her back.

Another drone floated into view beyond the broken window.

"I'll get it," Alisa snarled. She swatted Abelardus away and fired through the broken window. "You figure out a way to open the hatch."

She struck the drone dead on, but it only stuttered in the air, seeming to absorb the energy of the bolt. She fired twice more, growled, and pulled out her Etcher. Maybe bullets would do something.

The drone shot back. Fortunately, it aimed at the locking mechanism instead of through the window, or it would have taken Alisa's head off. As if that lock wasn't already mangled. She stood on her tiptoes and fired three rounds with her Etcher.

A wing flew off with her first shot. The second two hit it directly on the nose. This time when the craft stuttered, it did not recover. It pitched to the deck.

A boom came from the direction of the cargo hold. Alisa glanced at the view screen. Had Leonidas and Beck been forced back onto the *Nomad?* More smoke than ever filled the hold, and she couldn't see a thing through the haze.

"Abelardus," she said. "The hatch?"

"You're a demanding woman, Captain." He was crouching next to it, his hand on the warm metal, his face tilted in a thoughtful, or perhaps focused, expression.

"Yes, I am. Maybe you should have taken the time to find that out before going on a date with me."

He smiled up at her. "Fortunately, I can meet the demands of any woman." He stood up and grabbed the latch.

He had to heave, his shoulders quivering under his robe, but the hatch finally groaned open.

Smoke flooded into NavCom, and Alisa coughed. That did not keep her from striding into the corridor. She intended to make all of those robots suffer for blasting up her ship.

Abelardus caught her by the arm, pushing her to the side so he could pass her.

"You don't have armor," he said at her irritated look.

"Neither do you."

He smiled, waved his staff, and trotted toward the cargo hold.

Another boom thundered through the ship, the deck quaking under Alisa's feet.

"A secondary hull breach has been detected," the computer voice announced, and the alarm seemed to intensify.

A breeze whispered past Alisa's cheek, and the smoke streamed toward the cargo hold. Her stomach sank. They were venting the ship's atmosphere.

CHAPTER TEN

As Alisa and Abelardus passed through the mess hall and onto the walkway stretching over the cargo hold, two drones appeared out of the darkness. She jerked her blazer and Etcher up, one weapon in each hand, but the mechanical constructs were quicker. Crimson energy blasts streaked toward them. Alisa tried to dodge to the side, but knew she would be too late.

The blasts, however, never reached her. Abelardus, standing just in front of her, twirled his staff. He knocked one blast away, as if it were a ball instead of a scorching burst of energy. The other one never touched the staff. It seemed to be absorbed in midair by a forcefield.

Abelardus sprang forward, attacking one of the drones with the staff, trying to club the thing. Alisa had an opening and fired past his shoulder toward the second. She unleashed both bullets and blazer bolts. This close, her aim was impeccable, but it took several rounds before the drone faltered. It wavered in the air, wingtips shivering, and smoke wafted out, adding to the pall filling the corridor. Finally, it crashed to the deck.

Abelardus's staff connected with the first drone. Something like silver lightning sprang from the weapon where it touched the metal. The lightning enshrouded the drone, and a noisy crack sounded over the ongoing alarm, like something short-circuiting. Metal plating flew off the construct, and it tumbled to the deck beside the first one.

Instead of continuing along the walkway, Abelardus paused, looking through the smoke in the direction of the airlock—and the other ship. The sounds of weapons fire drifted through the tube.

"Beck and the cyborg are in the engineering section over there, and they're fighting another android," Abelardus said.

"Are they winning?"

"I don't think so. The android has more robots and drones helping him."

"Great." Alisa pointed at the smoke spiraling past, heading toward the wall near the big cargo hatch door. "Let's check on the breach, make sure there aren't any more drones, and find Mica."

Alisa was tempted to go to Mica first, but she ought to be safe in engineering with the hatch closed right now. She wanted to make sure all of the drones were done before calling for her to come out.

When she and Abelardus reached the part of the walkway where the stairs should have been, the metal sagged and groaned under their weight. Abelardus hopped over the edge, the smoke so thick that he disappeared from her sight as he landed. A grunt and a crunch came up from below. He had probably landed on some of the wreckage.

Alisa holstered her weapons for long enough to sit on the edge, turn, and swing down. Abelardus reached out and steadied her as she landed. She wanted to say that she did not need help, but this wasn't the time to be snippy. Besides, if more of those drones showed up, she *would* need his help. That staff and the shield he could generate would be all that stood between her and those energy weapons.

"This way," she said, following the stream of smoke. It ran over their heads now, and she could make out a faint whooshing sound over the wailing of the alarm.

Abelardus sprang to the side as another drone zipped out of the smoke, zeroing in on them. He thwacked it with his staff, and that lightning burst into existence again, engulfing the automaton. Alisa fired twice and finished it off. As soon as it hit the deck, she hurried on, stepping over other destroyed drones and pieces of debris that looked like they might have flown off that tank. Some of the drones were half melted, as if by acid, and she remembered the rust bangs Mica had been making. Leonidas and Beck must have found them useful.

When she reached the wall, she followed it, shaking her head at the blast marks and soot coating it. A figure appeared in the smoke ahead, and she halted, raising her Etcher.

The figure spun toward her, lifting a hand. "Captain?"

"Mica?"

"It's about time." Mica lowered her hand, one of her homemade rust bangs gripped in it.

Alisa lowered her Etcher. "I thought you were in engineering."

"There are *holes* in the ship." Mica waved at open patch kits sprawled on the deck by her feet, along with a soldering iron and a few other tools. "Someone has to do something about them."

Abelardus took up a guard position, putting his back to them and peering into the smoke.

"I thought the grab beam might help hold the atmosphere in," Alisa said.

"It *is* helping. This could be worse. You watching my back? Good." Mica shoved the rust bang into one of the big pockets in her baggy coveralls and returned to the breach.

"Something else is down here with us," Abelardus said quietly, the words barely audible over the alarm.

"More drones?" Alisa drew the blazer pistol with her left hand again.

"No. I believe it is—there!"

A humanoid figure shambled out of the darkness toward them. An android, the one Alisa had seen earlier on the camera, the one Leonidas had fought.

It was armored, more of a hard exoskeleton than bulky combat armor, but that outer layer was burned and mangled. The android dragged one of its legs as it walked. A piece of pipe was thrust through its chest, sticking out on the other side. The side of its face had been destroyed, half torn off. Despite all of its injuries, it headed toward them, a rifle in one hand and something that looked like a grenade in its other.

Alisa started to fire, but Abelardus leaped toward the android, getting in her way. She cursed and thought to move to the side, but decided to hold her ground. Someone had to protect Mica's back while she worked.

The android burst forward, meeting Abelardus several feet away. Abelardus swung his staff, but his inhuman foe lunged in and caught his arm before the weapon landed. Using his grip on Abelardus's arm, the android hurled him across the cargo hold. He disappeared into the smoke, so Alisa did not see him land, but she heard the thud and his pained gasp.

She did not hesitate to open fire. The android started to turn after him, but when her bullets and blazer bolts slammed into its side, it shifted toward her. Grimly, she kept firing, wondering if she had just strung a noose around her neck.

The android strode toward her, her weapons fire bouncing off that exoskeleton. She lifted her aim to its head. It flinched as a bullet cracked into its cheek, gouging a hole into the faux skin and revealing a metallic skull underneath. The android continued forward. She backed up as far as she could, bumping Mica.

"Rust bang," she blurted.

Mica turned, a rust bang in hand, but their enemy was too close. The android reached for Alisa.

A wall of air seemed to slam into their foe, and it was hurled from its feet. Alisa stumbled as the tail edge of the force struck her shoulder. She dropped to one knee, almost falling over Mica. The android hit the bulkhead with a thud, but rose to its feet immediately. Mica threw her rust bang at it.

"Get back," she blurted, grabbing Alisa.

Alisa staggered to her feet as Abelardus ran out of the smoke toward the android.

"Careful," she warned. A rust bang might be designed to eat through metal, but the spatters hurt like the hells when they landed on human skin.

Something skidded and clanked along the floor toward Alisa. At first, she thought the android had thrown the rust bang back, but this was a different weapon, the grenade it had been clutching.

Alisa started to dive away but saw that Mica had turned back to the breach, determined to patch the hole. She hadn't seen the grenade.

"Look out," she barked and grabbed Mica, pulling her and turning her away from the grenade.

She tried to kick it away before it could go off, but was more focused on getting them both out of there. She barely clipped it.

They raced several feet, Alisa pushing Mica ahead of her. The grenade exploded.

A wave of power slammed into Alisa's back, carrying her into the air. She crashed into Mica as pieces of shrapnel struck her, burrowing through her jacket and blasting into her skin. She screamed as she fell, pain lighting up her body in a hundred places. She and Mica grew tangled, and Alisa's shoulder struck the deck hard as she landed. A crunch sounded, and agony sprang from the injury.

The ship's voice sounded, warning of another breach, and Alisa almost cried in frustration. Knowing the android was still back there and might be charging toward her, she tried to get her feet under her, but as soon as she moved her arm, the pain increased. Her shoulder would not take her weight. Blackness washed over her when she lifted her head. She gasped, willing it to go away. She was *not* going to pass out, not when her ship was in trouble and that cursed android was still alive.

Footfalls thundered into the cargo hold, and bright red armor appeared through the smoke. Leonidas veered toward the wall where Alisa had last seen Abelardus and the android. They were grappling there—she could just make it out as more smoke—more of their precious air—streamed toward the breach Mica had been trying to fix.

Leonidas descended on the android like a jackhammer. Alisa let herself fall back to the floor. She didn't know if they were safe, but seeing Leonidas filled her with hope. If anyone could flatten that android, he could.

Beck came running into view. He looked toward Leonidas but then spotted Alisa and Mica and raced toward them. Behind Alisa, Mica moaned. She must have hit hard and perhaps taken some of that shrapnel too. Alisa hurt too much to roll over and look.

A clang sounded from the direction of the airlock. Alisa could barely make out Abelardus in his robe over there, closing the hatch. The smoke continued to destroy the visibility, and it irritated her nose and eyes. She tried to take a deep breath, to deal with the pain coming from all over her body, but she ended up coughing. The shards of metal that had burrowed into her skin seemed to poke deeper with the coughs, and tears pricked her eyes.

Leonidas rose, lifting the android over his shoulder, and called out to Abelardus, "Wait."

He ran to the hatch and thrust his load into the airlock. The battered android did not fight him—maybe it was dead. Inoperable. Defunct. Whatever the right word was. Leonidas was not taking any chances. He tapped the controls, probably opening the outer hatch so the android would be dumped into the tube. Or into space if the *Nomad* succeeded in pulling away from the tube. Had Leonidas and Beck turned off the grab beam? Alisa had no way to know.

"Leonidas," she said. She meant to call loudly and strongly to him, to be heard over the alarm still ringing throughout the ship, but his name came out as a pained gasp.

He heard her and left the airlock, running toward her.

All she meant to do was ask about the grab beam, but he scooped her into his arms. She winced as the shrapnel was pressed deeper into her flesh, and tears streaked down her cheeks, warm and salty where they touched her lips.

"Beck," he called, his voice muffled by the faceplate of his helmet, "get Mica." Then he raised his voice to bellow for Alejandro.

Alisa had no problem hearing that.

"We'll get you to sickbay," he said, speaking more quietly for her.

She gripped his shoulder. "Is the grab beam down?"

"Yes. We left the other ship with substantial damage in engineering."

"Is the captain dead?"

"No, there wasn't time. We heard the fight back here." He strode toward the walkway. "We can talk about it in sickbay."

"No, NavCom."

"You're injured."

"We have to get away from the other ship while there's time, especially if the captain is still alive."

Leonidas hesitated.

"NavCom," Alisa said firmly.

Behind her, she could hear Mica having a similar argument with Beck. He wanted to take her to sickbay, and she was demanding to be put down so she could repair the breaches.

"NavCom," Leonidas agreed.

He stopped where the stairs should have been. Alisa was wondering how they would get up to the walkway when he simply bent his legs and sprang with her still in his arms. She gasped, flinging her uninjured arm around his neck. They landed on the metal with a clank, the framework shuddering beneath them.

Leonidas jogged through the mess hall and toward NavCom, kicking aside fallen drones as he went. "Looks like you had a little trouble up here."

"Just a little. Abelardus was actually useful."

"I see," he said, his tone growing cool, his expression frosty behind the faceplate.

Those two, Alisa decided, were even less likely to become friends than Leonidas and Beck.

Alejandro was still in NavCom, watching the camera feeds. Yumi sat at the sensor station.

Alisa stretched her hand toward the pilot's seat, wanting Leonidas to deposit her directly in it.

"What's going on over there, Yumi?" she asked as he did so, setting her down with impressive gentleness for a big man in combat armor.

"Their engines are overheating," Yumi reported. "The grab beam let us go a couple of minutes ago. Alejandro and I were debating if we should try to pilot the ship away without your help."

"No need." Sitting on the edge of the seat so her back would not touch anything, Alisa reached for the controls. Or she tried. The pain in her left shoulder was too intense. She clenched her jaw and handled the controls with her right hand. It wasn't efficient, but she made do.

"Get your med kit, Doctor," Leonidas said. "She needs help. So does Mica."

"What about you?"

He hesitated. "Later."

Alisa grimaced. She hadn't realized he was injured, too, but how could she be surprised? His armor might have protected him from blazer bolts, but if the android had thrown him around as he had thrown Abelardus that one time, he could have internal injuries.

She guided the ship away from the *Explorer* and put them on course toward Leonidas's coordinates. She did not know if that was the wisest choice, but they were closer to that destination than to anything else. It would take more than two days to reach the nearest space station where they could dock for repairs, assuming someone on board could *afford* repairs. She dreaded hearing about all the damage the *Nomad* had taken. The cargo holds of freighters weren't meant to serve as the fields for space battles.

The alarm continued to complain about the breaches, but Alisa waited until they were well on their way before she overrode and silenced it. She wanted to ask Mica how the patches were going, but she trusted her engineer to do her job without monitoring.

Alejandro returned and pressed his auto injector to her neck. A soft hiss sounded, and she felt a sharp tap.

"Painkiller," he said. "But you're bleeding all over your chair."

"Even worse than sweaty butt prints," Alisa muttered. She hadn't realized she was bleeding that badly, but if he could tell through her jacket, it must be substantial.

"We'll deal with it in sickbay."

"Is the autopilot on?" Leonidas asked.

Alisa hated to leave NavCom when they were still so close to their enemy, but both Alejandro and Leonidas were giving her expectant looks.

"I can turn it on now," she said.

"Do it," Leonidas said, his tone making it clear it was an order.

Maybe later, she would remind him that she was the captain. Now, all she wanted was for someone to pull those metal shards out of her back. And fix her shoulder. She must have dislocated it.

"Done," she said, lowering her good arm from the controls.

She turned, intending to stand up and walk to sickbay herself, but Leonidas swooped her into his arms again, being mindful of her injuries. If she did not feel like sharp-fanged snakes were burrowing their way into her kidneys, she might have found the gesture romantic.

"Someone's on a spacewalk on the enemy ship," Yumi said, scanning through the various screens of data the sensor display offered. "Doing repairs."

Alisa let Leonidas carry her out of NavCom, but she knew she would be back up here shortly if the android captain got his ship working. Even with his engines operating at half-capacity, he could catch up with the *Nomad*. And if he did...she didn't know what they had left to throw at him.

CHAPTER ELEVEN

Alisa's shoulder itched like mad. She lay on the exam table in sickbay while Mica and Beck sat on a bench, waiting for their turn. Beck had removed his armor, and he had some impressive bruises on his arms and torso, though he was chatting amiably, in good spirits. Mica wore her usual glower and winced whenever she moved. At her insistence, she and Beck had finished patching the breaches before making their way up here. Nobody could fault her dedication to duty.

Leonidas was also in sickbay, still wearing his armor, except for his helmet, as he stood next to Alisa. He watched quietly as Alejandro worked on her bare back, removing dozens of pieces of shrapnel and applying QuickSkin to pull the edges of the wounds together so they could heal. By now, she had received enough drugs that she did not feel any pain, but they did nothing to suppress the itching within her shoulder. Alejandro had injected repair nanobots to work on the torn ligaments and cartilage.

A clank sounded as Alejandro dropped yet another piece of shrapnel into a bowl on the table next to her hip. Alisa had lost count of how many that was. Fortunately, Alejandro was quick and efficient as he removed them. It was strange to think of a man with a penchant for hiding under the control console as being good at anything, but he was in his milieu here.

"Next time, you can just yell at me, Captain," Mica said. "I can fling myself out of the way of a grenade as quickly as the next person."

"I'm sure you *can*," Alisa said. "I wasn't sure you *would*. You seemed intent on fixing that hole."

"It's important to fix little holes before they become big holes. It's also important not to wage battles from *inside* your spaceship."

"I've heard that. Odd how hard it is to avoid. Is Yumi still in NavCom, Beck?"

He had been the last one to join them in sickbay, stopping in his cabin to peel out of his damaged armor first. He had probably peeked in on her.

"Yes," Beck said. "She said she'd let us know if that other ship starts moving again. Especially if it starts moving in the same direction we're going."

"Good. I'm glad someone is up there." Alisa almost added that her small sickbay was quite crowded, with Alejandro having to step around Leonidas as he worked, and with Beck's and Mica's knees encroaching on the space around the table. But she did not want Leonidas to leave, so she kept the thought to herself. She twisted her neck to look up at him. "Do you have any injuries that the doctor should be looking at that are more important than mine?"

By now, she knew him well enough to believe he would stand there, half dead and only held up by his armor, before admitting to her that he was in pain.

"No," he said.

She couldn't tell if he was lying. "So, you're just here for moral support?"

"Yes. And also for Dominguez's drugs."

She smiled at his propensity for calling people by their last names, no matter how many times they corrected him. A byproduct of twenty years in the military, she supposed. She and her fellow pilots had usually used call signs. Maybe that wasn't much different. First names were so personal. The military probably preferred it when people distanced themselves from each other, so it wasn't such a blow when one's comrades dropped in battle. As if names could make a difference in thinking of someone as a comrade, a friend.

Leonidas's hand hung near the exam table, so she reached over and clasped it, hoping he hadn't had too many close calls with those androids. Having to watch from a distance, from a camera that hadn't even recorded him for much of the battle, had been distressing. He could have fallen, and she wouldn't have seen how it happened or even learned about it until later.

She had hated that about losing Jonah. Watching him die would have been horrible, but it seemed a crime not to have been there in the end. To have someone be dead and to not even be aware of it. Weren't lovers supposed to have a psychic link? To sense when something was wrong with the other person? Maybe the Starseers had that ability. Starseers who actually had power, not just mutated blood.

Leonidas pulled his hand away, and she felt a stab of disappointment. But he only removed his red gauntlet, then returned it to the table, offering it again.

"Are you feeling much pain?" He tilted his chin toward her back where Alejandro was working on yet another shard.

Maybe he thought she had grasped his hand because she needed something to squeeze. No, she just...liked having it.

"Not really. I'm fairly numb. The doctor has good drugs."

"Yeah, he does," Beck said. "I can barely feel my neck now. Wrenched it bad when I hit a bulkhead. What's with all these overly muscular people hurling you into walls? How is that a respectable thing to do to an opponent?"

"It's slightly more respectable than straight-up shooting a person," Alisa said.

"Is it? I feel that's arguable."

"We're lucky we didn't all get blown out into space," Mica said. "Next time, you fierce armored warriors need to take the battle to the other ship sooner."

"We'll keep that in mind," Leonidas murmured.

"Did you call me a fierce armored warrior? I like that." Beck beamed a smile at Mica.

Maybe Mica should give up on finding Yumi cute and see if Beck was interested in sharing his fierceness with her.

"Did you tell the captain about the box, Leonidas?" Beck asked.

"No."

"What box?" Alisa asked, wincing as Alejandro extracted a long piece out of her back—it might not hurt that much, but the sensation was even worse than the itching. She found herself squeezing Leonidas's hand. He squeezed back lightly. "And did you just call him Leonidas?" she added.

"Apparently, that's his name," Beck said. "Well, actually it's not, according to that wanted poster, but he seems fond of it."

"Yes, and he's been fond of it since the week we all met, but I haven't heard you use it."

Leonidas rotated his head toward Beck, and Beck met his gaze, his expression turning wry.

"He pulled an android off my chest plate," Beck admitted. "I thought I was about to be ripped into a thousand bits."

Huh. Maybe it had been worth having the *Nomad* poked full of holes if it meant that Beck and Leonidas had bonded in that battle. Now if she could just get Abelardus to stop calling Leonidas a mech and insulting him.

"There was a lead box in engineering," Leonidas said. "It was sealed, and we didn't have time to break into it, but our suits detected some radiation leaking from it. A small amount. The sides of the box appeared quite thick."

"You think there might have been some more artifacts in it?" Alisa asked. "Radioactive artifacts?"

"I believe non-radioactive artifacts go in a display case," Mica said, "not a lead box."

Alisa gave her a flat look. "I just meant that we don't know what was in there if they didn't look inside."

"There wasn't time," Leonidas repeated, but he looked distressed that he couldn't give her an itemized list of the contents.

She squeezed his hand again. "I'm sure there wasn't, especially if Beck was in danger of being ripped into bits."

"I knew I shouldn't have admitted that," Beck grumbled.

"If the androids *did* have radioactive artifacts aboard," Alisa said, "were they the artifacts from the pilgrim ship? Or were they different artifacts?"

"You're being loose with that term, aren't you?" Mica asked. "Artifacts? I saw a plaque and a bunch of space junk."

"*Old* space junk." Alisa remembered the helmet. She could imagine it in some collector's display case, a radiation-squelching display case. "Abelardus called everything there an artifact, and he's our expert on Starseer things."

Mica did not look impressed.

"Are you implying that the android ship might have been following us?" Alejandro asked, plunking another piece of shrapnel into the bowl. "That it came upon the pilgrim ship and then veered off to track us?"

"I don't know," Alisa said. "That shouldn't be possible. We destroyed that homing beacon back on Arkadius, so nobody should be able to follow us."

"Maybe the androids are out here collecting artifacts independently of us," Beck said.

"Or maybe someone leaked the news of their existence to numerous people," Alejandro said.

"I know we've talked about that and blamed Abelardus—and you've blamed me—but does that even make sense? Why would he want anyone to get there before we do? Before *he* does? I don't know who those androids work for, but I doubt it's Lady Naidoo or the Starseers."

"Why not?" Beck asked. "They had money, as evinced by the tips I got for my duck skewers, and they didn't seem to be afraid to use technology."

"True, but they're so secretive. It seems like they would handle artifact hunts on their own." Alisa shrugged, admitting that this was nothing more than intuition. She had no proof.

Abelardus poked his head through the hatchway. He seemed to be one of the few who had escaped the battle unscathed. He must not have landed on *his* shoulder when the android had hurled him.

He looked toward Alisa, frowned at her handclasp with Leonidas, and said, "I came to see if you're all right, Alisa."

Leonidas frowned back at Abelardus, or perhaps at his use of her first name.

"Just me?" Alisa asked, tilting her head toward Beck, Mica, and Leonidas.

"You're the one getting pieces of metal pulled out of your back."

"Ah."

"It looks painful. Too bad your bodyguard didn't get back a few seconds sooner, eh?" Abelardus flicked his fingers at Leonidas.

Leonidas's grip tightened on Alisa's hand, but he seemed to realize it right away, because he loosened it, extracting his fingers. She lamented that Abelardus's words made him want to do so, but also would not want him holding her hand if he got angry and inadvertently squeezed hard. She well remembered him smashing that drone with his grip, a drone that had been sturdy enough to withstand a lot of hits from blazer bolts and bullets.

"If you're referring to Leonidas," Alisa said, "he was busy disabling the android's ship so we could escape."

"A shame for your back that he couldn't have done it faster."

Alisa started to shift up onto her elbows, tempted to point out that Abelardus had been the one who she'd been depending on to help her in the cargo hold, but Alejandro touched her back, pushing her back down. It was just as well, since she did not have a shirt on.

"I'm not done yet," he said. "Relax."

Relax. As if that was easy with Starseers and cyborgs around.

"We came as quickly as possible," Leonidas said.

"I guess," Abelardus said. "It's not your fault you're not that quick anymore. You probably were when you were younger."

Leonidas's eyes closed to slits.

Alisa almost rolled her own eyes. The last thing she needed was for them to get into a fight in the middle of sickbay.

"Abelardus, could you go check on Yumi and the other ship?" Alisa asked. "See if it's still being repaired?" She doubted the *Explorer* remained within range of their sensors, but it was as good of an errand to send him on as any other.

"Actually, that's what I came to see you about," Abelardus said, "in addition to wanting to check on your well-being."

"What is it?" Alisa asked, far more concerned about those androids than her well-being.

"The ship finished its repairs and is flying again."

"I don't suppose Captain Echo is flying back to his employer."

"He's coming after us." Abelardus shrugged. "Sorry."

He withdrew from the hatchway, disappearing up the corridor.

Alisa let her forehead thump down onto the table and groaned.

Leonidas touched the back of her head. "I do regret that I wasn't quicker and didn't make it back before you were injured," he said quietly. "I should have known you wouldn't stay in NavCom."

"Not when there are holes in my ship, no."

She lifted her head, but he was walking away. He looked back as he ducked through the hatchway, the regret he had spoken of visible in his eyes. She clenched her fist as he disappeared, wishing she could punch Abelardus for saying those things. It wasn't as if Leonidas or anyone else was her keeper. If she got shot—or filled with shrapnel—that was her fault, not anybody else's.

"Captain?" Yumi asked, speaking over the comm. "The enemy ship has come into sensor range again. It's following us."

"So I've heard," Alisa muttered, letting her forehead thump down on the table again. "So I've heard."

CHAPTER TWELVE

Alisa gingerly put on a fresh shirt, trying to do it without lifting her left arm. The painkillers kept her back from hurting too much, and her shoulder itching had subsided somewhat, but she did not want to jostle the patches of QuickSkin all over her back. She felt like the *Nomad*, all patched up but far from one hundred percent. Mica lay on the exam table now, about to receive some of Alejandro's ministrations.

Alisa needed to get to NavCom to check on their pursuer, but she made herself pause and say, "Thank you for your services, Alejandro."

He grunted at her, busy sanitizing the instruments he had used for plucking shrapnel from her back. Mica hadn't received nearly as many pieces, but she had a couple.

"You're as talented as you are gracious," Alisa said.

"Go make sure that other ship doesn't get my orb," Alejandro said, waving toward the counter where the box sat. Somehow in all of this, Abelardus had let him start toting it around again.

"I wasn't going to blow it up," Alisa said.

Alejandro grunted again. Was that a sign of acknowledgment? Of agreement? Of something lodged in his throat?

"I suppose Captain Echo knew that too," she said, buttoning her shirt. "He didn't seem that worried. Are androids programmed to be good at poker?"

"I was not overly worried either," Alejandro said. "Perhaps you are not a good poker player."

"You weren't worried? Is that why you were foaming at the mouth, and Abelardus had to restrain you?"

"Even the penitent man is ultimately uncertain of his place in the heavens."

"Captain," Mica said, "I believe I hear the NavCom computers beckoning to you." She made a shooing motion.

"So long as that other ship isn't beckoning."

Alisa grabbed her jacket, scowled at the holes in the back and the blood staining it, and left sickbay. She swung past the laundry chute and dropped it in, hoping the automated system could clean and repair it. Even if the Alliance had been even more of a problem to her lately than the empire, she would hate to lose her flight jacket.

Yumi and Leonidas were in NavCom, pointing at the sensors and talking.

"Any new developments?" Alisa asked, slipping past Leonidas to take her customary seat.

"The *Explorer* isn't traveling as quickly as it was before," Yumi said, "but it's still gaining on us."

"Everybody gains on us. Freighters aren't meant to be fast—or to be used for secret missions into dangerous space."

"We're getting close to the coordinates," Leonidas said. "They should be scannable by the long-range sensors soon."

"At which point, we get to find out if there's anything there, or if you've led us into the middle of nowhere."

"If it's the middle of nowhere, an odd number of people are finding it alluring right now." He tapped the display. "Another ship just popped onto the sensors."

Alisa propped her arm over her backrest and looked, though there wasn't much to see yet.

"Make that three ships," Yumi said, as the *Nomad* continued to fly in that direction.

"Four," Leonidas said a few seconds later. "Five."

"Just give me the final tally," Alisa said, trying not to feel bleak and overwhelmed.

She had expected to find ships at the coordinates and told herself not to be surprised. The Alliance had been out here to place those warning buoys, so it was reasonable to assume some of their ships would be inside, investigating whatever had caused them to create the quarantine.

"And let me know as soon as you can tell if they're Alliance ships," Alisa added. "I'm assuming they are, but we could be dealing with more corporate-sponsored treasure hunters too."

She did not know which would be worse. The Alliance could shoot at the *Nomad* because it was ignoring the quarantine. Treasure hunters could shoot at them because they were competition—or because they, too, had excellent scanners, such as the android ship, and could detect the orb aboard.

Long minutes passed with nobody speaking. The *Nomad* drew closer to the armada of ships, and the *Explorer* drew closer to it.

"They *are* Alliance ships," Leonidas confirmed. "There are one, no, two warships."

"And the others?" Alisa asked.

"Those look like imperial research vessels." He touched the display, and details popped up in a column of text. "That's a medical ship. Also imperial. Presumably these were all stolen by the Alliance."

"You mean they were taken as spoils of war."

"I know what I mean," he said, giving her a cool look.

Alisa almost made a joke, but stopped herself. He might be willing to hold her hand while a surgeon was poking around in her back, but their pasts and their loyalties were always going to stand between them. Insurmountably so? She didn't know. She still hadn't figured out if he thought of her as any-thing more than a friend. A friend whose hair he sometimes touched.

A beep came from the control console. Alisa spun back to face it.

"Anyone want to tell me why the proximity alarm is going off?" She hadn't realized the *Explorer* was closing so quickly. From its previous course and speed, she had expected to reach the coordinates before it caught up.

"It's the *Explorer*," Yumi said. "It sped up."

"Because it's feeling perky, or because it doesn't want us and the orb to reach the Alliance?" Alisa tapped a button and took the ship off autopilot. There wasn't much she could do that it couldn't when they were flying in a straight line, but she tried to nudge more power out of the engines.

"Perhaps it perkily doesn't want the orb to reach the Alliance."

"I'm hoping the Alliance doesn't know about the orb and doesn't know about us." Alisa supposed that was too much to hope. "Or at least that it's too busy doing what it's doing to notice us. Though it would be nice if I could convince them to get the androids off our butts."

"How are you going to do that?" Leonidas sounded wary.

Maybe he was wondering if she thought she could barter him to the commander again in exchange for help. No, that did not sound like a good idea, perhaps because Abelardus wasn't up here, fiddling with her mind.

She glimpsed movement in the corridor in her peripheral vision. Abelardus walked into NavCom with his staff.

"Great," she muttered.

"He's getting close enough to fire," Yumi said.

Alisa raised the shields. She drummed her fingers next to the comm button as she debated on reaching out to the Alliance ships. What could she say to convince them to help instead of shooting her? She had no way of knowing if they had shot that first disabled ship they had seen, or if the salvage tug had attacked it before looting it, but she would like to think the Alliance wouldn't blow people away without a warning. Perhaps that was naive thinking, considering they'd had no trouble trying to annihilate the Starseer temple as soon as they had found it.

"One of the Alliance warships is turning away from the coordinates and heading in our direction," Leonidas said.

"*Our* direction? Not the *Explorer's* direction?"

"Our direction," he repeated firmly.

"Abelardus, if we need you to, are you ready to trot your mind powers out?"

"Always ready for that." Abelardus smirked at Leonidas, not appearing worried about their situation.

Alisa shook her head. Every male on this ship had dubious sanity.

The *Nomad* shuddered slightly as the first energy blast tapped the rear shields. The *Explorer* was not yet in optimal range for firing, and the blow was barely more than a nudge, but the attacks would only get worse from here. And who knew what the Alliance ship planned?

"I'm not reading anything *at* the coordinates," Yumi said in a puzzled tone. "Those ships are all sitting around, looking at empty space."

"A mystery I'll be happy to join you in contemplating once I'm sure we're not going to be blown to atoms." Alisa tapped the comm. Instead of saying anything, she sent out the preprogrammed distress call.

She adjusted the *Nomad's* course slightly, heading straight toward the warship. She tried not to feel like she was heading into the muzzle of a cannon.

The *Explorer* fired again, several times. Alisa cursed, torn between taking evasive action, insomuch as she could in the bulky freighter, and simply keeping the best speed possible and continuing toward the warship.

"What ship is that?" Alisa asked, checking the shield power. The hits were coming harder now as the *Explorer* closed.

"According to its digital ID…the *Storm Fury*," Yumi said.

Alisa started. "We ran into them last month at Perun. That's Commander Tomich's ship." A hint of hope stirred in her breast, but she squashed it, having no idea if Tomich would help her a second time. "Assuming he's still there and didn't get transferred or demoted after letting us go," she added in a mutter.

Another e-cannon blast struck the rear shields, this time with enough power to make the ship quake.

"I can't do anything to convince androids to leave us alone," Abelardus said, making a disgusted noise. Maybe he had tried. "And we're not close enough for me to fiddle with the ship's weapons and try to render them inoperable."

"How close would we have to be for that?"

"Close."

The shields dropped below fifty percent power. Alisa took the *Nomad* into a series of evasive maneuvers that would work wonderfully with a tiny Striker. With the freighter, it probably looked like a lumbering cow rolling around in a field.

The warship was taking its time reaching them, and she still didn't know if it would help them or hurt them.

The comm flashed. Alisa pounced on it. It was the Alliance warship.

"Captain Marchenko here." She tried to sound calm instead of frantic. "If you'd care to lend your assistance, *Storm Fury*, we would be most grateful."

"You are illegally trespassing in a clearly marked quarantine zone," an unfamiliar female voice said.

Alisa winced. What if Tomich wasn't the commander anymore?

"We had no choice," Alisa said. "We were chased into it by that civilian ship. It's attacking us without provocation."

She wondered if Captain Echo was on another line with the warship, giving a different version of the story.

"If you could lend us some help," Alisa added, when nobody responded, "we would be extremely grateful."

The *Explorer* fired again, sticking to her rear like a zit. Her wild maneuvers caused the e-cannon blast to merely clip them instead of hitting them full on, but the remaining shield power dipped inevitably lower.

Alisa veered toward the warship, which was close enough now to see on the cameras. It loomed ahead of them, huge and imposing. She wished she knew if it would help.

"Abelardus," Alisa whispered. "Is there any chance you could find a susceptible mind at the weapons console over there?"

"I think the warship is about to fire," Yumi said, her eyes wide as she leaned back from the sensor display. "Am I correct in assuming that our shields won't withstand that?"

"You're correct."

Leonidas frowned at the camera display that held the warship, scrutinizing something.

"Abelardus?" Alisa asked. "That gunner?"

"I'm trying to pick him out," Abelardus said. "They have dozens of people on their bridge."

Twin torpedoes launched from the bow of the warship. Alisa's breath caught in her throat. Were they heading toward her? Toward the *Explorer*? Toward *both*?

"They'll pass us," Leonidas said.

And they did. They streaked past on either side of the *Nomad*, close enough to make even the bravest captain see her life flash before her eyes.

The torpedoes chased down the *Explorer* as the ship dodged away, trying to move in time. Alisa knew better than to get smug, but it felt good to see their pursuer engaged in the same evasive maneuvers it had forced the *Nomad* to use. The projectiles had far enough to travel that the *Explorer* almost slipped away from them, but the torpedoes turned at the last moment, tracking its energy reading. They slammed into the ship's shields, exploding with flashes of white.

The *Explorer* survived the assault, but it immediately turned back the way it had come.

"I'd like to be relieved," Abelardus said, "but I doubt I should be."

"No," Alisa said, watching their forward camera as the warship flew closer, its massive body blocking out the stars, blocking out everything. "I wouldn't be."

She hit the comm button. "*Thank* you for your assistance, *Storm Fury.*" Sounding grateful couldn't hurt, especially since the warship's weapons were still hot. "Is there anything we can do to help you?"

Leonidas snorted.

"Well now, that's an interesting question, Captain Marchenko," a voice spoke over the comm, a *familiar* voice.

"Are you here to take me up on an offer of sake, Commander Tomich?" Alisa asked, wanting to feel relief, but not certain that she should. Tomich sounded contemplative, even wary. This time, it wasn't the tone of an old squadron mate—an old friend—greeting another.

"I believe we need to have a chat, Alisa," he said. "Sake is optional."

"I'm open to chatting." She was open to anything that didn't involve the *Nomad* being blown to bits.

"In person."

She hesitated. Was he wondering if she was still being influenced by Leonidas? Or someone else? Did he want to see for himself if anyone was looming behind her when she spoke? Or was he hoping that *he* might influence her if they spoke in person? He must know all about the orb now. She wished she could tell him the truth, that she cared very little about it or whether any of her passengers found this staff—she would prefer it if they did not. She would be happy to dump Alejandro and Abelardus into one of Tomich's cells, so she could fly off to Cleon Moon and find Jelena.

"Really," Abelardus murmured quietly from behind her.

Three suns, was he in her head again? Didn't they have a deal about that? She glared over her shoulder at him briefly before responding to Tomich.

"Your ship or mine, Commander?" she asked.

"That depends. If we come to visit you, are you going to sic your cyborg on us?"

Leonidas's eyebrows rose.

"I suppose that depends on whether you really just want to talk or if you're coming aboard to take him prisoner."

"He's not my priority right now," Tomich said. He sounded truthful.

"What *is* your priority?"

"I'm not authorized to speak with anyone about that, unless..." Tomich sighed. "Alisa, do you know more about all of this than I do? I understand your passenger has some kind of key to the station."

"The station?" She tried to sound knowledgeable rather than puzzled, but so far, all she had seen was that plaque. She certainly did not see a station anywhere ahead of them. They were close enough now to see all of the Alliance ships on camera—when the warship wasn't blocking their view. The four other vessels were sprawled out around Leonidas's coordinates, but there was absolutely nothing *at* those coordinates, nothing that she could see and nothing that the sensors could detect.

"You'll see it if you stay here long," Tomich said grimly. "Of course, my admiral is telling me to make sure you *don't* stay here long. It's dangerous to be this close. I doubt your freighter has the special hull that our science ships have."

"Uh, no. There's not much special about this freighter, but we do need to do some repairs. If we could have twenty-four hours without anyone firing upon us, that would be wonderful."

"Do you still have the key?" He lowered his voice. "I may be able to get you a reprieve if I can tell Admiral Moreau that I'm getting information about something that will help with our problem."

"What problem? The radiation?"

"More the *source* of the radiation."

"I'm open to talking to you about what I know," Alisa said.

For once, Alejandro was not breathing down her neck when she communicated with the Alliance. Might she find a way to explain everything to Tomich? And if she did, would he believe her? Or had she done too much lately for the Alliance to ever see her as anything more than a troublemaker—if not an enemy—again? Even if Tomich believed her, would it be enough? He might command a warship now, but he was only one commander in a large fleet with many senior officers above him.

Alejandro might not be in NavCom, but both Leonidas and Abelardus were regarding her warily, Leonidas because he did not know what she was thinking—and Abelardus because he did.

She shrugged at them, muted the comm, and said, "We need to go along with them."

They could not escape, and they certainly could not fight.

"For now," Abelardus said. "I want whatever information they have. They've been here longer than we have, studying the…phenomenon."

Why did she have a feeling Abelardus knew much more than she did? He turned toward the view screen, toward the warship, a distant look entering his eyes. Maybe he was poking around in people's heads over there right now.

"Let's talk on your ship, Marchenko," Tomich said. "Are you going to let us board without a problem?"

Alisa un-muted the comm while watching Leonidas's eyes. "Who's us?"

"Myself, my science officer, and Admiral Tiang. He's a doctor and a research specialist, not the fleet commander."

Which meant he had at least two admirals over there that he was dealing with, two admirals who outranked him and could give him the order to make the *Nomad* disappear.

"Is that Dr. Longwei Tiang?" Leonidas asked, an odd intentness taking over his face.

This wasn't some past enemy of his, was it? Alisa remembered the way he had reacted with that Commander Bennington during the Perun moon skirmish.

"It is," Tomich said. "Who's speaking, Alisa?"

"That's—"

"Adler," Leonidas said.

"The cyborg," Tomich said, his voice going flat.

"*A* cyborg, yes," Alisa said. "I have a Starseer too. I'm collecting interesting people."

Abelardus, still wearing that distant expression, did not look at her.

"You have a Starseer?" Tomich asked.

"Yes, I do."

Long seconds passed, and Alisa suspected that Tomich was the one muting his comm this time. Telling his superiors all about it? Maybe she shouldn't have said anything. Maybe she should have gotten Abelardus to change into normal clothing and then simply presented him as another security guard. He could have rifled through people's thoughts and reported back to her, assuming she could convince him to do so. Now, everyone would be on guard.

She growled in disgust at herself.

"All right," Tomich said. "To answer the question, yes, Tiang was an imperial medical doctor. He defected to our side late in the war, for a promotion and because we promised him that he could keep doing his research without being bothered. I gather the latter was more important to him. He's our top person out here working on this right now."

"Your top person for working on...what was it exactly?" Alisa prompted.

"I assume you would prefer it if we didn't bring your ship into one of our bays," Tomich said, ignoring her question. "We'll attach to your airlock and be over in fifteen minutes with the people I listed and a handful of troops to protect the admiral. Just protocol, understood? Nobody's looking for a fight."

Alisa grimaced. People who weren't looking for fights seemed to be inspired to find them when they saw red cyborg armor. Maybe she should try to convince Leonidas to stay away from the meeting. Alejandro could teach him how to hide under the console in NavCom.

"I assure you, we're tired of fighting," Alisa said.

He sighed. "I've heard cyborgs never get tired."

"If you give us thirty minutes, my head of security can make something nice for dinner."

"Your security officer? I'm not sure what's more alarming, the fact that you have a crew large enough to warrant a head of security or that he cooks."

"Technically, he's my only security officer," Alisa said. "But I assure you his food is wonderful, not alarming."

"Do I need to bring someone to taste it to make sure it's not poisoned?"

"Tomich, if I could afford fancy poisons, I wouldn't be piloting a seventy-year-old freighter."

He snorted. "You sure that scow is only seventy years old? Someone might have set the odometer back on you."

"Keep insulting my ship, and I *will* arrange for something special in your food."

"Poison?"

"I'd be foolish to poison an Alliance officer while I'm surrounded by Alliance ships. I do, however, have access to chicken droppings."

"Dastardly," Tomich said. "You know, I miss the days when you were working on my side."

"So do I," she said too softly for anyone to hear.

Almost anyone. Leonidas gazed down at her.

"Thirty minutes then," Tomich said. "We would prefer not to be met at gunpoint."

Leonidas said nothing but folded his arms over his chest.

"Thirty minutes," Alisa agreed, then hit the internal comm. "Beck? Where are you?"

"Finishing up with the doc in sickbay."

"We have guests coming to dinner. Can you make something nice in thirty minutes?"

"Thirty minutes? That's not enough time for a good marinade or rub. What are you trying to do to me? And who's coming to dinner? Not those androids, I assume."

"A commander, an admiral, a science officer, and a bunch of grunts."

"An admiral?" Beck's voice got a little squeaky. He was out of the Alliance now, but he might still find an admiral intimidating. Hells, Alisa found an admiral intimidating, and she wasn't intimidated by many people.

"Yes, one who used to work for the empire and defected, apparently." Alisa looked at Leonidas again. Did he have any intelligence on the officer that might be useful? She would have to see what she could get out of him in the next half hour.

"I'm not sure if that makes him more scary or less scary," Beck said.

"Neither am I." Alisa was tempted to ask Yumi if she had any special incense that might soothe nerves around the dinner table—or around the airlock hatch. When those soldiers came in, that would be the tensest moment, assuming Leonidas was standing at her side in his armor. She thought again of asking him to stay out of sight. "Yumi?"

Yumi's eyes were locked onto the sensor display, and she did not seem to hear her. She hadn't spoken in some time. Maybe she was running scans of the Alliance ships. Alisa wouldn't mind knowing if the research and medical vessels had any interesting capabilities in addition to their special hulls.

"Something interesting, Yumi?" she asked.

"I'm reading an anomaly."

"What kind of anomaly?"

"I don't know exactly. Your sensors are limited, but there's definitely a disturbance in space, with a growing amount of energy coming from an area roughly focused at the coordinates that Leonidas gave you."

"Are the Alliance ships moving away from it?"

"They're getting closer."

This might not be Alisa's mission, but she couldn't help but be curious. Curious and wary. Would her ship be safe if the energy anomaly grew? Was it the source of the radiation that had imbued those artifacts and ultimately killed everyone on that pilgrim ship?

"Invite me to dinner," Abelardus said, "and I'll get some answers from the officers."

"Won't you get those answers whether I invite you or not?" Alisa asked.

"Yes, but this way, I can sample Beck's food. I've heard grand things about it, but he hasn't offered me any yet."

"Odd."

"Yes."

"All right, gentlemen." Alisa made a shooing motion toward the corridor. "Let's go set the table. Yumi, keep me apprised, will you?"

Judging by the way her nose was to the sensor display and her eyes never wavered, she wasn't interested in going to dinner. "I will."

CHAPTER THIRTEEN

A clank sounded as the warship extended its airlock tube and fastened it to the *Nomad's* seal. Alisa shifted her weight from foot to foot. She stood between Leonidas and Abelardus. Abelardus had his staff, but was not otherwise armed. Leonidas wore his full combat armor, helmet included, and he carried two rifles, one cradled in his arms and one slung across his shoulder on a strap. Beck was in the mess hall, scrambling to get his meal together. Alisa hoped this was not all a ruse and that she wouldn't regret having her security officer in an apron instead of armor.

She also worried that seeing Leonidas armed would send Tomich's men reaching for their triggers. He had only given her a flat look when she'd suggested that he might find different attire more comfortable for dining. She had no idea if he intended to eat. If the scents of barbecuing meat and spices wafting into the cargo hold delighted his taste buds, he gave no indication of it.

Another clang sounded, followed by a knock. Alisa almost laughed. That had to be Tomich.

She started forward, but Leonidas stuck his hand out to stop her and strode toward the hatch. She went with him, determined that her unarmored face be the first thing that the soldiers would see.

The inner hatch already stood open, and she tried to slip past Leonidas to enter the airlock chamber so she could unlock the outer one.

"Alisa," he said softly, again stopping her with a hand out. "You can't assume that past relationships will play a role here. He will have his orders. This may be a trap. Like all the others, he may simply want the orb."

"If that's the case, you can shoot him just as easily from over there—" Alisa pointed to a spot three feet behind her, "—as you can from here." She pointed at the floor of the airlock chamber.

"You would be in the way of my fire," he said stubbornly. "And in the way of theirs. They could easily grab you."

"I appreciate your concern, but as the captain of this ship, I insist on greeting visitors personally. I'm afraid that if they see you first, there will be a scuffle. Or an all out war. And my cargo hold can't handle another battle." She waved to indicate the patches on the walls and the destroyed stairs—the mangled remains had been shoved under the walkway, and an improvised rope ladder hung in its place for now. "If you're going to work for me, you'll have to accept me as the captain and take orders. That's how it works. Chain of command and all that. I trust you're familiar with the concept." She wiggled her eyebrows at him.

He frowned. She waited for him to point out that he hadn't taken the job yet, or for him to simply scoff at the idea of taking orders from a lowly freighter captain. Instead, with his face grave, he stepped back. He didn't step back as far as the spot she had pointed at, but he did give her the space to open the hatch first.

The knock came again. Alisa turned and, with snakes slithering about in her stomach, pressed the hatch release button. Even though she wanted to trust Tomich, a part of her worried that Leonidas was right, that the Alliance soldiers might snatch her, take over her ship, and take anything they wanted.

The hatch opened, and Commander Tomich stood there, looking dapper in his uniform, a bottle held in one hand and the other pointedly held away from the blazer pistol holstered on his belt. He grinned at her, a roguish grin that always made him look closer to twenty than to forty and that won many ladies to his bed. Not that she'd ever been one of them. He was notorious for pursuing higher-ranking women. She wondered who he was luring to his bed these days. Leonidas's Admiral Tiang had sounded male.

"It's good to see you, Alisa," Tomich said, though his grin faltered when his gaze shifted toward Leonidas. "It is so odd seeing you with a cyborg standing at your back."

"I'd say it's odd seeing you with a bottle of alcohol in your hand, but we both know it's not."

The grin returned, if slightly more forced now. "No, it's not. Though I don't usually imbibe during duty hours. Our superiors frown upon that, as you may remember. This is for you." He thrust the bottle of clear liquid toward her with both hands. "A dinner gift."

"Thank you." Alisa accepted it, relieved he had brought sake instead of weapons. "Is this the part where I invite you in to enjoy the luxuries of my humble ship?"

She peered past his shoulder. Several young soldiers in combat armor were lined up behind him, though nobody was pointing a weapon in her direction. A couple of older officers waited at the far end of the airlock. The admiral and the science officer, she presumed.

"Luxuries?" Tomich looked at the patched walls. "You have luxuries here?"

"We have good food, if nothing else."

"That would be a welcome reprieve from our cook's rehydrated offerings."

Alisa turned to lead Tomich and his people into her cargo hold. Having all of those armored soldiers striding after her made her uneasy, but she felt better knowing that Tomich was between them and her. Leonidas stuck close, never straying more than a couple of feet from her side.

When the soldiers strode out of the airlock, they spread out, looking all over, presumably hunting for threats to their admiral. Every one of them gave Abelardus a long look, an even longer look than Leonidas received.

"Didn't you say a *few* soldiers?" Alisa asked, watching more than she expected enter the hold. "That looks more like twenty or thirty to me."

"Does it? Huh."

She propped a fist on her hip.

"Admiral Moreau only agreed to let Admiral Tiang come over if he came with a suitable guard," Tomich said.

"Moreau wasn't worried about you having a guard? Or your science officer?"

"Not really." He grinned again. "Tiang has a brilliant mind. He's not expendable."

"What does he do with his brilliant mind?" Alisa hadn't gotten much out of Leonidas when she had asked how he knew the doctor. He'd simply said he had been briefly involved in the military's cybernetics research division.

"Whatever he wants. He's published groundbreaking articles in thirteen different fields." Tomich waved toward the walkway as the last of his troops filtered in. "Nice ladder."

"The ship you drove away caught us in a grab beam and spewed drones, tanks, and androids in our direction."

"Its commander wanted the key, I presume?"

"You seem to know more about that now than the last time we met," Alisa said.

"I've been briefed." He looked down at her. "I'm sorry about your husband."

"Thank you," she said quietly, watching the soldiers stalking about, waving their weapons.

Tomich bumped her arm with the back of his hand. "If I give you a hug, will your bodyguard punt me across the room?"

Alisa looked up at Leonidas, but his faceplate was turned toward the soldiers, his hand resting on his rifle as he watched them.

"Probably not," Alisa said, "as long as you keep your pistol in your holster while you do it."

His grin was more of a leer this time. "That's a hard thing to do when talking to a pretty girl."

She swatted his arm, aware of Leonidas's faceplate turning toward them.

"You say things like that, and I'll tell Commander Kristia that your eyes are roaming," Alisa said.

"Alas, Commander Kristia and I are no more. I've got my eye on Admiral Fukusaku now."

"You don't have *another* admiral out here, do you?"

"No, she's back on Arkadius."

"How old is she?"

"Sixty, but she's very fit for her age." Tomich winked at her.

A throat cleared in the airlock tube. The two other officers had come forward, the white-haired one with medical insignia on his collar frowning slightly as he regarded Alisa and Tomich. Admiral Tiang, she presumed. He had dark, sharp almond-shaped eyes, and Alisa fought the urge to squirm. She almost saluted before remembering that she was a civilian now. The science officer wore captain's rank pins and appeared to be about fifty, a dark-skinned woman with wiry black hair shorn close to her head, and a perky yellow and orange earstar hooked over her helix. It was displaying a compact holodisplay in front of her eyes, data scrolling, and she only looked at Alisa briefly before returning focus to the display. Perhaps she was receiving updates about the energy anomaly that Yumi had noticed.

"Admiral," Tomich said, "this is Captain Marchenko. She was one of our fighter pilots during the war."

"Yes." Tiang's gaze passed over her with indifference before scanning the rest of the cargo hold and settling on Leonidas.

Leonidas lifted his hands to his helmet and unfastened it. A few of the soldiers who had been keeping an eye on him fingered their weapons uneasily, but nobody pointed one at him.

When Leonidas's helmet came off, the admiral nodded to himself, as if he expected nothing less. Tomich's mouth opened, surprise flickering in his eyes. Alisa was surprised too. She had assumed Leonidas would remain fully armored in the presence of the Alliance soldiers.

"Dr. Tiang," Leonidas said.

"Colonel Adler. I heard you were over here. It is good to see you."

Leonidas inclined his head. "I should like to speak with you if you can make time this evening, sir."

What was this? Leonidas hadn't mentioned pulling aside admirals for private chats.

"I—if there's time, certainly." Despite his cordial greeting, Tiang appeared slightly uncomfortable under Leonidas's gaze. It was far from one of his worst gazes. Leonidas almost appeared affable, which Alisa found strange. Shouldn't he be irked that such a high-ranking imperial officer had gone over to the other side?

"Good." Leonidas inclined his head once.

"Something smells tasty, Alisa," Tomich said. "Is that the dinner you promised?"

"Yes, follow me."

Alisa led the officers to the ladder, lamenting the awkward way that they had to get to the upper portion of the ship. Mica was toiling away in engineering, making more permanent solutions for those patches. Alas, stairs weren't high on the repairs priority list.

Alisa? Abelardus spoke into her mind as she led the procession up the ladder.

She almost missed a rung and fell. *What?*

I can't read the admiral's thoughts.

Alisa wished Abelardus had that problem when it came to her. *Is that highly unusual, or does it happen sometimes?*

It happens sometimes, but I also can't read the commander's thoughts. I believe they may have taken some drug to inhibit me. There are a few things like that out there.

Yes, Alisa remembered Yumi saying that she had something in her cabin that would befuddle telepathic Starseers.

You get anything from the rest of them? The soldiers? Alisa climbed onto the walkway and waited for her guests to join her.

Nothing duplicitous, Abelardus said. *They believe they're here to guard their officers during this dinner.*

It could be that Tomich and Tiang didn't want you to be able to learn about the anomaly and what the Alliance has been researching out here.

Once again, Alisa wished she hadn't warned Tomich that she had a Starseer onboard. If she hadn't, they wouldn't have thought to take precautions, and Abelardus would now have free rein to surf through their thoughts and discover all manner of secret information. As much as she hated it when he was in her head, she had to admit that it was useful to have an ally with such powers.

Of course it is, he said smugly. *As to the rest, I suspect you're right, but you may want to watch them carefully, see if your simple intuition might be useful in detecting treachery.*

My simple intuition and I will do so.

Tomich brushed his hands off after he climbed onto the walkway and came to stand next to her. "Your ship took a lot of damage, didn't it?"

"I wasn't lying when I said we need time for repairs," Alisa said.

"I'll do my best to see that you get it." Tomich glanced at his admiral and stepped away from her.

Leonidas jumped up to join them without using the ladder. The damaged walkway shivered as he landed on it. A few of the soldiers below started, fingering their weapons. Alisa waved for the officers to follow her, not wanting to test how much weight the damaged walkway could withstand, not until Mica had time to look at it.

More than a dozen of the soldiers scrambled up the ladder after their officers. A few took Leonidas's route, eschewing the wobbly rope and using the extra power from their combat armor to jump the twelve feet. The looks they gave him seemed to hold a challenge, as if they were pointing out that they, too, could do inhuman feats, at least while in their armor.

"Evening, Captain," Beck said, saluting her with tongs when she walked into the mess hall. He wore his apron, but a sheathed dagger and a blazer pistol hung from his belt underneath it.

As her guests filed in, Alisa did her best not to cringe at the mismatched and dented cups and plates set at the table. They were clean but that was the highest accolade she could give them. As with everything else on the *Nomad*, upgrades were needed. She imagined the admiral being accustomed to lavish dinners on flagships, both imperial and Alliance, with dedicated mess soldiers scurrying about, keeping crystal wineglasses full.

Yumi must have been recruited for this service because she walked about the table, filling the cups with tea. Alisa almost wished she had suggested that Yumi put something more potent into people's beverages, something that might make tongues flap freely and put people at ease. She hoped the officers wouldn't invite any of the soldiers to dine with them. There were only ten plates, those representing the extent of the *Nomad's* tableware collection. She also was not sure how the benches would stand up under the weight of armored butts.

Four jars of some kind of liquid—sauce?—with homemade labels sat in the center of the table amid platters of food. Two were a normal-looking reddish color. One was green, and one was blue. Alisa could already imagine the admiral regarding the blue with skepticism. Hopefully, Tomich was not thinking of poisonings.

"Come on in, everyone," Beck said, waving his tongs in invitation, appearing as casual as always, though Alisa had come to know him well enough to recognize nervousness in the pinch of his brows. He licked his lips and glanced at her when the admiral walked in. "Sit anywhere," he offered. "We've got Arkadian sausage, Senekda short ribs, beans, and slaw. Pan-grilled cornbread with jakloff butter and honey too."

As far as Alisa had noticed, Beck cooked everything on the grill if he could. The *Nomad* had an oven, and it usually worked with minimal fiddling and prodding, but he did not feel a dish was complete unless it claimed some char marks.

"What is this, Marchenko?" Tomich asked, picking up a cup. "Tea? It's a good thing I brought the sake."

"It is," she agreed. "I haven't had an opportunity to shop for alcoholic provisions yet." She decided not to mention that the modest fares that her three passengers paid her did not go a long way toward outfitting a ship with luxuries. Or basics. That was probably apparent from the dented plates.

The admiral sat at one end of the table and sniffed at the substance in his cup. Tomich smiled easily, though he also seemed to scrutinize everything around him, and he nodded for several of the soldiers to stand in the corridor that led toward crew cabins and navigation. Alisa watched, trying not to feel fenced in. Several of the soldiers leaned against the walls, appearing more bored than alert. She decided to take that as a sign that they were probably not planning anything inimical.

Yumi finished pouring cups and sat at the far end of the table from the admiral. Mica arrived, elbowing soldiers aside to get inside. From the way her gaze devoured the plates on the table, hunger had likely prompted this appearance rather than a desire to be sociable. Alejandro wasn't around and did not join them. Alisa thought about calling for him—maybe he would appreciate talking shop with another doctor—but she could understand why a loyal former imperial citizen might not want to fraternize with Alliance officers. Especially when one of those officers had switched sides.

"Let me do a few introductions," Alisa said, waiting for everyone to be seated before she picked a spot next to Mica. Leonidas stood near a counter, his helmet back on, a rifle resting in his arms. He might wish to chat with Tiang, but apparently, he wouldn't let his guard down to do it while they ate. "This is Yumi Moon, my science-loving passenger," she said, waving at Yumi. "This is my engineer, Mica Coppervein. That's another passenger, Abelardus Shepherd." He had chosen a spot in the middle of the table, his fingers intertwined in front of him. "Our cook for the night is my security officer, Tommy Beck. And you've met Leo—Colonel Adler."

Normally, she wouldn't break his cover, but Tiang had already addressed him by his real name.

Alisa settled into the empty spot between Mica and Abelardus and across from Tomich. Aside from the dubious blue liquid, Beck had done a wonderful job preparing a meal, especially given the short notice. She only hoped that the admiral would appreciate the food and that his and Tomich's questions would not be too invasive. She was secretly glad that Alejandro wasn't around, because she would like to explain everything to the Alliance officers, in the hope that it might filter upward, and any black marks on her record could be removed. All she wanted was to find Jelena, not become an outlaw.

"I'm Commander Brad Tomich," Tomich said, nodding to the various people Alisa had introduced, except for Leonidas, "and this is Admiral Tiang, and that's Captain Onobanjo, one of our science officers."

The captain's holodisplay still scrolled before her eyes, but she gave them all a cordial nod.

"Are you going to tell us about that energy surge?" Yumi asked brightly, sitting across from the science officer.

Abelardus started shoveling beans and slaw onto his plate. Leonidas settled in behind Alisa with his back to the counter, where he could see both doorways and keep an eye on the soldiers. In addition to those that had positioned themselves around the room, in similar guard stances to his, several more were visible out on the walkway, along with the handful in the corridor that led to NavCom. The rest had stayed down in the cargo hold—at least Alisa hoped they were down there and not wandering around engineering.

Mica left a no-trespassing sign on the door to engineering, Abelardus informed her.

And they're obeying it?

For now.

"I believe the answer to that question is classified," Onobanjo told Yumi, folding her hands on the table and eyeing the coils of sausage on a platter.

"Another hour, and it won't matter," Tomich said.

"*If* this ship is still here then," Tiang said, his eyes narrowing.

"Yes, my superiors aren't quite sure why we didn't drive you away, Alisa," Tomich said, "but I've been wondering how you got mixed up in all of this. I wouldn't have guessed you to have an interest in Starseer artifacts." He glanced at Abelardus.

"It's a long story." A story that Alisa was prepared to launch into, but apparently, her words led Beck to believe that she wouldn't do so, because he stepped up to the end of the table and spoke.

"Friends, old and new," he said, "I thank you for joining us for dinner. I've already informed you as to what you'll be eating, and I particularly recommend the spicy arangwa pepper slaw, but I also invite you to try all of the sauces you see before you." He smiled at the admiral. "I left the meats only lightly seasoned so you can appreciate the various flavor profiles."

Flavor profiles? Alisa plastered her hand to her face. What kind of chef-speak was that? And why was he doing it *now?*

"This one is a simple barbecue sauce sweetened with apple cider," Beck went on, pointing to the first jar. "It's a perennial favorite. For more of a kick, the next one is my infamous beer and molasses sauce. Highly recommended."

Tomich and the admiral exchanged perplexed looks. Alisa tried to catch Beck's eye and make a cutting motion, but he only had eyes for his sauces—and for the admiral. For some reason, he was giving Tiang a lot of attention.

"My third offering is an extra spicy sauce, also flavored with the aromatic and excellent arangwa pepper. Lastly, we have one of my favorites, blueberry balsamic sauce. You'll find it extremely tasty on the ribs, and some people like it on the cornbread, though the cornbread is delicious all by itself."

"Thank you, Beck," Alisa said, hoping to stop him from going into further details. She could understand his pride in his cooking, but they had headier matters to discuss.

"You're welcome. All of the sauces are available for purchase," he went on, "and I also have samples available. Ah, Admiral?"

"Yes?" Tiang asked cautiously.

"I'm sure you're a man of influence and power back home."

"He's a man of influence right at this table," Tomich said, while giving Alisa a what-is-your-chef-doing look.

She shrugged back at him. Explaining Beck's passions and dreams for the future, not to mention his fear of having the mafia catch up with him before he could achieve them, was too much to bring up now.

"Of course," Beck said. "But back home, I imagine he goes to fancy dinners with government officials and other important military officers, people who might enjoy samples of excellent sauces from the far reaches of space."

"Think those flavor profiles are getting a boost from the radiation leaking out of space nearby?" Tomich asked, smirking.

Yumi's eyebrows rose. "We're not able to read radiation on these sensors, not very effectively. Is the source of it the same as the source of the energy I've been reading?"

Alisa gave her a silent thank-you for getting the conversation back on topic. Beck looked like he might try to finagle another chance to sell his condiments to the admiral. Alisa caught his eye and made a sit-down motion. Deflated, he removed his apron and slid in at the end of the table. The seats near the admiral had been taken, fortunately. Tiang might go to official military functions, but he did not look like the kind of man who went to a lot of social gatherings—or bought souvenir barbecue sauces.

"If you *could* read the radiation levels, you wouldn't have dared come this close," Captain Onobanjo said, her voice still distracted. She leaned close to the admiral and whispered something.

Alisa looked at Abelardus, hating to depend on him but wondering if he had any insight to what they had said. Normally, she would look to Leonidas for deciphering whispers, but that would be more obvious—and he couldn't speak the answer into her mind.

No, I'm handy. Abelardus smiled at her. *Her thoughts are clearer. She's been studying the phenomenon, along with the admiral and several Alliance experts in—oh, that's interesting.* He tilted his head, gazing at Onobanjo. *I wondered if it might be something like that, but I don't have the science background to know what's possible and what isn't.*

What?

He kept gazing at Onobanjo, apparently reading her mind like a scintillating book.

Alisa elbowed him.

"Colonel," Admiral Tiang said, spooning beans and sausage onto his plate. "Won't you join us for this meal?"

"I'm on duty, sir," Leonidas said.

"Duty? The empire is no more, as I'm certain you've noticed." Tiang let out a wistful sigh. "As I regret. I had little choice but to switch my allegiances if I was to continue my research."

Alisa watched him, trying to use her simple intuition, as Abelardus had called it. He had struck her as a reserved man, someone difficult to read, so that sigh seemed strangely emotive. Of course, she had only spent ten minutes in his company. It was early to make assumptions about him.

"I work here now," Leonidas said.

"On this dingy, dented freighter?" Tiang looked at the dented cabinets and wrinkled his nose in Alisa's direction.

Surprisingly, Mica glared frostily at him. She was usually the first one to mock the *Nomad*, but maybe it was different when the insults came from an outsider.

"Are you trying to imply that Tomich's warship is a better home?" Alisa asked. "Because I've seen him land ships before. If that one is any less dented than this one, it's only because he has a fast-acting team of mechanics with welding torches and hammers."

"Now, now, Alisa," Tomich murmured. "You know commanders don't have to land their own ships."

"Is that why they promoted you? To save hangar bays all across Alliance space?" She shut her mouth before she could say more. She felt defensive about her ship, but she did not truly wish to insult Tomich. The snobby admiral, on the other hand...

"That might have played into Command's decision," Tomich said.

"Seriously, Colonel," Tiang said, ignoring the jibes and focusing on Leonidas. "Please, join us. Did you not wish to speak with me? Before I was called out to this situation, I was working on something you might find interesting. Did you know the Alliance is investing funding into creating a cyborg program? Perhaps you could offer some feedback, based on your own experiences."

Alisa expected Leonidas to scoff and say that he had no interest in helping the Alliance with anything, but after a moment of hesitation, and a last look around the room at the soldiers, he lifted his hands to his helmet. A soft snap sounded as he undid the fasteners. He set the helmet on the counter next to him.

None of the soldiers reacted strongly, but a couple of the men who had been leaning nonchalantly stood straighter now.

"You worked with Dr. Bartosz for a time, didn't you, sir?" Leonidas asked.

It was strange hearing him call someone sir. Even though he must have done it to superior officers in the fleet, the *Nomad* had yet to run into any of those on its adventures.

"I did," Tiang said. "When I was a younger doctor, before I got so heavily into research, I even assisted with a few of the surgeries."

Leonidas stepped forward, his eyes intent. Did he think the admiral had some of the answers that he had hoped to find on that station?

Tiang's eyes were also intent, almost calculating. He wasn't up to something, was he?

"Sit," Tiang offered, waving for his science officer to scoot aside. "Have some food with me. Tell me if you've experienced any troubles over the years, things we should avoid if possible if we do another generation of military cyborgs."

Leonidas took another step, and Alisa found herself noticing his helmet, the way it was now several paces away from him. Maybe it was nothing. Maybe the admiral was truly curious about him, but her senses, her simple intuition twanged.

"Leonidas," she said. "Perhaps you and the admiral could discuss this later. I believe Tomich wanted to tell us about what his people are doing out here."

"That's not exactly why we came over," Tomich said dryly.

"Colonel," the admiral said, rising to his feet. "Let's talk privately for a few moments, shall we?" Tiang gestured toward the corner of the mess hall.

Leonidas hesitated, and Alisa wondered if he shared some of her suspicions about the officer's intentions. But for some reason, a gleam of hope brightened his eyes, and he followed Tiang around the table and to the corner. They started talking softly, the admiral gesturing expansively.

"Alisa," Tomich whispered. "Are you working *with* them or *for* them?" He nodded toward Leonidas. "I can't help but notice that nobody has you tied up."

"Not yet," Mica muttered. "I think she's hoping for that eventually."

Alisa elbowed her. "I'm just a captain carrying passengers," she told Tomich. "I'm not quite sure how it happened, but I got involved in a quest I have no interest in. All of this is getting in the way of my own… mission."

"So, you'd consider it a favor if we got rid of some of your passengers for you?"

"No. They paid their fare."

Tomich squinted in puzzlement. Alisa groped for a way to explain that she did not want Alejandro or Abelardus here, but she wasn't willing to betray them, not when Leonidas was tangled up in the equation.

"Even the cyborg?" Tomich asked, nodding toward Leonidas.

"Especially him."

"In taking them on, you've been working against our people." Tomich leaned forward, his hands doing something under the table. Fiddling with a napkin? "What happened at Arkadius? The reports say that you fought with the Starseers against the Alliance."

Alisa took a deep breath. This was her chance to come clean, to explain everything. "I—"

A faint clink came from under the table. Alisa started to lean back to look under it, but Leonidas barked, "Gas!"

"Get them," Tomich ordered his men, surging to his feet.

Leonidas whirled toward his helmet, looking like he would leap over the table and everyone sitting there to get at it. Admiral Tiang lunged away from him, and Leonidas switched directions. He caught the man by the throat.

"No," Alisa blurted, confused as to what was happening, but if he killed an Alliance officer...

The soldiers in the room and in the corridors raised their weapons at him. Leonidas put his back to the corner, pulling the admiral against him to block the soldiers' line of fire. The men did not shoot, but they all looked ready to do so at the first opportunity.

"Are you truly going to kill me, Colonel?" Admiral Tiang asked, his voice only slightly affected by the hand around his throat. Leonidas wasn't grasping him tightly. "I believe I know what you want. I may be the only one who can give it to you."

Leonidas eyed his helmet on the other side of the mess hall. Alisa worried about moving with all of those fingers on triggers, but she slid under the table and crawled toward the other side. If she could reach the helmet and throw it to Leonidas, he could protect himself from whatever gas he had detected—and protect his head from fire.

She bumped something as she navigated between moving boots—Tomich and the science officer were shifting to stand, to get out of the way. A spherical canister rolled away from her. Tomich had dropped that—she was sure of it. Nothing to be done now. She held her breath as she crawled out from under the table on the far side and leaped to her feet. She lunged for the helmet, but someone caught her from behind.

Instinctively, she drove her elbow back, not bothering to look at who had her. It sank into someone's stomach with satisfying force, and a pained male grunt sounded in her ear. She jabbed her would-be captor again, stomped on his instep, and whirled, following the attack with a palm strike to the sternum.

Tomich stumbled back, his legs catching on the bench. He crashed down to the deck, leaving Alisa with a view of Leonidas and Tiang as Leonidas pushed the admiral down and leaped away from him, toward the soldiers.

The squeals of blazer fire erupted, and streaks of crimson and orange leaped through the mess hall. Those without weapons and armor dropped to the deck. Alisa started to grab Leonidas's helmet, but he would never see her, never catch it if she threw it. He had hurled himself into a knot of armored soldiers in the corridor, trying to drop them while also keeping them in the way of their comrades' fire.

A *hiss-clink* came from the other corridor, and smoke started spewing into the mess hall.

Benches toppled to the ground. Alisa crouched, trying to stay out of the way as she reached for her Etcher. The weapon wasn't there. She hadn't brought it to dinner.

Tomich recovered and scrambled for the corridor that led to the cargo hold. With Leonidas battling the soldiers there, he couldn't get through, so he pressed his back to a wall. He dug something out of his pocket and stuck it into his nostrils. Filter plugs. He had come prepared. The soldiers might not have known this was an ambush, but Tiang and Tomich surely had.

Alisa took a step toward him, not caring that she had no weapon. She would punch him again if she had to, rip out the plugs and make him breathe his own gas. So far, she did not feel the effects of anything, but smoke rolled into the room, and she still didn't know what was in the canister Tomich had unleashed under the table.

More soldiers charged into the room. Beck roared and leaped toward one, his dagger in one hand and his pistol in the other. His apron flapped about his thighs. The weapons would be useless against men in armor.

Mica and Yumi made their way over to Alisa, crouching beside the counter to try and stay out of the way of fire. Abelardus reached a corner, putting his back to the wall, and took a deep breath, his eyes narrowing as he focused on the battle.

A soldier jumped out of the corridor, escaping Leonidas, and reached for Alisa. She kicked out, but only connected with an armored shin. Striking it hurt, even through her boot. A hand latched onto her shoulder.

Beck was flung onto the table. He bounced off, upending it as he fell, all of his food pitching to the deck. Alisa tried to twist away from the man grabbing her shoulder, but he only tightened his grip. Then an invisible force struck her, hurling her into the air, along with the soldier and two more men. It seemed like the entire contingent of soldiers was in the mess hall. Why hadn't Leonidas flattened them by now? What were ten to one odds to him?

As Alisa flew over the table and neared a wall, something invisible softened her landing. The soldiers hit hard, armor crunching, but she only bumped it and slid to the deck. Abelardus saluted her from across the room, then focused on another group of soldiers.

Alisa spun toward NavCom. If she could get up there, she could fly them away from the airlock, strand Tomich and his admiral here, and keep the *Alliance* from getting what it wanted.

She ducked the grasp of a soldier reaching for her, but he was fast, his speed enhanced by his armor. She had to turn the duck into a drop down to the deck. A wave of energy slammed into the man, helping her escape. She scrambled to her feet, again veering toward NavCom.

A soldier ahead of her gripped Mica from behind. She thrashed wildly, kicking at anyone who came close, but she could not escape.

Alisa hesitated, wanting to help, but what could she do? She glanced back, expecting to find that Leonidas had mowed down most of the soldiers and was running in to help them. Instead, he lay on his back on the deck, his eyes staring upward, unblinking.

She stumbled and nearly fell. What the hells? They hadn't... They *couldn't* have... killed him?

Tomich leaped over Leonidas's fallen form, pushing the admiral ahead of him. The science officer had already disappeared, heading back toward the cargo hold and the airlock. Alisa wanted to run after them. *They* weren't armored. She could pummel them senseless. But two soldiers lunged toward her. Another was on the deck, wrestling with Abelardus amid a mess of spilled food. She hated to leave Leonidas and the others, but she would only end up captured if she stayed.

She whirled and sprinted through the smoke choking the corridor and to NavCom. It was full of even more smoke, a grayish-green miasma.

She reared back, holding her breath and clamping her mouth shut as soon as she realized the threat. She couldn't smell anything, but that did not mean much.

Footsteps thundered on the decking behind her. Alisa lunged into the murky smoke, spinning to grab the hatch. She tried to shove it closed, but an armored hand reached inside, clasping the wall. The owner of it struck the hatch with his shoulder, and it was thrown open. It bumped into Alisa hard enough to throw her back. Her head cracked against the bulkhead near the sensor station, and her precious air escaped.

A soldier jumped inside. She tried to dive away from him, still hoping to reach her controls, to veer away from the warship, but he caught her easily. He had his armor to assist him, and she had nothing. Worse than nothing. Her movements felt sluggish, and she feared she had already inhaled some of that gas.

He hefted her over his shoulder as if she weighed nothing and turned back toward the corridor.

"Tomich," Alisa yelled, giving up on the idea of avoiding breathing the gas. "You're a worse dinner guest than you are a pilot!"

She lamented that nothing snappier came to mind. It probably did not matter. Was he even on the ship anymore? Or had he and his duplicitous admiral escaped?

As the soldier maneuvered her through the hatchway, she caught a glimpse of the view screen through the smoke. Before, only stars and the hull of the warship had been visible on it. Now, out where the other ships hovered, something new was visible. Or something very old.

A dark space station spun in place, the axis-and-wheel design that had been common after the Order Wars, after mankind returned to space but still had to use fancy tricks to create artificial gravity. It had been at least three hundred years since anything like that had been built.

Alisa tried to get a better look, but her captor toted her into the corridor. She growled and thumped her fists on the soldier's back. Even without his armor, she doubted it would have done anything. She thumped him again out of frustration.

"Let go," came a cry from the direction of the crew and passenger cabins. Alejandro. Such an anguished and drawn out, "No!" followed that she thought he was in true pain.

Then a soldier said, "Got it," his voice muffled by his helmet, and she realized what had happened. More than that, she realized what this entire chat must have been about. Getting the orb. Tomich and his people were no better than the treasure-hunting androids. At least the android captain had been upfront and honest about what he wanted.

Her captor dropped Alisa in the mess hall next to Beck and Mica. Both of them lay sprawled amid the spilled food, their eyes closed. Abelardus was unconscious in the corner next to two armored soldiers who also appeared to be out. Alisa lifted her head—it was so heavy she could barely manage it. Her eyelids kept trying to droop shut. It would be much easier to lay her head on the deck than to continue to fight. What was the point? The Alliance had won. Shouldn't she be happy? What did she care about Starseer artifacts?

Except she *did* care about Leonidas, and he still lay in the mouth of the corridor, his frozen eyes staring upward. His helmet was uselessly back on the counter where he had left it. Where that damned admiral had tricked him into leaving it.

"Don't be dead," she whispered. Her lips and tongue were so numb that it came out in a jumble.

Someone dropped Alejandro next to her, a gag in his mouth and ties binding his hands behind his back. His form blocked her view of Leonidas. She tried to lift her head again, to see over him, but she couldn't manage it.

Her eyes shut, and she slumped to the deck, succumbing to unconsciousness.

CHAPTER FOURTEEN

Alisa awoke to someone nudging her shoulder. She opened her eyes, squinting against light that seemed far too harsh. Her first thought was that she had woken in some blindingly lit brig or interrogation cell, but she soon realized she was still on the deck in the mess hall. The lights only seemed blinding because she had a hellish headache. Her throat also felt thick and phlegmy. She did not know what gas the soldiers had used on them, but she hoped to shove a giant canister of it down Tomich's throat one day.

She forced her eyes fully open, trying to focus on the blurry red figure in front of her.

Red! Leonidas?

"Alisa?" he said softly.

It *was* him.

"You're alive," she croaked.

He sighed. He did not sound nearly as enthused about the fact as she.

"Tyranoadhuc gas," he said. "They came prepared to deal with me."

"Yeah," she said, struggling to sit up even though her head throbbed. Leonidas helped her. "Tomich dropped it. I saw him fiddling under the table, but I wasn't nearly suspicious enough. He was one of the commanders at our Perun moon skirmish. He must have heard all about you from the crew of that salvage tug."

"The smoke that came later was a sedative," Leonidas added. "That's what got you and the others. I don't think I breathed in as much, since I was flat on my back with my lungs barely working." He made a disgusted noise, directed more at himself than at the situation, she guessed.

Glad for his arm holding her upright, Alisa peered around the mess hall. There was food spattered everywhere, including on the walls and even the ceiling, but someone had turned the table and benches upright. Leonidas must have been waiting for someone to wake up. Abelardus, Mica, and Beck were still out. Alejandro was awake and had been untied, but he hadn't moved from the spot where the soldiers had dropped him. He sat with his knees drawn to his chest, his hands over his head, his position one of utter dejection.

"I should have kept him as a shield," Leonidas grumbled.

"Who?" Alisa asked. "The admiral?"

"Yes. But I couldn't—I didn't want him getting hit." He sighed again. "I shouldn't have left my helmet behind. I was lulled—I let myself be led aside, because I wanted to hear what he had to say. He used to be one of our people, and he's one of the researchers familiar with cyborg tech. I wanted to trust him, even though I doubted..." He shook his head.

"I was surprised you seemed to care about the Alliance starting up a cyborg division."

"I didn't. What I want from him is personal."

Beck groaned, and his fingers twitched.

"Dominguez," Leonidas said. "Take care of the others." He stood, lifting Alisa to her feet. "You should see this."

Alejandro did not acknowledge him, but Leonidas guided her toward NavCom. Her legs barely worked, but his arm around her waist kept her upright.

"They got his orb," Leonidas said.

"I heard. At least the android treasure hunters won't have a reason to attack us now, right?"

His expression grim, Leonidas did not answer.

"Are all the soldiers off my ship?" Alisa wished she had gotten that chance to punch Tomich.

"Yes. They were gone and the warship had already moved away by the time I was able to move and get up."

He ducked through the hatchway leading into NavCom and guided her inside, sitting her in the pilot's seat. He pointed at the view screen, to the space station visible in the center of the Alliance armada. Tomich's warship had moved closer, to join the others, though she noticed that it and the other large warship were staying farther back than the medical and research vessels. Maybe they had less shielding against radiation than the other ships? Or maybe the space station was emitting more than radiation? Yumi had mentioned energy.

Alisa turned and shifted through the various displays at the sensor station, trying to find what she had been looking at. There was a lot of data, and she did not know how to interpret all of it. She could tell that the station's wheel was spinning and that it was maintaining a stationary position. Some of the more modern stations had repositioning thrusters and the capability of travel. This one did not. If it had possessed something like that, it might have explained how it could have moved into the area, but it was old and basic. And inexplicably there.

"You don't look surprised," Leonidas remarked.

"No, I had a glimpse of it earlier. Albeit, I was dangling over someone's shoulder at the time. I'm beginning to wonder why men always carry me like that when they're capturing me."

He smiled faintly. "You're a good height for it. And they can grab you around the waist to anchor you down."

"Waist, please. You mean they can grab my ass and enjoy themselves while they're squishing me."

His gaze drifted toward her backside. It was more skeptical than intrigued.

"It's enjoyable. Trust me." Alisa flipped to another display. "There are odd readings coming from the space around the station, aren't there? Will you get Yumi, please? See if she's up?"

"Yes." He ducked back into the corridor and disappeared.

Alisa sneered at the jargon scrolling down the display, then turned toward the comm. There were answers aplenty on those Alliance ships. Could she convince someone to give them to her?

It occurred to her that she could simply steer the *Nomad* out of the quarantined area and turn her back on this mystery. Especially if Abelardus was still unconscious and Alejandro was indisposed by his depression. Who would stop her? Leonidas? She'd done what he had asked of her when he made his bargain, offering to work for her. Surely, the men could not expect her to stay now? With the orb—the key—gone, what could they do here?

Despite the thoughts, she tapped the comm to hail Tomich's warship. After tricking her, didn't he owe her an explanation?

"Yes?" came a cautious response.

Huh, Tomich himself had answered. She had expected a low-ranking comm officer. Or to be ignored altogether.

"What's the orb going to do for you?" she asked.

He did not answer, though she could hear the murmur of voices and beeping of equipment in the background. He must be on the bridge.

"Come on," Alisa said. "You might as well tell me. What am I going to do now? Besides, don't you feel guilty for coming over and enjoying our food and then ambushing us?"

"Moderately, but you're the one strolling around arm-in-arm with a cyborg. I'm only protecting the interests of the Alliance."

"Arm-in-arm? He's my employee, just like Beck. He's retired. He's no threat to you, or wouldn't have been if you'd left us alone and simply eaten your beans and sausage. By the way, Beck will want to know if you all enjoyed his sauces."

"Look, Alisa. I'm sorry. You're the one who got involved with something that's way over your head. And you said you don't care about it. Why bother asking now?"

"Well, there's a big old space station on my view screen that wasn't there an hour ago, so I'm curious."

"Curiosity gets pilots killed."

"Also, we saw one of the ships that came out of this quarantined area, Tomich. It flew right by those coordinates, and it had some radioactive junk inside, junk that was killing its people. We boarded it and saw the dead crew."

"You boarded it? You weren't...exposed to that radiation, were you?" He truly sounded worried. Funny how many of her old comrades cared about her and yet betrayed her all the same. "Alisa, three suns, why can't you just run freight like a normal civilian freighter captain?"

"I'm special."

"Oh, I know *that*."

"Tomich, the station? Please. I'd like to know why those people died."

Leonidas and Yumi entered NavCom, Leonidas supporting her much as he had Alisa. Yumi's face was pale, but her eyes widened and then intensified with sharp interest as she gazed upon the station.

"It's the station," Tomich said. "The entire thing is emitting intense radiation."

"How? Why?"

"I was studying the rift earlier," Yumi said when Tomich did not respond immediately.

"Rift?" Alisa kept the comm open, still hoping Tomich would enlighten them further, but she turned toward Yumi.

"A dimensional rift, I believe. I wasn't sure what to expect when the massive energy surge was building, but this isn't surprising."

"It is to me," Alisa said.

"Dimensional rifts are not without precedent, but this is, from what I've read, the first time it's happened in our system. The mining corporations have been experimenting and trying to create such rifts, or doorways into other dimensions, so they could exploit the nearby resources that might exist in dimensions similar to this one. That could potentially be more feasible than interstellar travel, since humans have yet to figure out how to travel between stars, aside from our trio of closely linked ones, in a timely manner. The original colonists for *our* system spent centuries in cryogenic sleep to arrive here."

"I know *that.* Tell me about these dimensions."

"If you're unaware of the multiverse theory, which has all but been proven now, it's the notion that multiple universes exist in addition to the one in which we live. We call them parallel universes or dimensional planes. They rarely interpenetrate of their own accord, but astronomers looking into distant parts of the galaxy have discovered rifts that may represent possible doorways."

"You're saying that's a doorway?" Alisa pointed at the space station.

"The space around it could be, yes."

"What made the station pop through that doorway, right now? And did that doorway exist a month ago? A year ago? It couldn't have. When Leonidas gave me these coordinates, I looked them up. Sys-net had absolutely nothing to say about them. No mention of rifts or doorways to interesting new dimensions."

Yumi spread her arms. "I have no way of knowing why it's there now and wasn't before."

"We believe the Starseers made the rift," Tomich said, startling Alisa. She had forgotten he was still on the channel. "And when I say *we*, I mean my scientists informed me of their hypothesis."

"I assumed that," Alisa said. "As I recall, your hobbies are drinking, women, and gambling, not astronomy."

"I also enjoy needlepoint, to calm my nerves after a battle."

"Ha ha. What do you mean the Starseers made the rift?" Alisa pointed toward the hatchway, about to ask Leonidas to get Abelardus, but he was already walking up the corridor toward them, steadying himself by leaning on his staff.

"It's their station," Tomich said. "Or it was. After centuries of floating in unclaimed space, it's arguably open for salvage operations to anyone who can get to it."

"So we could fly over there and take a look for ourselves, and the Alliance wouldn't stop us?"

Abelardus stopped in the hatchway and looked toward the view screen. It should have been his first time seeing the station, but he did not appear surprised by its presence.

"We *would* stop you," Tomich said. "For your own safety, as we've been stopping every ship that comes close."

"Our own safety, huh? And so you can keep whatever's in the station for yourself?"

"Alisa, your ship isn't shielded enough to withstand the radiation coming from it. We would stop you for your own good. You said you already saw what happens to people who get close."

"To people who get close and take glowing plaques out of it, yes."

"Those likely came from the hull or were debris floating around outside of the station, being pulled into and out of the rift with it. Nobody's gotten in yet."

"Because a key is required, by chance?"

"Our people have been working on the hull, trying to cut a way in," Tomich said, "but it's surprisingly sturdy, and they have limited time in which to work. The station comes in and out of our dimension. Our first group of people disappeared with it, and when they came back…they were dead."

"You shouldn't be tinkering with what you don't understand, Commander," Abelardus said.

Alisa frowned at him and made a shushing motion. "I'm sorry for your loss, Tomich." Even though she was irritated with him, she didn't want him to close the channel and stop talking to her. Nor did she want to make light of lost soldiers, men and women who may have been directly under his command.

Tomich did not respond to either of their comments.

"Yumi," Alisa said, lowering her voice, "any idea as to why it's radioactive?"

"Presumably, the dimension it's coming from has a radioactive phenomenon nearby, or it's possible that the entire dimension has a much higher level of background radiation than our own."

"That's what our scientists believe," Tomich said. "We've watched the station shift into and out of our dimension five times now."

"How long does it stay each time?" Alisa asked. "Is it regular?"

"You'll forgive me if I don't tell you," Tomich said. "I've already shared too much. I know you, Marchenko. You might be planning to go take a look at it right now."

"Not if we'll get irradiated if we get close. I'm fine looking at it from here."

"Good," Tomich said. "Stay safe."

He cut the comm.

"Seven hours, thirty-seven minutes," Abelardus said. "It's as regular as clockwork."

"The station told you that?" Alisa asked.

"I saw it in Commander Tomich's mind."

"Ah." She considered him, the calmness with which he gazed at the station, the lack of surprise on his face when he first walked in. "Did you expect this to be here, Abelardus?"

"Since we saw the plaque, yes. The presence of a station explains some of our history in regard to Alcyone and her staff."

"Such as?"

"When she knew she was dying, she and her most trusted aides found a way to hide the staff," Leonidas said, speaking for the first time in several minutes. He had been standing and listening, absorbing everything.

Abelardus glanced at him in surprise.

"It was in the nursery rhyme," Leonidas said. "The same one that gave us the coordinates. It spoke of the fall of Kir and of the famous villain-traitor Alcyone, along with her final resting place."

"Hundreds of years ago, the Starseers had power enough to make an inter-dimensional rift?" Alisa asked.

"It likely took many of them to do so, but I'm not surprised," Abelardus said.

"I doubt they could do it now," Yumi said.

For a moment, Abelardus looked like he wanted to sniff in derision at this slight toward his skills, but he finally shrugged and said, "That's probably true. Our blood has been diluted through the generations, as we've mixed with mundane humans."

He looked at Alisa, an odd speculation in his eyes.

She did her best to ignore it. Beck and Alejandro had come up the corridor and were peering past shoulders and toward the view screen. Alejandro looked like the survivor of an all-night drinking session, but his mouth opened in something akin to awe as he gazed at the station.

"Is that the resting place of the saint?" he whispered, not questioning the station's presence. Maybe he believed the gods had brought it back.

"None of this explains why that place started popping in and out of space, just as we decided to come to visit," Alisa said, jerking her thumb at the station. "And are all these ships here because someone blabbed Leonidas's coordinates? Or did they find it independently of us? Was someone simply flying by when the station happened to be there?"

"You'd have to ask Commander Tomich," Leonidas said.

"I'd be happy to if he hadn't closed the comm on us."

"He doesn't know," Abelardus said, his eyes distant. Whatever Tomich had taken to thwart Starseers from seeing into his thoughts must have faded. "He simply received orders from his superiors to come out here."

"Does anyone else on his ship know?" Leonidas asked. "The admiral in command?"

"I don't know. There are limits to my range." Abelardus touched his temple. "It's easier for me to link with people I'm familiar with and when I know where to look for them."

"Since we are in a remote part of the system, it's possible that the station could have been coming in and out of space for a long time before anyone discovered it," Leonidas said.

"But for centuries?" Alisa asked.

"Perhaps not, but for weeks or months, certainly. Of course, once one ship discovered it, the word would have gotten out."

"Until even pilgrims were making stops?" Alisa frowned, wondering if the people on that ship had truly been seeking some kind of enlightening experience. Had they heard that this station had possibly been the resting place for Alcyone? Had they simply wanted to come and look for themselves? Perhaps, they had gathered the artifacts out of religious fervor rather than from any desire to cash in on the loot. If so, she found their deaths even more lamentable.

"It would be interesting to study," Yumi said, "but it might be best if someone found a way to send it back to where it came from and close the rift, to keep any more people from being hurt, or killed."

"I'm still waiting for an explanation as to why this rift opened up *now*," Alisa said.

Yumi could only shrug.

"My guess would be the orb," Abelardus said.

"That seems like a stretch," Alisa said. "I know it can raise the hairs on my arms, but are you suggesting it's also raising space stations from other dimensions?"

"I have no idea where the orb has been for the last three hundred years—none of my people knew—but it seems likely that it was squirreled away in someone's private collection somewhere. Or maybe the imperial heirs had it all along, kept safe in some vault on the other side of the system. As long as the key was buried, there was no reason for the door and the lock to be present." Abelardus nodded toward the station. "But when the key came out of that vault and started roaming the system, maybe the station woke up."

"How would it know what was going on in another *dimension*?"

"My ancestors could create powerful artifacts, artifacts few of us alive today understand and that none could replicate."

Leonidas stirred. "If what he suggests is true, we may have been the ones to...rouse the station. I feel silly saying things like that."

"Because colonels are only supposed to use their command voices to say stolid and staid things?" Alisa asked.

He narrowed his eyes at her. "Because treating a space station as if it has sentience and can be awakened seems ludicrous."

"Why? We have all manner of artificial intelligences in the system."

"This sounds more like a hibernating bear than an A.I."

"It may be neither," Abelardus said, "simply a tool programmed to react when certain stimuli are applied."

"But if it's feeling stimuli from all the way across the system..." Alisa said.

"We weren't actually that far from here when we visited the Trajean Asteroid Belt," Leonidas said.

Alisa did the rough calculations in her head as to how far they would have to travel if they flew straight there. "More than three days."

"Relatively close. Much closer than the orb would have been if it was being held on one of the core worlds."

The comm beeped, and Alisa reached for it without looking, thinking Tomich might want to talk to them again.

Instead, it was Mica. "Did you see this, Captain?"

"The station?" Alisa asked, assuming Mica had found a porthole.

"The what?"

Or not.

"Never mind," Alisa said. "What do you have?"

"A huge pile of ahridium ingots, spare parts, and raw materials for making less temporary patches. It's all sitting stacked in the cargo hold. I might even be able to make a new set of stairs if I can get some help."

"The Alliance soldiers left all that?" Alisa asked, puzzled.

"I doubt it was the spare-parts fairy. Maybe your Commander Tomich is hoping you won't hold a grudge. Or maybe he considers this fair trade for the orb."

"The orb wasn't mine to trade."

"Is this a new laser welder?" A clunk came over the comm followed by a delighted laugh. "It *is*!"

"Mica isn't concerned about the morality of my quandary, I see."

Leonidas raised an eyebrow, and Alisa thought he would point out the times she herself had failed to worry about morality.

All he said was, "I've never heard your engineer laugh."

"No, I don't think I have, either. She's even dourer than you most of the time."

"I'm not dour," Leonidas said.

"I'm not dour, either," Mica said. "I'm practical. Give me twenty-four hours and some of Beck's sausage, and I can have this box functioning as efficiently as possible outside of a complete overhaul and an extended stay in a repair dock."

"Is the sausage to keep you fueled," Alisa asked, "or are you implementing it into your repair strategy?"

"Engineers don't share their secrets, lest they find themselves replaced by junior officers."

"I thought you wanted to be replaced. That's usually what happens when you accept a position elsewhere."

Something whirred near the comm, and Mica laughed again, then closed the channel.

"Hm, maybe all I have to do is get her a pile of tools and parts to entice her to stay on the *Nomad*," Alisa said.

"Do we have a plan to recover the orb and investigate the station?" Alejandro asked, his gaze riveted to the view screen.

"No. We have a plan to sit here and help Mica repair the ship while the properly equipped Alliance team investigates the station."

"That's not acceptable." Alejandro raised his eyebrows in Leonidas's direction and tilted his head toward Alisa.

What was that supposed to mean? That Leonidas should force her to do something? Hadn't she already done enough? She was more than ready to abandon this quest and go find Jelena. Better for the Alliance to have the staff than the empire.

Leonidas gave her a sad look, and she almost wondered if he had developed mind-reading skills. No, he was probably lamenting that his loyalties were divided, that she had come to be a friend and muddled things between him and his empire.

"The next twenty-four hours should be enough," Abelardus said, "to see whether the Alliance succeeds or if they need our help."

"Why would they need our help?" Alejandro frowned at him. "They have the key."

Abelardus smiled cryptically.

CHAPTER FIFTEEN

Alisa slept a few hours, woke in the middle of the night, and lay there, unable to fall back to sleep. She got dressed and headed to NavCom, curious about the station, curious about what the Alliance ships were doing, and even more curious as to whether she would escape this place without getting involved again.

More than once, she had considered piloting the *Nomad* away from the station—there was no reason that Mica could not do her repairs elsewhere—but the men might lynch her if she tried. This might not be her mission, but she did not seem able to escape it.

Unfortunately, even if she somehow separated herself from the men and headed to Cleon Moon, she would not have much of a lead. She had checked Abelardus's messages during a quiet moment before bed and had been disappointed to see that Durant hadn't yet returned any of them. What if something had happened and Durant was dead? What if Jelena was alone out there somewhere? Hurt or injured, with no way to find her way home, with no one to help her, care for her? She could be anywhere in the system, hungry, cold, and lost. Scared. And Alisa wasn't there to put her arms around her, to tell her it would be all right, the way she had done when Jelena had been four and scared of thunderstorms.

Would it be all right? She knew nothing about Durant. What if he was cruel? Or a pervert? Or some zealot so caught up in his own world that he would neglect to care for Jelena? Alisa couldn't imagine him being a decent human being, not when he had thought kidnapping a child was a good idea.

With these thoughts plaguing her, she had a lump in her throat by the time she headed into the short corridor leading to NavCom. She almost turned right back around again when she saw the back of Abelardus's head in the co-pilot's seat, his braids dangling about his shoulders. He gazed at the station on the view screen, the zoom pushed to maximum. He looked back before she could retreat. She thought about leaving, regardless, since she did not want to spend time alone with him, but he waved for her to come in.

"I'm watching the soldiers in spacesuits crawling around on the station," he said.

Alisa hesitated, but finally decided to have a look. If there were soldiers out there, that was a new development.

"They've been back and forth in shuttles, and they're attempting to force their way in," he said. "They've tried using the orb. There's a slot for each of the four individual pieces, and they've inserted them, but the big double doors won't open for the soldiers." He smiled smugly.

"You think a Starseer needs to operate the key?" Alisa asked.

"That's my belief, yes."

"How long until the station disappears?" Alisa looked toward the digital clock in the console, thinking of the seven hours and however many minutes Abelardus had plucked from Tomich's thoughts.

"Less than an hour."

She looked closer at the view screen. "They truly are out there in spacesuits and with blow torches, aren't they?" Even with the zoom, the soldiers looked like ants crawling around on the surface of the station. "Do those look like special suits to you? Something to deal with the radiation?"

"Likely so."

Since Abelardus appeared to be more interested in talking about business than personal matters, Alisa let herself be drawn inside to continue the conversation. She stood behind her seat instead of sitting in it, resting her hands on the backrest.

"It's a shame the *Nomad's* sensors aren't better," she said.

"Yes. My sensors—" he smirked and tapped his temple, "—are fairly useless at such long range too."

"Unfortunate."

"I'd like to go over there. I never had any great interest in the legend of Alcyone or in hunting for her staff, but now that we're here and might be so close…I thought about calling up your Alliance buddies and asking to join their team. I figure if I helped them find something, I could find a way to reacquire it later." He looked over at her. "Would you mind?"

"Mind what?"

"I know you don't want the empire to have it. I don't either. Would you object if I had it?"

"You?" Alisa did not want to see a super weapon in Abelardus's hands any more than she wanted to see it in the hands of some spoiled ten-year-old prince. Hells, she didn't want to see it in anyone's hands. Maybe it should remain buried in that station and in another dimension. Or maybe it should simply disappear forever. She wondered if there was any way she could convince Tomich to take his warship in and blow up the station.

Abelardus laughed. "I see you *do* object."

"I thought we had a deal about you staying out of my mind."

"Sometimes your thoughts are so visible on your face that I don't have to delve into your depths." He smirked again.

Alisa wondered if that had been an innuendo and decided she did not want to comment on it even if it had been. That would only encourage him.

"If the staff is as powerful as you all seem to believe, nobody should have it," she said. "Look what happened the last time it was floating about in the system. Someone used it to destroy your home world."

"Yes." Abelardus gazed toward the view screen again. "It would be unfortunate if history repeated itself. But there used to be twelve of those staffs on our planet. Our people managed to keep from blowing up worlds for centuries before a traitor turned against us."

"Funny how one person's traitor is another person's hero, isn't it?"

"Funny, yes." Abelardus pushed himself to his feet.

Alisa watched him, hoping he simply meant to head to bed. She never felt comfortable around him, not with those smirks and the way he looked at her.

"Yes, and that's unfortunate," he murmured, leaning his hip against the back of his seat, facing her.

"What is?" she asked, though she suspected he was reading her thoughts again.

"That you're not comfortable around me. If I were you, I'd be a lot more worried about being alone with the cyborg."

"Because if you were me, he wouldn't like me," she said, then debated whether that had made sense.

Abelardus snorted. "Perhaps. But you have to admit, I'm the more logical choice."

"Choice for what?" she asked, glancing toward the hatchway, making sure she still had a direct path toward it in case Abelardus did something... untoward. She didn't have any weapons with her, not even her multi-tool, and she was aware that he was a large, strong man, mental powers notwithstanding.

"Alisa," he said softly, holding out his hands, his palms open. "I'm not an animal. I...I'm sorry if I've made you uncomfortable. I haven't dealt much with non-Starseers, to be honest. When everybody knows each other's thoughts, reading people isn't really an intrusion. It's just something everyone does. And as far as choices..."

He shrugged and stepped forward.

Alisa thought about walking out, but her feet did not move. She found herself curious to know what he would say.

"If you were looking for someone to go along with you on your journeys, to help you find your daughter, I would be the logical choice, wouldn't I?" He tilted his head, nothing but warmth and concern, even innocence in his inquiry. "I would be the one who could teach her once you found her. I wouldn't mind. I've taught before. I like kids."

She stared at him, realizing that he was making a good point. She was almost puzzled that she hadn't thought of it before. As much as she liked Leonidas, he wouldn't know how to help raise a girl gifted with Starseer talents. Besides, he had not said he wanted to do anything like that. He hadn't made it clear at all if he was interested in her in a romantic sense.

Abelardus took another step forward and reached toward her, clasping her hands gently in his.

Uncertainty entered her again, and she reminded herself that she hadn't wanted to end up in this position, hadn't wanted to be alone with him.

"I'll help you find her," he whispered, gazing into her eyes. "I know Durant, know where to look even if he doesn't answer his messages. I can make some guesses as to what he was up to and where he might be."

"Why?" she whispered. "Why would you bother? The staff—"

"Isn't what I'm interested in." Abelardus lifted a hand to her cheek, keeping his other hand down, hers captured within it.

Captured, an odd word choice. Was she a prisoner here? Surely not. In fact, she should be delighted with his attention. He was a handsome man, strong, talented, well connected in his society, able to protect her from the threats out in the system.

Abelardus's head bent toward her, his eyes suddenly closer to hers. His lips brushed her lips, and she did not draw back. Why would she draw back? He might be cocky, but he wasn't a bad man. Maybe he would even be a good father. A teacher and protector for Jelena. He shifted closer, the length of his body pressing against hers, his kiss deepening, growing more certain. Maybe she could even see having more children with him, children who would have strong genes, who might have the potential to become—

Alisa frowned at the thought. It was so foreign to anything she cared about.

With a flood of adrenaline, she realized what was going on. The bastard was manipulating her. And kissing her. What the hells?

She pulled her mouth away from his, stepping back, her shoulder blades bumping the sensor panel. She was torn between shouting at him and punching him, and in that moment of hesitation, she noticed someone else standing in the hatchway, someone who must have just arrived, someone who was staring at them with a shocked expression on his face.

Leonidas.

As soon as their eyes met, he jerked back as if stung. He disappeared before she could blurt a wait.

Fury surged through her, and she planted her hands on Abelardus's chest and shoved him away.

"You asshole," she growled.

He glanced toward the hatchway, then back to her and licked his lips. "Alisa, you know I'm right. The right choice."

"You're not the right anything," she said, pushing away from the sensor equipment, her hands balling into fists. "And you can take your staff and shove it up your ass. Don't you ever touch me again."

He lifted a hand toward her. She punched him in the eye. Pain flared from her knuckles, but she was half-tempted to do it again. He hadn't tried to block, and now, he merely gaped at her, lifting his fingers to his eye.

She stalked out, shaking with rage and indignation. She couldn't believe he had been trying to brainwash her, maybe to rape her, damn it. How far would he have taken that? The sun gods knew there was a reason her people had gone to war with his and been behind blowing up their home world.

Trembling, she turned down the corridor toward her cabin, wanting to jump inside and lock the hatch, afraid Abelardus would follow. What would she do if he did?

When she drew even with Leonidas's hatch, she stopped there. Had he gone back to his cabin? He would be far more protection than anyone else if Abelardus *did* follow her. More than that, she wanted to explain what that had been, that she hadn't willingly kissed Abelardus. She might not know if Leonidas had romantic feelings for her, but she knew she didn't want him thinking that she had romantic feelings for *Abelardus*. He would surely think less of her. And if he *did* have feelings for her, she wouldn't want him thinking that she had chosen that ass over him.

She knocked on his hatch, looking toward the intersection, still afraid Abelardus might stalk after her. The right choice. A good man. Please. All she knew was that he hadn't paid her a lick of attention until he'd decided she had Starseer genes. Now, all of a sudden, he thought she would be a good choice for making babies?

"Ass," she growled again, almost missing that Leonidas's hatch had opened.

"Not me, I trust," he said quietly, warily.

"That wasn't what you think," she rushed to say.

"It's none of my business," he said. "I heard people talking in NavCom and thought something might have changed. With the station. I didn't mean to intrude."

"You weren't intruding. Trust me. Can I come in? Please?" She glanced toward the intersection again, though it remained empty.

Leonidas stepped aside.

Alisa hurried in, almost amused as she remembered there had been a time when she hadn't wanted to be alone with *him*, when she had been worried about going into his cabin by herself. He shut the hatch, and she spun toward him. She meant to speak, to explain what had happened, but instead found herself flinging her arms around him, burying her face in his shoulder.

At first, he did not move, did not seem to know what to do, but eventually, his arms came around her. She hugged him tighter, clenching her eyes shut, tears leaking out. She wasn't sure why the tears were there, just that she was frustrated that she had been so weak-willed as to let Abelardus get as far as he had.

"That wasn't my choice," she said, her voice muffled since her lips were pressed against his shoulder. "He made me—I mean, he was in my head, trying to *convince* me. I can't stand him. I'd never kiss him."

Would he believe her? She worried he wouldn't. Or that he would think she was pathetic for succumbing to that mind manipulation. Or he'd ask *why* Abelardus would have any interest in her, and then she would have to explain her newly discovered genes. Leonidas hated Starseers. Would he hate her too?

"He tried to force you?" Leonidas asked, his voice like ice, his body growing tense, like a coil on the verge of snapping.

"He tried to *trick* me," she said, abruptly wanting to downplay the situation, lest he stalk off and try to kill Abelardus.

Too late, the rage in his eyes said. More than rage. There was *murder* in their hard blue depths.

He released her and spun for the hatch.

"No, Leonidas—"

He didn't stop. He yanked open the hatch.

Desperate to stop him, Alisa leaped onto his back, wrapping her arms and legs around him. At the least, he would have trouble murdering someone with her attached.

"Stop," she whispered in his ear, not wanting to wake everyone—or alert Abelardus. "Please, just listen."

Her weight on his back did not affect him whatsoever, but he paused, one hand gripping the jamb. "I'm listening."

"He's the only lead I have for finding Jelena. If you kill him, that'll make things harder, if not impossible for me. Not to mention that you'll end up incurring the wrath of all the Starseers if they find out that you killed him."

She hung from his shoulders, neither of them moving as she waited for his response. Maybe she had been wrong, and he'd only intended to beat up Abelardus, not kill him. Maybe she was being overly dramatic.

"I don't care about the Starseers," Leonidas said, not denying that he'd had murder in his thoughts.

"What about me? Don't you think you all have delayed me enough on my hunt to find my daughter?" She winced, wishing she could retract the question as soon as she asked it. The last thing she wanted was to make him feel guilty, especially when he wanted to charge out to her defense.

Leonidas lowered his head, his chin to his chest, and she felt even worse.

"I'm sorry," she whispered and pressed her face to the side of his neck.

He was still tense, his corded muscles rock hard against her cheek, but some of the blind fury seemed to have faded.

"Can I at least beat him senseless?" he asked.

"I already punched him," she said.

A feeble effort compared to what Leonidas could do, but she flexed her hand without letting go of him, wondering if she would have bruised knuckles in the morning. They already ached. She distinctly remembered her unarmed-combat instructor telling her to use palm strikes instead of punches, but that punch had felt good. It had been worth it.

"Did you?" he murmured, sounding pleased. "I suppose you can handle your own battles." His fingers tightened on the jamb, and she imagined he was still thinking of pummeling Abelardus.

Maybe she should let him. But she would much rather keep hugging him, however odd the hug, than let him run off to get into a fight that could end up in serious injuries, for Abelardus *and* him.

"When I've imagined riding you before, this wasn't quite how I pictured it," she said, making the joke in the hope of further lightening his mood. They could both use some humor right now, whether he would find it appropriate or not.

"What?" He sounded more puzzled than amused as he turned his head, looking at her out of the corner of his eye.

"Leonidas, you're oddly oblivious for a handsome man who's old enough to have had many women fling themselves at him during the course of his life."

"I—oh."

She kissed him on the neck and released him, sliding down to the deck. Her knuckles brushed against his clothes, and she winced, shaking her hand. Yes, that definitely smarted. Punches should be avoided in the future.

Leonidas faced her and caught her wrist, his grip gentle as he turned her hand to look at her knuckles. "Wait here," he said, gesturing to his bunk. "I'll find you something in sickbay."

"Just not one of the doctor's potions, please. They all make me have to use the head."

"I was thinking of an ice pack."

"Ah, that sounds good."

He left, closing the hatch behind him. Alisa hoped he did not cross paths with Abelardus. Even though he had calmed down, she could envision his rage returning at a glimpse of that smug face.

She wiped away the remnants of her tears and sat on the edge of Leonidas's bunk. She ran her hand over the rumpled sheets, wondering if he had been resting well or having nightmares. Something must have woken him—she and Abelardus hadn't been talking that loudly, not until *after* Leonidas had come in. She now wished she had knocked on his hatch and joined him instead of going to NavCom. Even if Abelardus hadn't gotten far with his advances, she felt dirty and disgusted with herself for letting him even touch her. A squeeze bottle of water rested in a wall nook next to the head of the bed, and she pulled it out, dribbling a few drops into her hand. She rubbed the water on her lips, then scrubbed them off with her sleeve, wanting all trace of the bastard off her.

The hatch opened. Fresh relief came over her when Leonidas walked in. She wondered what he would say if she asked to sleep here, on the floor if need be. Abelardus would not bother her in here, not with Leonidas nearby. But he might pester her if she went back to her cabin and he could get her alone again. She hoped that pestering would only take the form of an apology, but she did not want to deal with even that.

Leonidas handed her a squishy cold pack, then poked into his duffel bag. It leaned against his crimson armor case in the corner of the room. He pulled something out and came over to sit beside her.

"Is that chocolate?" Alisa asked, catching a glimpse of a cherry and what might have been a cacao bean on a wrapper.

"Yes." He unwrapped the end of the bar, handed it to her, then took her wrist again. He rested it on his thigh and positioned the cold pack across her knuckles. "I got it on Arkadius Gamma," he said, "while Dominguez was talking with a contact."

"For me?" Alisa smiled and leaned against his shoulder. Even if he had purchased it for himself, she would be inordinately pleased at his ability to produce it to share at this stressful moment.

"For you," he agreed, meeting her eyes.

"Thank you."

Alisa melted a little inside, the gentleness in his gaze making her want to kiss him. Or to cry. Or maybe both. She could feel the warmth of his thigh under her palm, contrasting with the chill of the cold pack. She could also feel the musculature beneath the soft togs he wore to sleep in. It would be easy to run her hand along his leg, to inch closer. But his obliviousness, as she had called it, made her hesitate. He hadn't corrected her or offered an explanation. More than once, it had crossed her mind that he might be gay. But he didn't drool over Beck either. Of course, Beck called him *mech* and daydreamed of collecting his bounty.

Maybe he was just shy. It seemed almost ludicrous from someone who had no shortage of self-confidence and no reason to feel uncertain about himself, unless one counted his discomfort about being labeled anything less—or more—than human.

Hells, maybe she should just kiss him and find out if he would allow it, or if there was even a spark between them. Or if kissing someone—without someone subverting her mind—would bring thoughts of guilt rather than arousal, thoughts that it was too soon and she was betraying Jonah's memory. She knew he wouldn't begrudge her going on with her life, but she also didn't know if she should wait longer, if this was inappropriate. She was good at being inappropriate. She certainly wouldn't have gone out and sought someone so soon of her own accord, but Leonidas's appearance in her life had been unexpected.

"Alisa?" he said softly.

"Yes?" She pulled her wandering thoughts in and realized she was leaning her chest against his arm, her chin almost resting on his shoulder. She could feel the hardness of his body beneath the thin material of his shirt and couldn't help but think of slipping her hand under the hem and stroking his warm skin, of tracing the contours of his stomach.

Leonidas lifted his hand to her face and cupped her cheek. Her heart nearly lurched out of her chest as anticipation ricocheted along her nerves, making her even more aware of his body—and of hers. His thumb brushed her lips, and she shivered, thoughts of crawling into his lap and kissing him rampaging through her mind. Only the expression on his face made her hesitate again. It wasn't lust or ardor. No, there was the faint crinkle to his brow, as if he was trying to figure her out.

Damn it, what was there to figure out? She wasn't complex.

"Leonidas," she said, her voice somewhere between exasperation and passion.

He opened his mouth to respond, but she decided in that instant that she would make her intent utterly clear, make it so even the most oblivious man would understand it. And more than that, she wanted to kiss him, out of pure, selfish hunger and desire.

She lifted her hand, not caring that the cold pack tumbled to the floor. She clasped the side of his head, twining her fingers into his hair, noticing its softness, the only soft thing about the man. His lips remained parted, whatever words he'd had in mind unspoken, and she lifted herself up to meet them, finally pressing her mouth against his.

He did not draw back. For a moment, he did not move at all, but then one of his arms slid around her waist, and triumph rushed through her, mingling with her desire. He wouldn't push her away. He wanted this. He kissed her back, his mouth gentle, his concern for her coming through in the gesture.

She closed her eyes, sliding her tongue along his lips, enjoying the taste of him, the pleasure of being close to someone she cared about. It had been so long since someone had held her, kissed her, protected her. Cared about her.

It did not take her long to realize she wanted more than a kiss. She shifted her weight, sliding her leg over his lap, smiling as she imagined demonstrating what she'd had in mind with her comment about riding him.

But he drew back, his lips leaving hers. Her fingers tightened in his hair. What was it? She didn't want to stop. She wanted to push him back onto the bed and bring some pleasure to both of them. There were enemies and betrayal everywhere they turned, but couldn't they have this? Couldn't they have each other?

"Alisa," he said, regret in his voice. "We need to talk."

"*Talking* isn't what's on my mind right now," Alisa said.

"I know. I'm sorry."

"Don't be sorry. Just—" She stopped at the anguished look in his eyes and dropped her face to his shoulder, struggling not to feel disappointed. She wanted to keep kissing him, to do *more* than kiss him, not to talk. Whatever he had to say couldn't be good. Nobody ever started good news with the words, "We need to talk."

He did not let go of her, but he shifted her off his lap.

"I can't be with you," Leonidas said softly.

Alisa tried not to feel rejected, but it took a Herculean effort. The urge to slink off to her cabin came to her, Abelardus be damned, and she looked toward the hatch.

"I can't be with *anyone*," he amended.

She frowned, meeting his eyes. "What?"

"No cyborg can, not the ones made for the military."

Made. As if he were some machine, like one of those androids, and not a human being.

A human being who had agreed to a lot of unpleasant surgery for the empire. The first inkling that it had involved more than replacement bones and implants came to her.

He was watching her warily, and she realized that he, too, must be worried about rejection.

She rested a hand on his chest and scooted back on the bunk so she could lean against the wall. "Tell me."

He hesitated, but then scooted back with her, shoulder to shoulder. "It's part of the surgery. They tell you about it, and it's a deal-breaker for a lot of the men. There's a reason that enlistment bonus is so high. Others think that it won't be real, that they're virile enough to find a way around it." He snorted. "Others are just…motivated to join the Cyborg Corps, no matter what the repercussions."

Alisa remembered his story, how he'd needed the money to save his mother.

"I don't understand," she said. "I mean, I get why the men would be forced into accepting the deal, but why did the military do it to start with? What could be gained?"

"Any number of things. When the Cyborg Corps program was first started, the fleet used a lot of convicts, offering them a life in the military as an alternative to life in prison. In the beginning, the military scientists were worried about giving a lot of power to people who might abuse it. They didn't want their cyborgs raping women, enemies or otherwise. Later, I think they also realized it was useful not to have their super soldiers having divided loyalties between wives and lovers and the outfit, and it also meant they wouldn't be susceptible to pretty spies or assassins seeking to seduce them. Either way, it continued to be a part of the program, even after the fleet started taking regular men with no criminal pasts. They made them—us—physically incapable of penetration by tying off something somewhere—" he waved vaguely toward his groin, "—but there's a mental component, too, an adjustment to the brain chemistry, so you don't even think of sex or arousal. I'm not sure what, exactly—I was unconscious for the surgery. It's not hormonal—if anything, the increased production they give us in that department ought to make us *more* interested in sex, not less."

Alisa rested a hand on his forearm, not surprised they had tinkered with his hormones. Every cyborg she'd seen had the proportions of a body builder. She wondered what the long-term side effects were and what the life expectancy was for them. For him. She blinked, finding tears in her eyes again as she looked at him.

"Everything is still *intact*," Leonidas said, giving her a concerned look, probably misinterpreting her moist eyes. "And I have the hope that it may be reversible. Now that I'm not working for the empire anymore, at least not directly, I have the freedom to look for a solution."

"*That's* what you were looking for on that research laboratory? And that's why you were interested in Admiral Tiang?"

"Yes. Dr. Bartosz performed my original surgery. I figured that if any-one knew how to undo what had been done, it would be him."

"All that for—uhm." She stopped herself, not wanting to make light of his problem, but she had expected that something more grandiose had been motivating him.

"I'd like to have a family," Leonidas said. "Children."

"But you could have children without having sex. There are any number of ways that could happen."

"I'd like to have a wife and mother for my children too," he said dryly. "I imagine she might be disappointed if the marital relationship didn't go beyond hugs."

"Depends on the woman," Alisa said. She had known plenty of women who wouldn't mind not having sex with their husbands of many years. Some had never been that interested in it to start with.

Leonidas looked frankly at her, his eyebrows raised. "*You* wouldn't be disappointed?"

"Uhm." She was tempted to say it wouldn't matter, that she could see accepting him as he was, but was that the truth? It wasn't as if he was unappealing in any way—quite the opposite, rather. And yes, she would be disappointed to sleep next to him every night and not sleep *with* him. Early on, she might have told herself that he wasn't her type, and maybe she had believed that, but even before he had saved her life and stood up for her all those times, she had found herself thinking of him with his shirt off. And imagining other things coming off too. "Yes, I'd find that…frustrating."

He nodded, as if he had expected nothing else. She wished it wasn't the truth, and felt selfish for her greedy desires.

"Losing the orb is for the best, then," Alisa said. "Now I can continue my mission and you can continue *your* mission."

He snorted, but a wistful expression entered his eyes. He might be loyal to the empire, and he might be willing to help Alejandro, but she'd never gotten the impression that he cared much about the orb—or this staff, now that he knew about it. Maybe he, like she, realized that giving a boy such a weapon—or giving it to *anyone*—would be asking for trouble.

She clasped his hand, threading her fingers through his, and leaned her head against his shoulder.

"Alisa, I hesitate to ask anything of you, or to say anything at all, because it's not fair to you…but it makes me moderately crazy when you joke with other men, especially knowing that I can't…" He sighed. "Apparently, cyborgs are perfectly capable of feeling possessive and jealous."

She bit her lip, secretly pleased at the admission. "Then you probably need to show greater appreciation for my humor so I don't feel the need to share it with others."

He grunted. "I don't think you would ever lose that need. You share it with everyone, even enemy commanders."

"Hm, it does seem to be a compulsion. But I don't want to share more than humor with them." She met his gaze again. "I would like to share the rest of myself with you."

His eyes continued to hold a touch of wariness, of concern. Did he worry that he would never find a solution? And that she would eventually seek someone else who could satisfy her? She didn't know what promises she could or should make to alleviate his concerns. *Would* she wait indefinitely? She didn't know.

Leonidas finally smiled and said, "Good. I'll work on showing greater appreciation for your humor."

"I look forward to it." Pushing aside the worries for another time, Alisa grinned, grabbed his arm, and pulled him down onto the bed. "In the meantime, can I sleep here?"

She meant to point out that they could at least cuddle and spend time together, but the concerned look returned to his eyes, and she remembered his nightmares, the fact that he seemed to lash out in his sleep. Indeed, now that she looked, she could see dents in the bulkhead where objects—or maybe his elbows—had struck it.

"Or we could forego sleep," she said. "The day cycle isn't that far off. Perhaps we could share this chocolate and try out that massage I've been wanting to give you for some time now." She slid her hand up his arm to his shoulder and wriggled her eyebrows.

"Or I could give *you* a massage," he offered, almost shyly.

"Oh, that does sound appealing. We could take turns."

"I would like that."

CHAPTER SIXTEEN

When Alisa opened the hatch and stepped out of Leonidas's cabin a couple of hours later, she did not see anyone in the corridor, though she did hear someone talking in NavCom. The voice was muffled, the speaker having his back to the hatchway, and she was trying to decide if it was Abelardus when Leonidas came out behind her. He only listened for a couple of seconds before pursing his lips and shaking his head.

"The doctor is communicating with someone," he said.

Alisa had been thinking of getting something to eat, but she veered toward NavCom instead, having no trouble imagining Alejandro making a deal with an android treasure hunter or someone else who might help him reacquire the orb. She would have preferred to enjoy a leisurely breakfast in the mess hall, a chance to sit in peace and appreciate her delightfully relaxed muscles as she sipped coffee with Leonidas. He could probably use some coffee too. He had been careful not to doze off during his massage. She did not know if that was because he also worried he might be dangerous to someone sharing a bunk with him or if he just didn't want her to witness his nightmares, the way he tried to keep her from noticing when he was hurt and in pain. She hoped he had a plan of action for those nightmares, the way he did for his other problem. Maybe he would eventually grow comfortable enough with her to talk about them. Perhaps that would help.

"...don't have everything you need, I assure you," Alejandro was saying to someone over the comm. The forward camera was still displayed on the view screen, but only the Alliance ships were visible in it now. The space station had once again disappeared. It must have happened recently. Several shuttles were flying away from the area, en route to the larger ships. "I've consulted with our Starseer resource, and he's positive you need him. I'm also well versed on the lore surrounding the station itself, and I believe you'll also need me." Alejandro sat alone in NavCom, his robed butt in *her* seat.

Alisa could have growled at him for that alone, but she restrained herself, stopping in the corridor to listen for the response.

"If that's true, then we know where to find you," came the reply, an older man's voice.

Alisa did not think it was Tiang, and it definitely was not Tomich.

"I offer my services with no strings attached," Alejandro said, "my services and those of the Starseer."

Alisa stared, surprised he was speaking on Abelardus's behalf, and even more surprised that those two would be planning something together. Had they decided to join forces to keep the Alliance from getting the staff? And would they later play a game of Asteroid Bang to decide which one of them got to walk away with it? Maybe they each had plans to deceive the other.

"I shall discuss your offer with my science people, but as I told you, I doubt we have any need for your services. We'll be in contact if I'm proven incorrect."

"This offer isn't on the table indefinitely," Alejandro said.

Leonidas touched Alisa's shoulder and passed her, heading for the co-pilot's seat. Alejandro flinched, looking guiltily at Leonidas and then noticing Alisa in the corridor. His lips flattened together. Alisa almost sighed at Leonidas. She wouldn't have minded listening in for a while longer before announcing their presence. Apparently, cyborgs were above eavesdropping.

"I trust we can find you whenever we wish if we need you," the man on the other end of the channel said.

Alisa leaned through the hatchway so she could see which ship Alejandro was communicating with. It wasn't Tomich's warship, but it was an Alliance vessel, the research ship.

Abelardus walked up the corridor from the mess hall, some of Beck's leftover cornbread in his hand. Alisa clenched her jaw, fresh irritation flooding her and threatening to undo the relaxation from her massage. Her only modicum of satisfaction came from seeing the black mark around his eye. She hoped he realized he deserved it and was not planning any retaliation.

Abelardus bobbed his head at her, murmuring a subdued, "Alisa," to her.

"Captain," she said.

"Pardon?"

"I never invited you to use my name, and I'd prefer it if we kept our relationship professional."

Abelardus lifted a finger, a protest on his lips, but then he noticed who sat in the co-pilot's seat. Leonidas came to his feet, turning to face him, his jaw clenched and his eyes like ice chips. He looked to be undoing the effects of his massage too.

Alisa grew aware that she stood between the two men, two large and muscular men. If they started throwing punches—or mental attacks—she might end up smashed into a bulkhead.

But Abelardus did not puff up and glare back at Leonidas. He nodded toward Alejandro.

"Did they say anything, Doctor?"

"Just that they don't think they need us."

"They'll regret that."

"I hope so." Alejandro seemed oblivious to Leonidas towering inches away from him, still glaring fiercely at Abelardus. He dropped his chin onto his fist and stared at the armada. "To have come this far only to watch the Alliance walk away with the prize." He made a choking sound. "It would be intolerable. That staff could turn the tides. It could—" He glanced back at them and fell silent.

"I don't care how clever they think they are," Abelardus said. "I can almost guarantee it'll take a Starseer to get into anywhere important, and the staff will be somewhere important. A vault, perhaps. Or even a tomb."

"The Tomb of Alcyone?" Alejandro said, reverence in his tone.

"Her final resting place was never revealed in our histories, but she was known to carry her staff with her late in life."

Abelardus turned his attention to the view screen, eyes closing to slits as he watched one of the shuttles flying toward the research ship. Alisa did not find it that fascinating and was wondering if she could entice Leonidas to the mess hall for shared cups of coffee when a white flash lit up the screen.

"What was that?" she asked, pulling down the sensor-station seat and sitting.

"One of the shuttles," Alejandro said. "It just…"

The light faded, leaving nothing but black space behind it.

Alisa focused the sensors on the area. "All I'm reading is wreckage."

"That's all that's left." Abelardus had that abstracted, distant look that came over him when he was using his mental powers.

"What happened?" Leonidas asked Alejandro. "You've been up here, watching. Weren't the shuttles just flying back to their mother ships?"

"That's what it looked like," Alejandro said, then turned back to look at Abelardus.

"I can't look back in time. I have no way to know what was going on before that explosion occurred."

Alisa squeezed between Alejandro and Leonidas and opened the *Nomad* to all of the common comm channels. Maybe she could catch some unsecured chatter.

Even as she tried, another shuttle exploded, white flashing on the screen against the black starry backdrop.

"…stay back," came stern words on one of the open channels. "Whatever you've picked up, don't bring it aboard."

"It wasn't a *disease*, Captain," someone replied—that was coming from one of the three remaining shuttles. "I was in contact with the Gamma Shuttle lieutenant just a moment ago. She mentioned a malfunction."

"You're telling me that two shuttles malfunctioned and spontaneously exploded within seconds of each other?"

"I don't know, sir, but it could be something from the station. That place is creepy."

"Wait where you are. We're not letting you back into the hangar bay until we know for sure."

"You're not letting us in, sir?"

"Not now. Not until we see what else happens."

"You mean if we blow up too?"

"Stand by."

The channel fell silent after that. Alisa left it open in case more words were exchanged.

"Malfunctions that caused spontaneous explosions?" Leonidas wondered.

"Perhaps they did, indeed, pick up something from the station," Abelardus said.

"Like what?" Alisa asked. "A disease wouldn't blow up a ship. And what virus could be alive in there after hundreds of years of radiation exposure?"

"I do not mean to suggest that there's a disease. Rather, such a valuable artifact is inevitably booby-trapped. If they tried the key several times and were lacking in some particular component, then the station may have deemed them unworthy of accessing the interior."

"If that was true, why wouldn't they have been blown up right outside the door?" Leonidas asked. "The station is back in the other dimension."

"I could only make guesses," Abelardus said. He did not share any of his guesses aloud.

"Comforting," Alisa said, running her hand along the back of one of the seats. She hoped the *Nomad* was far enough away that it wouldn't be included in any vengeful attacks from the station.

"No, it's not comforting," Abelardus said, "but these accidents could be to our advantage. The Alliance may be asking for our help soon, Doctor."

He smiled faintly. It chilled Alisa. She remembered how the Starseers back on Arkadius had caused some of the combat ships attacking their temple to crash. Was it possible *Abelardus* had done something to those shuttles? That the malfunctions had nothing to do with ancient booby traps?

She looked at Leonidas, trying to catch his eye. He was also scrutinizing Abelardus. Did he have the same suspicions?

The comm flashed, and Alejandro answered it before Alisa could.

"This is Dr. Dominguez," he said.

"This is Commander Tomich. I heard you're offering to help us get into the station."

———

The second time Tomich's warship came to visit the *Nomad*, Alisa did not give Beck any orders regarding meal preparation. She told him to suit up, grab all of his weapons, and join Leonidas in the cargo hold. There would be no casually dropped canisters of gas this time.

Abelardus also stood in the cargo hold, his staff in hand, and a kit of some type slung over his shoulder. Yumi and Alejandro watched from the walkway, staying near the corridor, where they could duck for cover if needed. Mica was whistling and trotting back and forth from the pile of equipment and materials left in the center of the cargo hold, carrying selected items into engineering. If she worried about needing to duck for cover, she did not show it.

The warship did not attach to the airlock. Instead, the Alliance sent a shuttle over, one that appeared uncomfortably similar to the two that had blown up. It was a boxy transport with a thick hull, the outside of which gleamed and reflected light away from the craft. According to the nomenclature on the side, it belonged to the research ship.

When someone knocked at the airlock hatch, Alisa propped a fist on her hip, her knuckles brushing the handle of her Etcher. Tomich wouldn't have come himself again, would he? If he had, she would be tempted to shoot him.

Leonidas strode forward and opened the hatch. He looked at whoever was on the other side for several long seconds, his broad armored form blocking Alisa's view.

"Is it someone we want to see?" Alisa asked.

"Doubtful." Leonidas finally stepped back, revealing Tomich, who now wore a bulky spacesuit, the helmet tucked under his arm.

"That's not a nice thing to say about the man who insisted on leaving everyone alive and the ship better supplied than he found it," Tomich said, meeting Alisa's eyes. "How are your repair goodies?"

"My engineer likes them," Alisa said, as Mica walked toward the pile again, still whistling. "How's your orb?"

"Not as pleasing as we had hoped. The admiral believes we got the short end of that trade."

"It wasn't a trade. It was theft. And Admiral Tiang is lucky that Leonidas didn't break his neck."

"I believe he's aware of that," Tomich said, "and the admiral to whom I refer is Admiral Moreau, the mission commander. I have to answer to him. Admiral Tiang doesn't care much about the orb. I believe he's more interested in studying the dimensional rift."

"So sorry your dinner date didn't turn out the way you wished," Alisa said, peering past him to movement in the airlock tube. He'd brought a squadron of soldiers along with him. *They* wore combat armor rather than spacesuits, very nice, high-powered armor like Leonidas's. Probably radiation-resistant too.

Suspecting some of them were the same men who had made a mess of her dinner party, Alisa curled a lip in their direction.

Tomich looked back, lifted a palm toward the men, then faced her again. "We weren't sure what our reception would be so I brought troops."

"I'm surprised you came yourself. Beck is thinking of stripping you down, putting you on the grill, and slathering you with sauce."

"Which sauce?"

"The blue one."

Tomich shuddered visibly, which had to be difficult to do with all the padding of that suit.

"The blue one is *good*," Beck said, managing to sound plaintive through his faceplate. "Nobody gives it a chance."

"My men and my Starseer are ready to go with you," Alisa said, feeling strange taking possession of any of them except perhaps Beck. "And the doctor up there is willing to go along too. He's done a lot of research on certain Starseer artifacts." She didn't mention the staff in case they didn't know what it was that they were looking for. She had no idea if it would even end up being inside of the station.

"Actually," Tomich said, raising a finger, "we need all of you to come."

"What?" Alisa asked.

Yumi's eyebrows lifted. Mica paused in the middle of one of her treks, a crate of bottles in her hand.

"What?" she echoed Alisa.

"And I'm afraid I'll have to insist," Tomich said. "Admiral Moreau's orders."

"Insist?" Leonidas asked, his voice dangerous.

Alisa walked forward to stand next to him and so she could more effectively frown at Tomich.

"I'm the pilot," she said. "Why would I leave my ship? Why would we all leave my ship? You're not planning to hijack it, are you?" Who would even want her old freighter?

"We're not *that* desperate for ships." Tomich smiled.

Alisa was not amused. "Then what's the ploy?"

"No ploy. We—Moreau—doesn't want your team to grab valuable artifacts and run. If all you have is our short-range shuttle, that won't be possible."

"I don't want any artifacts."

"Others here do." Tomich looked to Abelardus and Alejandro. He had them all figured out, did he? "And they seem to have the disturbing ability to influence you."

Alisa almost snapped and said nobody here except Leonidas could influence her, but she doubted that would be a good thing to admit.

"Fine," she said, "I'll go with you, assuming you have a way to keep me from keeling over from radiation sickness. But Yumi and Mica can't fly the *Nomad*. You can leave them here. They're not going to take off on their own or swoop in to pluck us off the station."

"Nobody stays," Tomich said firmly.

Alisa scowled at him.

"I have my orders." His visage softened slightly. "Believe it or not, this is a better scenario for you than Moreau wanted. I argued on your behalf."

"What'd he want to do? Torture us for what we know?"

Tomich did not nod or say yes, but his expression grew grimmer.

"Glad to know the Alliance isn't adopting imperial policies," Alisa said.

"Will you come? I know you can make trouble if you want to." Tomich eyed Leonidas who was eyeing him right back. "But I advise against it. My warship isn't far away."

"Oh, why not?" Alisa asked. "I'm sure this will be fun."

Judging from Yumi's perked ears, she was interested. She might have been the only one.

Mica's whistling had halted, and she glared over at Tomich and Alisa. "Is this a joke? Give me new tools and materials, and then take me off to die before I can use them?"

"I'm hoping we'll all live," Tomich said.

"There are a lot of previously hopeful people in graveyards."

"Your Starseer and your doctor implied they have the knowledge to get us in and out."

Mica waved toward Alejandro and Abelardus. "Do those look like the faces of honest people?"

No, Alisa thought. Neither of them had been completely forthright with her. Maybe that was why neither of them appeared offended by her question.

"Then this mission should be interesting," Tomich said, tapping the chest of his spacesuit, perhaps to let her know he was going onto the station himself.

"Interesting," Mica said, "that's just how I want to die. Being interested to death." She glared at Alisa, as if this was her fault.

Alisa shook her head and walked toward the airlock tube. She didn't know what else she could do.

CHAPTER SEVENTEEN

"I hope there won't be bears," Beck said, his shoulder pressing against the shoulder of the baggy spacesuit Alisa had been given. He, too, wore one of the radiation-proof spacesuits that Tomich had issued them. Only Leonidas and the Alliance soldiers had combat armor sturdy enough to protect them from the intense radiation. Not that Alisa expected combat to be required inside the station. What could possibly be alive to fight?

"I doubt we'll run into bears or anything else," Alisa said.

"We shouldn't run into anything living after so many centuries," Abelardus said.

He sat across from them, a porthole displaying the stars behind his head. He, too, had been stuffed into a spacesuit, which had required removing his bulky robe and leaving it on the *Nomad*. If Alisa's team was going to retake the freighter after this, they would have to do it in their underwear.

Alejandro sat next to Abelardus, a medical kit resting in his lap. If Alisa got a cut, there was no way she would take off her spacesuit to attend to it, not on that station. The kit itself would be contaminated, as far as she knew. Maybe he had something besides bandages in there.

"Eight minutes to destination," the pilot said in a professional monotone voice. He sounded like an android.

Alisa snorted.

Leonidas looked down at her. He sat on her other side, his helmet in his lap. She could have used his shoulder for a pillow if he hadn't been wearing all that armor. Right now, it would be like laying her head on a hunk of metal. Of course, his shoulder wasn't that different *without* the armor. She grinned at him, and his eyes closed partway for a suspicious squint.

"Are you contemplating inappropriate humor?" he asked.

"Usually. Why do you ask? Do you want to hear it?"

"I don't know."

"I was thinking that the pilot should enjoy his job more," Alisa said. "Add some flair to his announcements. And maybe his flying too. He's extremely cautious. I think we're going at the minimum speed possible to keep from going backward."

"How would you handle the approach to a dangerous space station that could kill us all?"

"I'd add a few barrel rolls to let the station know I'm not afraid of it. Maybe throw in some jokes about how our destination will soon be a hot new tourist spot in this end of the system and how wise it is to visit now before the crowds show up. If you can't have fun with your job, you should get another job."

"Hm."

Alisa closed her mouth. That had been a thoughtless comment to make to a man who killed people for a living—and who spent a lot of time with people trying to kill *him*. Someday, she would remember to edit her thoughts before they spewed out of her mouth.

She patted his thigh in silent apology, figuring she could make such gestures now, since they had a relationship of sorts. At the least, she knew the truth about his reticence, and that his subdued interest had nothing to do with her. That ought to make her actions toward him less complicated. Or maybe it would just make them complicated in a different way.

She searched his face, wondering if he minded the familiarity. Did he even feel her pat through all that armor? She would much rather pat him without it on, without *anything* on. An action that would ideally lead to him ravishing her.

He gazed fondly at her, which was promising, but he was probably oblivious to the fact that she was imagining him nude. And daydreaming of being ravished. No, this wasn't going to be less complicated at all.

"Do I get my thigh touched too?" Beck asked. "On account of us going into a dangerous situation?"

"Mica is sitting on your other side," Alisa said. "Maybe she'll touch it."

"I doubt it. She only touches her tools with that kind of fondness."

"Tools are useful," Mica said. "It's hard not to feel fondly toward them."

"Did she just imply that my thigh *isn't* useful?" Beck asked.

"I'll agree to that," Leonidas said.

"Says the cyborg who sucked down eight sausages for breakfast this morning. Where's the appreciation?"

"Was your thigh integral in the sausage-making process?" Alisa asked.

"Of course. You can't make decent sausages sitting down."

"What about the stuff in the blue jar? If your thigh was integral in making that, it could explain a few things."

"The blueberry balsamic sauce is *amazing*. I can't believe you're mocking it."

Alisa caught a wistful expression on Tomich's face as he gazed in their direction. Was he regretting that he did not work on the flight deck anymore, exchanging barbs with fellow pilots? His crew probably did not try to include their commander in their banter. Maybe she ought to try to suborn him, get him to leave the Alliance and work for her. That would make recovering the *Nomad* easier, and she could promise plenty of banter. Of course, it had taken her weeks to suborn Leonidas, and he'd surely only agreed to become her employee because the empire was mostly dead. She had better work on another plan for Tomich.

"Four minutes to destination," the monotone pilot said.

"The radiation warning light just went on," his co-pilot added.

"Finish dressing if you haven't already," Tomich said, as he plopped his helmet onto his head, "and make sure your seat buddy double-checks your kit. I haven't been over here yet, but I've heard from the scientists that the radiation *next* to the station will fry you if you have anything exposed. I can only imagine what it'll be like inside." He looked at Alisa. "It's going to be tough to sell the place as a tourist destination."

"I'm sure the Alliance can do it with slyly worded brochures," she said, then shifted toward Leonidas. "Will you be my seat buddy?"

She caught Abelardus rolling his eyes and resisted the urge to make a rude gesture. She would be crabby, too, if she had Alejandro for a seat buddy.

Alisa rolled her braid up behind her head and used a couple of pins to clip it back, then slid the helmet into place. The fasteners attached themselves with a *hiss-sluuup*. Leonidas stood up, waving for her to do the same, and checked the various fasteners around her helmet and boots.

"Do you want me to check you out?" she asked, waving to his armor.

"I thought you did that the first day we met him," Mica said.

"No, that took at least a week."

"I see. You wanted to be thorough."

"Very." She grinned at Leonidas, though the two faceplates between them muted the effect.

"Is she *flirting* with your cyborg?" Tomich asked Mica, sounding somewhat horrified.

"Yes," Mica said. "He's even more useful than my tools, so it was probably inevitable."

"That's high praise, Leonidas," Alisa said. "How do you feel about it?"

"My armor doesn't need a check. The internal sensors will let me know if anything is amiss."

"You feel strongly, you say?"

"We're almost to the station," he said, nodding toward the view screen in front of the pilots.

"So it's not the time for inappropriate humor?"

"Precisely." He grabbed the blazer rifles that he had brought along, slinging one over his shoulder and keeping the other in hand.

"Does the cyborg ever flirt back?" Tomich whispered to Mica, his expression of horror shifting to one of fascination.

"Not that I've noticed," Mica said, "but he does glare fiercely when other men get close to her."

"I thought that was just his normal expression."

"No, that's just his typical glare. He reserves the fierce one for special occasions."

Leonidas sighed as the shuttle glided beneath the wheel of the station, heading for huge doors on the hull of the axis.

"Do you miss the days when we were all afraid of you?" Alisa asked him.

"Occasionally."

The rest of the shuttle crew finished suiting up, then watched in silence as the craft approached the station. The bluish-gray hull filled the screen, no hint of lights or life visible on the exterior. No glowing plaques, to Alisa's relief. Despite appearing long-abandoned, the station did continue to spin on its axis. The shuttle matched its rotation, settling into an orbit that kept it alongside those big bay doors.

A bright yellow dot gleamed from atop the set of doors, and Alisa thought there might be lights on after all. Then she realized what she was looking at. A piece of the orb. It had been inserted into some alcove in the hull. She leaned to the side so she could see around the pilot's head and spotted another piece. This one was tucked into an alcove on the left side of the doors.

"We thought sticking the four pieces into the matching slots would unlock the doors," Tomich said. "But our research seems to have holes in it. We haven't had any Starseer advisors." He looked toward Abelardus.

Alisa thought about pointing out that Abelardus hadn't advised anyone on much of anything, but the pilot spoke first.

"We're lined up as good as it's going to get, sir. You can leave anytime."

"No airlock to latch onto?" Beck asked.

"No airlock that will let us in," Tomich said. "How do spacewalks make you feel?"

"A little queasy, to be honest."

"I'd advise against throwing up in your spacesuit. You're not going to be able to take the helmet off for a while."

"Thanks for the tip, sir," Beck grumbled.

A clink sounded as something bounced off the hull, some debris. Alisa remembered that the artifacts the pilgrim ship had found had been plucked from outside of the station.

"This way," Tomich said, walking past Leonidas and Alisa as he headed toward the rear of the shuttle.

Alisa started after him, but Leonidas made sure he went ahead of her. Abelardus jostled his shoulder, trying to go ahead of *him*, but jostling Leonidas was like jostling a mountain. It did not work, and Leonidas ended up at the airlock hatch right behind Tomich. Alisa let the men go first. What help was she going to be over there? Leonidas had given her a blazer pistol, but she couldn't imagine there being anything to shoot at. It wasn't as if energy bolts could clear out radiation.

"Isn't this exciting?" Yumi asked, coming up to her side.

"Being forced to go along on a mission you can't contribute to because the Alliance is paranoid?" Alisa asked.

"*I* might be able to contribute."

"Oh? Did you bring along something soothing to mix into the water reservoirs of our suits?"

Yumi frowned.

"Sorry," Alisa said, regretting her snark again. Yumi did not deserve it. "I'm nervous. And tetchy about my ship."

"I should have brought *you* something soothing."

"Undoubtedly so."

"There's enough room in the airlock for us to go across four at a time," Tomich said. "I'll go first with—"

"Me," Abelardus said. "If we can get the doors open, the shuttle and the rest of the people can fly in."

"I'm not sure we want the shuttle flying in, but all right. Abelardus, isn't it? You come in the first wave. You, too, Sergeant Croix. And…Colonel Adler."

Leonidas did not object. He strode into the airlock with the rest of the men.

"Should we be offended that we weren't picked for that group?" Alisa asked.

"I thought you didn't even want to go," Mica said, joining Yumi and Alisa. Alejandro waited behind them. Beck had maneuvered his way into the group of Tomich's soldiers.

"I don't," Alisa said, "but I like to feel as if I'm indispensable."

"Unless that space station can be flown somewhere, I doubt they'll need you."

"You're crushing my indispensability delusion."

"I would be fine staying here and playing a round of Banakka," Mica said.

Alisa looked at the proximity of the soldiers, made sure the comm was off in her suit, and lowered her voice to whisper, "How about instead, coming up with a plan for getting the *Nomad* back and escaping the pursuit of five Alliance ships that are faster than we are?"

"I don't see how that could happen. Don't you think they'll let us go once they have whatever treasure they're seeking in there?"

"I think…it's unlikely that Abelardus is going to let them have the staff. He and Alejandro both want it for their own reasons."

"What they want isn't going to matter much when they're surrounded by Alliance soldiers and ships."

"I bet Abelardus will try to influence Tomich, trick him maybe."

"You think that will work?" Mica asked.

"Not indefinitely. At which point, we have to deal with getting back to our ship and avoiding pursuit."

"Captain, the *Nomad* couldn't outrun a garbage scow, much less a warship."

"So you don't have any ideas for a plan yet is what you're saying."

Mica frowned at her. "Isn't that your job? As the captain of the ship?"

"Is it?"

"Yes."

"Damn, I was afraid of that."

"Next group," a sergeant at the airlock said.

Alisa took a step, but four soldiers pushed past her to go first.

Alejandro sighed.

Alisa climbed onto a seat to look out a porthole on the same side of the shuttle as the station. Leonidas's red armor was distinct as he stood above the door and perpendicular to the axis, his boots locked onto the hull. The rest of the soldiers, clad in matching combat armor, were impossible to identify, but only Tomich and Abelardus were out there in spacesuits. Alisa assumed the one fiddling with an orb piece was Abelardus. He had removed it from its niche and was studying it. She could now see the other three pieces of the orb, each nestled into niches at the cardinal points around the huge double doors.

She turned on her comm, and the chatter of the men filled her helmet. Most were making quips or complaints, nothing she would consider useful. Her spacesuit only offered her access to one channel, so she could not single out Leonidas to talk to him and get an update, at least not without everyone else hearing them.

A *ker-thunk* sounded, and the four soldiers who had gone into the airlock appeared outside of the shuttle. They pushed off to join the men on the hull of the station. Like Leonidas, they also carried rifles. One had a bandolier of grenades.

Alisa eyed a bag that Mica carried, wondering what she was bringing. Tools? Smoke grenades?

"Next group," the sergeant manning the airlock said.

This time, Alejandro held up his hand and made his way to the front. None of the remaining soldiers objected.

Alisa hopped down, following in his wake, and Mica and Yumi went with her. They passed a bank of decontamination showers and turned into the dim airlock chamber. The sergeant closed the hatch behind them, and they waited for the interior to depressurize. Soon, the outer hatch opened, and Alisa had her best view yet of the station hull. The oblong core stretched up and down, and the wheel shadowed them from the faint light of Rebus, the nearest sun.

Alejandro stepped into the hatchway and pushed off. The shuttle had pulled close, and the station was the size of a ten-story building back on Perun, so it would be hard to miss. Still, nerves teased Alisa's stomach as she floated through space, arrowing toward the red combat armor. She had always been fortunate that her stomach did not bother her in zero gravity, perhaps a side effect of having been born on a ship and spending so much of her life out here among the stars. But that did not mean that situations like this did not make her nervous.

Alisa landed next to Leonidas, her aim proving true. She shifted the soles of her boots so the magnets locked onto the hull.

Leonidas touched her back briefly as she stood upright beside him, the shuttle orbiting over their heads, but he did not say anything. He, too, might be cognizant of everyone else listening on the same channel.

"I think you're going to have to do more than touch it, Starseer," Tomich said. He was crouched above the doors next to Abelardus. "Nothing's happening."

"I assure you, I'm doing more than touching it," Abelardus said stiffly. His gloved hand rested on the piece of the orb, which he had inserted back into its niche.

"Fine. I think you're also going to have to do more than *fondle* it."

"I'm using my mind to try a few things. Honestly, I thought it would open for me, just because of my blood."

"Maybe your blood isn't as special as you thought," Tomich said.

"My blood *is* special. But I'm beginning to wonder if it will take someone with a closer link to Alcyone. If this was her station, her final resting place, maybe she didn't want just any Starseer getting in. I suppose that could make sense since she was ostracized from what remained of the Order in the end."

"Is that your way of saying that you can't open the door? Because we haven't had any luck cutting into the exterior. That hull is thick. It's as if they built this station to withstand being pelted by asteroids."

"I assume they didn't want anyone to cut their way in," Abelardus said. "Let me try a few more tactics."

All the interest was directed at the top piece of the orb, so Alisa scooted down the hull to look at the one on her side of the doors. She doubted she could do anything the others could not, but the glowing artifact tugged at her with some invisible power, as it had the other times she had seen it outside of its case. All the hairs on her arms stood up, and she could feel gooseflesh rising all over her body.

The urge to gaze into the orb's swirling depths was difficult to resist, and before she knew it, she stood above it, her eyes locked downward. The quarter piece lay snugly in a niche that appeared to have been designed to hold it. She remembered the puzzle-like protrusions on the inside of the pieces from the time she had seen the orb disassembled. Now, its snug and exact fit into the hole kept it from floating free. Or maybe some power she did not understand did that.

Drawn by something inexplicable, she reached down to touch the surface. For some reason, a memory flashed through her mind, the one where she'd been pressing a blazer pistol to the orb. She sensed something, almost a feeling of indignation.

She hesitated, her fingers a couple of inches from its surface. It would not zap her if she touched it, would it? She imagined herself being flung away from the hull and having to be rescued.

"Alisa?" Leonidas asked quietly. He had followed her along the hull and stood a couple of feet away.

Feeling more confident thanks to his presence, Alisa poked the surface with her finger. A tingle of power ran up her arm, but it did not hurt this time. She rested her gloved palm on the piece and felt warmth even through the thick material.

A flash of intense white light came from beneath her hand. Alisa stumbled back, almost losing her footing—and her boots' grip on the station.

Leonidas grabbed her arm, steadying her. "What did you do?"

"I—"

The rumble of machinery beneath her feet interrupted her, the reverberations coursing up from the hull. Several of the soldiers, including Leonidas, whirled toward the doors, their weapons at the ready. Alisa could only stand and gape. Had *she* done something? Or had she simply been touching this piece of the orb when Abelardus had done something to the other one? That seemed more likely.

With a grinding that she felt rather than heard, the ancient doors rolled open, revealing a pitch-black hangar bay inside.

Alisa looked toward Abelardus, expecting him to bow and take credit for finding a way in. But he was staring straight at her. The faceplate made it hard to see his expression.

"You might want to put some more effort into looking up Stanislav when you have time," he commented.

She stared back at him, puzzling through the ramifications of the words.

Leonidas was the one to respond. "What does that mean?"

"Nothing," Alisa said. She hadn't told him about her questionable genes, and she did not want to do so now, not with a bunch of unfamiliar soldiers—and their familiar commander—looking at her. "Who's the brave soul who's leading the way in?" she asked, hoping to divert their curiosity.

Leonidas was the one to walk over the threshold of the doorway, heading into the blackness.

CHAPTER EIGHTEEN

The hangar bay was empty.

The soldiers directed flashlight beams all over the place as the team entered. Some of the men pushed off the walls, floating through the cavernous space until they landed on a floor or ceiling, but most of them chose the conservative approach that Alisa favored, walking along the walls and making sure one magnetic boot sole was solidly locked to metal before taking each step.

Leonidas strode ahead of her, but he looked back at her several times. She couldn't help but think he was wondering about the doors. She was trying not to wonder herself. This was not the time to ponder how strange her life had become of late.

At Tomich's direction, the soldiers waited when they reached the far end of the bay where a smaller set of double doors led deeper into the interior, another pitch-black interior.

Abelardus waved the men aside, indicating that he would go in first. Or at least Alisa thought that was his intent, until he looked at her and gestured for her to join him.

"Oh, I get to lead now?" she asked.

"It seems like a good idea to put the person who the doors opened for in front," Abelardus said. "There could be traps."

"That *really* makes me want to go first."

"I meant to imply that the traps might not trigger if you're in front."

"Yeah, what you meant to imply and what's going to happen aren't necessarily related."

"You're sounding pessimistic, Captain," Mica said, coming up behind her.

"From you, that's a compliment, isn't it?" Alisa asked.

"Absolutely."

"I'll lead with you," Leonidas said, though he gave Alisa another of those curious what-is-this-about looks. Or maybe that was a concerned I-think-I'm-figuring-out-what-this-is-about-and-I-don't-like-it look.

"Let's do this then," Alisa muttered and stepped through the doorway. Leonidas stuck close, his rifle in hand.

Her spacesuit came with a built-in headlamp, so she flipped it on. She had expected a corridor, but another huge bay opened up, the ceiling at least three stories above them. She could not see to the other end because mountains of rubbish rose all around them, the peaks touching that high ceiling in places. An aisle meandered through the towering heaps, like a river snaking between hills.

"Looks like we have gravity," Tomich said, coming through the doorway with Yumi, Alejandro, and the soldiers.

"And radiation," a soldier carrying equipment for measuring the environment said.

"More than expected?"

"No, but we expected an alarming amount."

"I'm watching my helmet display," Tomich said, "but let me know if you read anything that suggests our suits won't be able to handle this and we need to get out."

"Yes, sir."

Abelardus stayed right beside Alisa, opposite of Leonidas. She felt like a controversial political figure who needed bodyguards to keep the assassins at bay.

Mica walked toward the closest pile and picked up a small piece of rubble. She tossed it high into the air, and it tumbled slowly back down for her to catch. "Partial gravity."

"Keep your boots magnetized," Tomich told everyone.

"Down the path?" Leonidas asked Alisa. "Or over the piles to avoid possible traps?"

As if she knew. This was Alejandro's quest. She looked back at him, and he shrugged.

"I thought you had some extra insight, Doctor," she said.

"From what I read, the unwelcome will be punished for trespassing," he said.

"I can feel the presence of Starseer artifacts," Abelardus said.

"Booby-trap artifacts?" Alisa asked.

"Possibly."

"Can you sense the presence of anything...significant?" Alejandro asked him.

Significant? Their Staff of Lore?

"It's possible it's among the things I sense, but..."

"You don't think so?"

"I would expect a greater presence from something so powerful," Abelardus said.

"So, it's not here?" Alejandro sounded more relieved than devastated. Maybe because he knew the soldiers would only take the staff if they found it now.

"I can't be certain yet. It could be muted by being stored in a vault."

Sensing that everyone was waiting for her—and what a lovely feeling that was—Alisa started up the path.

"May I see that?" Yumi asked, walking beside Mica.

Mica handed her the small lump of rubble she had been tossing. Yumi rubbed it with her gloved fingers.

As they followed the path, Leonidas kept his steps slow so that he did not pull ahead of Alisa. He probably wanted to, but if anyone would trigger traps in a station made by Starseers, it would be a cyborg.

"This is a gold coin," Yumi said, holding up the prize that she had cleaned of dust. "Pre-empire. Late Kirian, judging by the date and stamp."

Several of the men stopped to stare at the dust-shrouded piles with renewed interest.

"Are *all* of those coins?" one asked.

"If so, we've stumbled into some ancient dragon's treasure cave," another said.

"Just worry about the mission for now," Tomich said. "If there's treasure here, we'll come back for it later. The three suns know the Alliance can use valuables in its coffers to pay for the expenses of running a system."

Judging by the look the two soldiers exchanged, they weren't overly concerned about the *Alliance's* coffers.

"Not treasure," Alejandro said, rubbing off a piece of equipment that looked like it belonged in an engine room, a very old engine room. "Offerings for the dead. This is a burial chamber. *Alcyone's* burial chamber."

"Which makes me feel all the better about invading it," Alisa muttered. She continued along the winding path, the beam of light from her headlamp playing across the dusty floor ahead of her.

Something made the hairs on her arms rise again, and she stopped a second before Abelardus grabbed her arm from behind.

"Don't walk there," he said, pointing at a portion of the floor that looked the same as the rest. "That should be fine up there." He waved a few feet to the side, indicating she should walk over the lumpy base of a rubble pile.

"*Should* be fine," Alisa said.

Despite his earlier attempts not to get out in front of her, Leonidas walked in the indicated direction first. Rubble—*offerings*—shifted and cracked under his boots as he avoided the path. Alisa and the rest of the team carefully followed him.

A faint *clink-clunk* sounded from a far corner as Alisa stepped back onto the path. She froze.

"Do we have atmosphere in here?" Mica wondered. "I heard something."

"As did I," Abelardus said. "I think someone brushed that trigger."

"It wasn't me," a soldier in the back said.

"We may have just reached the point," Abelardus said, "where whatever sensors are still working on the station realized someone is here."

"Comforting," Alisa said.

Another clunk sounded from a corner that they could not see, not with the mountains in the way.

"Can you tell if something is over there?" Tomich asked Abelardus.

"I sense...not much in that direction. Machinery."

"Isn't machinery what you sensed when you tried to read those androids?" Alisa asked. "Androids that tried to kill us?"

"Yes."

"My sensors show a partial atmosphere," Leonidas said. "Not enough to breathe, but there might have been more once."

More sounds followed, the shifting and tinkling of pieces of rubble—or coins—being moved aside. It was coming from that corner.

Even though his only weapon was his staff, Abelardus walked forward to stand shoulder-to-shoulder with Leonidas in the path. Beck and several more soldiers also eased past Alisa.

A shriek came out of the darkness, so loud and startling that Alisa nearly fell over. Flashlight beams crossed in the air, seeking the source. Something flew out of the shadows, massive webbed wings flapping. Alisa thought it was a real animal—a real *monster*—but it clinked as those wings flapped, and dull, mechanical eyes stared out from its bat-like face.

"Fire, sir?" a tense soldier asked as it soared around the ceiling, looking down upon them.

"Abelardus?" Tomich asked.

"I've never heard of anything like it before," Abelardus said. "And it's not living, so I can't perceive its intent, though it does have…This is one of the artifacts I sensed."

Artifacts? Did that mean it would have some power beyond wings and talons? *Starseer* power?

"It's here to defend the tomb," Alejandro said, sounding certain.

"The tomb we aim to raid?" Alisa asked.

The creature screeched again, the ear-splitting noise more animal-like than mechanical. Then it banked and veered straight toward them, straight toward Leonidas.

He stood his ground and fired. The blazer bolts splashed off the creature's metal hide, as if they had struck combat armor. It continued toward him, plummeting, razor-edged talons extended.

Alisa, Mica, and Yumi scurried back as several soldiers leaped forward. Alisa felt cowardly for scrambling out of the way, but Leonidas and the soldiers were the only ones in true combat armor. The spacesuits were designed to withstand radiation, not talons.

Leonidas sprang out of the way an instant before the construct would have snatched him up. The long talons snapped at the air where he had been. Air beat at Alisa's chest as it caught itself with flapping wings, just keeping from crashing. Only now, with the great creature so close, did she realize how large it was. It had to have a wingspan of thirty feet.

She joined the soldiers in firing at it, but her little pistol did no more than their rifles. Someone switched to a grenade launcher.

"Abelardus," Alisa called. "Can you attack it? Throw it against a wall?"

"I'm trying to do something," he replied, his voice strained. He stood on the path, his staff pointed toward the creature, but only shook his head. "It's as if there's a barrier around it, protecting it."

"Alcyone, or those Starseers who entombed her here, must have expected that Starseers might one day invade her tomb," Alejandro said.

As the flying creature banked for another attack, Leonidas scrambled halfway up a treasure pile, coins skidding down under his weight. It headed straight for him again.

"Apparently, they were worried about cyborgs too," Alisa muttered, looking around, seeking inspiration. She felt useless.

This time, instead of springing away from it, Leonidas leaped *toward* the creature.

Alisa cursed. What was he *doing?*

He slammed into it hard enough that the great bird faltered. One of those talons grazed his armor, but he struck its chest, managing to find handholds as his legs dangled free.

The creature landed on one of the piles, using its wings to bat at Leonidas's armored back. Ignoring the battering, he clawed his way upward, toward its neck. The bird's sharp metallic beak plunged toward his helmet. Alisa fired at the same time as several other soldiers. She struck the construct's faded gray eye, and the head reared up instead of striking Leonidas. It screeched again, pinning her with its stare. Had that actually hurt it?

One of the soldiers launched something at the construct as Leonidas made his way to the neck and clambered aboard the creature's back. A grenade. It exploded as it struck the bird's chest, the flames contorting oddly in the weak gravity and atmosphere. Smoke stole Leonidas from Alisa's sight.

The creature leaped into the air, flapping away from the men.

"Watch where you're firing," Alisa yelled, wanting to shoot whoever had hurled the grenade. That could tear up Leonidas's armor as easily as it could tear up their enemy.

She let out a relieved breath when she spotted Leonidas, his head up as he straddled the creature's back. He lifted an arm and drove a punch between its shoulders. Another ear-splitting shriek came out of that metallic beak.

Leonidas appeared to have a good grip, but he was abruptly flung away from the creature's back. He spun through the air and struck the ceiling so hard that Alisa heard the thunderous thud from halfway across the chamber.

As he tumbled back down, the soldiers opened fire on the creature. It screeched and spun toward them, fearless—fearless and *pissed.*

The air seemed to shimmer, and a wave of power slammed into the men. They scattered like poker chips struck by an angry gambler. Darkness descended as flashlights flew from men's hands and hit the floor.

Alisa was on the edge of the wave, and she caught some of it, too, enough that it knocked her backward, her legs flying over her head. One of the treasure piles stopped her flight as her back struck it, blasting her breath from her lungs.

Though dazed, she rose to her knees and patted herself down, making sure none of her fasteners had been torn free. Her Starseer genes would not save her from the radiation in *here* if that happened.

Another grenade flew through the air as Alisa, assured that none of her body was exposed, climbed back to her feet. Where had Leonidas gone? The construct was still flying around, alternating between diving and flinging mental attacks. The men were scattered all about, a couple of them no longer moving as they lay among the dusty burial offerings.

The creature swooped down to attack someone blocked from Alisa's sight by another mountain. Leonidas?

"Mica?" Alisa called, looking for her friend. "Where are you? You didn't bring any rust bangs, did you?"

She had no idea if the corrosive acid would do anything against whatever shielding Abelardus said this creature possessed, but anything would be better than firing useless blazer bolts.

"Of course I brought rust bangs," Mica said from surprisingly nearby.

She crouched behind Alisa, waving a canister. "I've thrown two and completely missed both times. I *have* melted good-sized holes in piles of gold."

Alisa took the offered canister. "Let's hope Alcyone won't mind."

The creature came back into view, powerful wings stirring the air as they flapped. Alisa hefted her new weapon, but did not throw. Leonidas had found his way astride the great bird again. He gripped the back of its head and tore off a piece of plating, flinging it to the side.

The construct shrieked like a wounded bat, and Alisa expected Leonidas to go flying again, but he flattened himself to its back and wrapped his arms around its neck. His body jerked, as if he'd been struck by a giant hammer, but he did not let go.

The construct started to bank, turning away from a wall coming up in front of it. Leonidas's armored shoulders flexed and heaved. The long neck jerked to the side, and the head whipped along with it. The creature's flight faltered, and it did not bank in time. It struck the wall hard and went down. Leonidas kept his grip, going down with it. Both cyborg and creature disappeared from view.

Alisa scrambled to the top of the nearest pile, hoping to get a chance to use the rust bang—and hoping Leonidas was all right. She had seen before what those Starseer powers could do to him, harming him even inside his armor.

Several of the soldiers also ran over a ridge of offerings. They shot blazers, seemingly oblivious to the fact that they were ineffective, and the man with the damned grenade launcher looked to be ready to fire his weapon before seeing if Leonidas was next to the creature or not.

Abelardus passed Alisa as she ran, topping the same pile that she was on.

"It's down, but it's getting up," he called, and pointed his staff at it.

Alisa made it to the top and found Leonidas punching the creature in the side of the head, as if his fists were the best weapons he had. In this case, maybe they were. His power could bring down walls, after all.

"Get out of the way," Abelardus yelled down to him.

Leonidas glanced up, and Alisa waved her rust bang. He punched the construct a final time, leaving a dent she could see from her perch, and sprang away, leaping twenty feet before landing.

The creature struggled to rise, inching off the scattered offerings where it had come down. Abelardus growled, his staff quivering as he concentrated. The creature bowed its head, its legs also quivering. Was he holding it down?

Alisa threw the rust bang a second before Abelardus yelled, "Everything you've got. Use it now."

The soldiers needed no urging. Weapons fired, and another grenade spun through the air. It exploded next to the construct's head, flames and smoke bursting into the air. The rust bang also exploded, less spectacularly, but perhaps more effectively. Acid flew everywhere, spattering the metallic creature.

Leonidas ran up the mountain to join Alisa and Abelardus. He turned toward the creature, as if he might use this elevated perch to spring atop it again. But the smoke cleared, revealing that their foe was not moving. Its head had been torn off, wires and the remains of metal vertebrae spilling from the stump.

"It seemed to like you," Alisa said, swatting him on the chest playfully, though she was eyeing him up and down with her headlamp, hoping there were not any breaks in his armor. Dust dulled the usually shiny crimson, and it definitely had new dents.

"It saw me as the biggest threat," he said.

Abelardus snorted. "More likely, it shared the Starseer hatred for cyborgs."

"Alcyone worked alongside the fledgling imperial army and its newly minted cyborgs."

"Just because she fought with them doesn't mean she liked them. I'm fighting with you, and I don't like you."

Leonidas looked at him. "I have more reason to loathe and distrust you, Abelardus, than you have to feel that way toward me."

"But you don't?" Alisa asked.

"No, I do." Leonidas put his arm around her back and pointed down the treasure pile to where the soldiers were gathering around Tomich.

She let him help her descend. "Is your arm around me because you're a gentleman and you're assisting me, or because you're possessively removing me from Abelardus's company?" she asked quietly.

"I *am* a gentleman, and a gentleman removes ladies from the company of unsavory influences."

"Who told you that you were a gentleman, Colonel Adler?" Tomich asked over the comm.

A few snickers came in response.

Alisa flushed. She had forgotten that everyone was on the same channel, and their comms were open.

"Did someone tell you I wasn't?" Leonidas asked, deadpan.

He and Alisa joined the soldiers, a sour-faced Abelardus right behind them. Apparently, he did not care for being called unsavory.

"It's not the usual adjective we in the Alliance apply to cyborgs," Tomich said.

"I've heard Alliance officers have a limited vocabulary."

"Well, we all know I do." Tomich grinned and thumped Leonidas on the arm. "Nice riding up there."

Leonidas grunted indifferently, though he looked faintly pleased at this acknowledgment.

"Now who has a limited vocabulary?" Alisa teased him.

"Sir?" a worried voice asked, hurrying up to Tomich.

A couple of flashlight beams targeted the young soldier as he lifted an arm. Three parallel slashes in his suit revealed bloody cuts in the flesh beneath.

The soldiers fell silent.

"Get back to the shuttle and hit decon," Tomich said, all of the humor gone from his face. "Max, go with him."

"Yes, sir."

The two men hustled back the way the group had come. Alejandro watched, his expression also grim. Alisa almost asked if the soldier would be all right, but she was afraid to do so.

"This better be worth it," Tomich said, turning up the path they had been following. "Abelardus, you sense any other threats out there?"

"Yes."

"Wonderful." Tomich waved for Alisa to take the lead again.

Wonderful, indeed.

Not feeling brave, she made sure Leonidas and Abelardus were with her before heading down the path.

They had been at the halfway point through the chamber when the construct attacked, and it did not take long for another set of double doors to come into view, these also standing open. Alisa spotted a dusty staff sticking out of the bottom of one of the last piles of offerings. She paused, eyeing it sidelong, and an idea popped into her head.

Careful not to draw attention to it, she tapped her faceplate and turned toward the people behind her. Beck, Alejandro, and Mica. Yumi was lagging behind, wiping dust off things and examining them. She would be the ideal one to make an accomplice in this, if Alisa could get her attention.

"Anyone have any idea how to scratch your eye when it's behind a faceplate?" Alisa asked, when a dozen faces turned curiously toward her, people wondering why she had stopped.

"Let me know if you figure it out," one of the soldiers said. "I'm sweating like warts on a frog."

"That doesn't make sense," another man said.

"Unless they're sweaty warts."

Tomich sighed. "There may be a reason imperial cyborgs think we have a limited vocabulary."

"What, are we supposed to say perspiration instead of sweat?"

"Yumi, what's that you're looking at?" Alisa asked, hoping the conversation would distract the men for a minute—or at least keep them from growling at her to keep going.

She caught Abelardus's eye as she headed back toward Yumi and tried to give him a significant look. Since he liked to jump into her thoughts, he shouldn't have any trouble reading that as an invitation to do so.

Got it, he said into her mind. *I'll try to ensure they find this conversation ridiculously fascinating.*

It might take more than a Starseer to do that.

We'll see.

"It's some old medical equipment," Yumi said, as Alisa approached.

"Do you think Alejandro would like to add it to his collection?" Alisa turned off her comm and touched Yumi, pointing toward the staff. "Can you linger behind, dust that off, and see if there's a way to fancy it up? Leave it leaning against the wall by the door there, so we can grab it on the way out."

Yumi opened her mouth, but Alisa held a finger in front of her lips. She doubted Yumi had turned off her comm.

After a glance at the staff, Yumi nodded.

Alisa returned to the front of the group as the wart-sweat conversation concluded. She turned her comm back on. Leonidas was watching her suspiciously. That was fine. So long as the soldiers were not suspicious.

She shook her head as she resumed walking, scarcely believing that she was trying to arrange things so that her people got the staff. If they actually *found* the staff.

When she and Leonidas reached the double doors, he leaned his head through first, shining his built-in flashlight around the next chamber. The next and the *last* chamber, it seemed. There were not any visible doors on the other walls. Instead, a dais rested off to one side with a sarcophagus atop it. Several rows of black humanoid statues stood facing it, staffs held at their sides, as if they were Starseers eternally worshipping the one entombed there.

A mural was painted on the opposite end of the chamber, as dusty as everything else, but the details still visible. A woman with flowing black hair stood in the sky on an asteroid, pointing a staff toward a planet. A painted yellow beam showed energy shooting forth from the staff, slamming into the surface of the planet, which was already partially crumbled, pieces streaking out into space.

"The saint," Alejandro breathed as he leaned through the doorway. "We are in the presence of a divine hero." He touched his chest, his religious pendant probably dangling there underneath his suit. "May we prove worthy of her blessing and of being in her presence."

"She's a traitor, not a saint," Abelardus said from behind Alisa, his gaze also toward the mural.

Something stirred near the dais, one of the statues. Leonidas pointed his rifle at it. It turned to face them, revealing that it was not a statue at all, but some human-shaped robot. Layers of dust topped its shoulders and head and dulled the rest of its black body, but the centuries did not keep the eyes from opening in its expressionless face. They glowed a disturbing red, and the head turned toward the doorway, its gaze locking onto them.

The rest of the statues—robots—came to life, at least twenty of them, all turning toward Alisa and the others. They raised their staffs, their intent clear.

CHAPTER NINETEEN

Leonidas pulled Alisa out of the doorway, pushing her behind him. "Wait out here where it's safe," he said as he strode forward to meet the threat.

"Where it's *safe?*" Alisa asked, getting bumped as the soldiers pushed past her. "You mean in the room where we just got attacked by a giant metal pterodactyl that hurled you into the ceiling?"

He did not answer. The soldiers took over the comm channel, barking orders to fan out and find cover. The noise of unfamiliar weapons firing drowned out their words, something that sounded like a cross between her Etcher and a blazer. Were those staffs *shooting?*

Alisa glimpsed bolts of energy streaking through the air in front of the soldiers, but she obeyed Leonidas's wishes and moved back into the treasure room. Mica, Alejandro, and Yumi were there, and so was Tomich, who stood in the doorway, using the wall for cover. He fired into the fray, even though he wore only a spacesuit instead of combat armor. Beck and Abelardus had gone into the chamber with Leonidas and the soldiers.

Yumi held up the staff Alisa had pointed out a few minutes earlier.

"Guess I could have gotten that myself," she muttered, since none of the Alliance people was paying her any attention.

She took it and leaned it against the wall by the doorway. It felt like metal rather than wood and had runes engraved in the sides at either end. They did not glow or do anything interesting. In fact, it looked like a walking stick one might buy at some camping store. Would the soldiers believe it was Alcyone's legendary staff? Alisa blocked it with her body in case Tomich took his gaze from the battle.

"Any rust bangs left, Mica?" she asked, thinking of leaning through the doorway and trying to help.

"No."

"None at all?"

"Maybe you should bring your own weapons when you're heading into battle," Mica said.

Alisa barely heard her over someone giving orders and someone else shouting an earnest, "Look out!" She muted her comm so she would not distract them.

"I didn't think there would *be* battles here," she said.

"Shortsighted. You should have expected the worst."

"As any good pessimist would?"

"Precisely."

Alisa turned back toward the doorway and almost ran into Alejandro's back. Tomich had stepped inside—she could just see his sleeve as he fired at someone. Or something. Now Alejandro stood in the doorway.

She reached for him, intending to pull him back. Since he did not carry weapons, she assumed he simply wanted a good look at the dais and sarcophagus. That could wait until later.

But he slipped inside before she could grab him. What was that fool doing?

"Masters and Diaz are down," someone reported grimly.

Down? Did that mean injured? Or dead?

"They know to target the seams in our armor," another soldier said, "and whatever they're firing is as powerful as a pissed sun god. Do *not* get hit."

Alisa paused as the gravity of the situation pressed down upon her. How many people could be killed here trying to get something she cared nothing about?

Nothing at all? Are you sure?

Abelardus? she asked. What was he doing in her head when he was in the middle of the battle? At least, she assumed he was in the middle of the battle.

I'm getting the staff. Be prepared to pilot us out of here.

In what? The shuttle is the only thing nearby. And it already has *pilots.*

You're a better pilot. I prefer you.

Uh, thanks, but that's not what I was—

An explosion went off near the door, interrupting her concentration. Smoke billowed out, and Alisa stumbled back. She need not worry about breathing it inside of her suit, but her instincts said to get away from it.

An armored soldier flew backward through the door, just missing her as he landed on his back. Half of his chest had been blown open, his armor peeled away.

"Blessing of the Suns Trinity," Alisa whispered, the words coming out in a shocked stutter.

Join us in here, Abelardus urged. *We may not have much time.*

You better be helping them, she snarled back in her mind.

He did not respond. Another explosion sounded, this time from the direction of the dais.

Alejandro had disappeared inside. Alisa crept to the doorway, batting aside the smoke. Her instincts said to stay outside, but if Abelardus was about to do something stupid—or if he wasn't using his powers to help as much as he should—someone had to crack him on the back of his helmet.

Smoke filled the entire chamber, with occasional crimson slashes of blazer fire streaking through the area. Alisa glimpsed the back of a spacesuit near the wall ahead, someone moving along it. Alejandro?

Feeling like a fool, she crouched low and hurried along the wall after him. If she could get to the sarcophagus, she could hide behind it—and hope the robots did not notice her.

As she reached the corner, weapons fire ricocheted off the wall ahead of her. One of those black robots strode out of the smoke, its staff pointed like a gun. She was on the verge of sprinting back for the door but realized it was aiming at the person in front of her, not her.

"Alejandro, look out," she called.

He turned toward the robot and lifted his hands. As if *that* would do anything.

"Duck," she shouted.

He started to, but the robot fired. Alisa ran forward, as if there was time to pull him out of the way. She knew there wasn't.

But the projectile that flew from its staff diverted oddly and bounced off the wall next to Alejandro. The robot itself flew backward before it could fire again, disappearing into the smoke.

I protect my allies, Abelardus said firmly in her mind. *Come here. To the dais.*

Her feet obeyed before her mind decided if that was a good idea. Alisa snarled, certain Abelardus was influencing her again. Had it even been her idea to come in here and check on Alejandro? She thought about digging in her heels and doing her best to race back to the doorway, but reluctantly admitted she might be safest beside Abelardus and behind the sarcophagus. She assumed—*hoped*—the robot soldiers wouldn't fire at the very thing they had been left here for centuries to guard.

As the shape of it grew distinguishable through the smoke ahead, Alisa peered into the chamber, trying to glimpse Leonidas's red armor. Another explosion went off. One of the black robots flew toward her and smashed into the wall several feet above her head. She dove toward the dais, fearing it would crash down atop her. She wasn't wrong. It clunked to the floor scant inches behind her. Its head was gone, but its arm twitched as it tried to lift the staff still held in its grasp.

Imagining it targeting her, she sprinted the last few meters to the sarcophagus. She forgot about the raised dais and the toe of her boot slammed into it. The impact sent her sprawling, and she tumbled against the sarcophagus itself. Her fingers curled about the top, and she caught herself, managing to keep from cracking her helmet against the side. She hauled her body upright and found herself staring into an open coffin, the decaying remains of Alcyone, or whoever had been buried there, staring at her.

Alisa tightened her grip on the rim, barely keeping from screaming. The last thing she wanted to do was call everyone's attention to her.

"Just a dead person," she whispered. "Just a dead person."

A dead person whose skeletal hand looked like it had been pried open. Alisa did not see the staff. Had Abelardus already taken it? Several other items were in the sarcophagus, including dusty armor that looked like something an Old Earth knight would have worn. If these were truly the remains of Alcyone, she had been buried as a warrior.

A keening went up from different points in the room, the noise hurting her ears.

"What happened?" a soldier asked over the comm.

"I don't know, but keep shooting," Tomich said. "They're not moving now."

They know we have the staff, Abelardus said into her mind. *We have to get out of here.*

A hand gripped her from behind, and Alisa jumped.

It's me, Abelardus said, pulling her behind the sarcophagus.

Is that supposed to make me less alarmed?

He tugged her toward the wall behind the dais. The eerie keening continued, raising in pitch and growing in intensity. She did not want to take her gaze from the smoke, in the hope that Leonidas would stride out of it to join them. Only when they had gone several steps and when the smoke had started to swallow the sarcophagus did Alisa realize that the wall she had expected was not *there*.

From the doorway, the wall behind the dais had appeared solid, but Abelardus was pulling her into a tunnel. Alejandro walked beside him, holding the staff, one different from the one Abelardus bore. Alisa, seeing it for the first time, gaped at it. The long ebony weapon was similar to the one Lady Naidoo had carried, but in addition to having illuminated runes, a golden sphere on the top glowed softly, lighting the windowless passage they had entered. It looked like a smaller version of the orb that had brought them here.

Alejandro met her eyes, a triumphant smile stretching across his face. Abelardus looked triumphant too.

Alisa planted her feet. "Where are you taking me, and why didn't you call the rest of our people back here too?"

Alejandro leaned close, trying to hear her, but the keening noise was following them, still growing louder. Alisa had the uneasy impression of something about to overload and explode.

That's my guess too, Abelardus said, not needing to hear her words to understand her. *They may be enacting a last-ditch effort to save the staff. We have to get out of here now.*

And the others? Alisa jammed her fists against her hips.

I don't need them to fly the ship.

What ship? Alisa looked into the darkness behind Alejandro. Did Abelardus know where this tunnel led? Had he known all along?

There's a centuries-old ship back there, yes.

Why can't you fly it?

I've only flown Starseer Darts—they respond to mental commands and are intuitive. This looks as intuitive as a rock. But you fly that freighter. I'm sure you can fly this.

Fly *it*? You actually expect something that old to start?

We'll find out if it can, he said, pulling her again.

Alisa leaned back. *We're not leaving without the others.*

They can go back in the Alliance shuttle.

You'd send Leonidas back with them? They want him for questioning. Or interrogation. She shuddered.

Darn.

Abelardus gave up on pulling her and lunged in, trying to wrap his arm around her waist.

She jammed her knee into his chest. She wished she could have put it in his face, but the helmet precluded that. It didn't matter. The blow did not hurt him, and he succeeded in lifting her. She kicked him in the groin, but his spacesuit offered too much padding. He probably did not even feel it.

"Damn it." Alisa turned her muted comm back on. "Leonidas, behind the dais. There's a tunnel—"

Stop! Abelardus growled in her mind.

She did not want to stop, but her tongue obeyed him instead of her. She hissed in frustration.

Are you trying to give them the staff? Abelardus demanded.

Yes! she roared with her mind since she couldn't speak. *You think I want the empire to get it? Or the Starseers? If it has to be dragged out of hiding, I want it in the hands of people who can't use it.* In truth, she had no idea if the Alliance could use it. What if anyone could wield it? Or what if they found an Alliance-friendly Starseer to use it on their behalf? She gritted her teeth. Even if that happened, it would be better than whatever the empire would do with it. *I'm not flying you anywhere without Leonidas, Beck, Yumi, and Mica.*

By the gods' grace, you're frustrating, Abelardus said.

Are they coming?

He paused, then replied, *I told them to join us.*

"Hurry," Alejandro shouted, tapping Abelardus's shoulder. The word was barely audible over the keening. "If that continues to escalate, it'll rupture our eardrums."

"Eardrums aren't our primary worry here," Abelardus replied. "Trust me."

The smoke stirred behind them, and he set Alisa down.

She tensed, half-expecting the soldiers to burst into the hidden passage, firing blindly as they went. But Beck led the way, his spacesuit smoldering and charred but intact. Yumi and Mica followed him, Yumi waving the staff from the other chamber.

"Do we still need this?" she yelled.

"Yes," Alisa replied at the same time as Abelardus barked, "No."

"Yes," Alisa said again, waving for them to follow. "Abelardus, where's Leonidas?" she added as the others charged past.

Beck shone his headlamp into the passage ahead, and she glimpsed another chamber. Another hangar bay?

Your noble cyborg is carrying wounded Alliance soldiers out of the dais room before those robots blow themselves up.

"But he'll end up stuck with them," Alisa blurted.

His punishment for being noble. Come on. I will carry you if you don't come.

The smoke stirred again, and Alisa paused, hoping it was Leonidas. But a soldier in a spacesuit was running into the tunnel toward them.

"Marchenko," Tomich yelled. "You'll never see your ship again if you take that staff."

Abelardus flung out his own staff, and Tomich was hurled backward so far that he disappeared into the smoke again.

"Damn you, Abelardus," Alisa snarled.

He grabbed her from behind, this time not giving her any leverage with which to kick him. He hoisted her from her feet and sprinted away from Tomich and the Alliance soldiers. Away from Leonidas.

CHAPTER TWENTY

Abelardus did not set Alisa down until he could plant her in front of a small spaceship that she vaguely recognized from museum pictures. It reminded her of the first biplanes that had been invented back on Earth. It certainly wasn't much larger than one. Would it fit all of her people?

"Get in," Abelardus ordered. "Fire it up."

She would have stubbornly refused to fly, but that keening was growing louder and louder. If those robots blew up, who knew how much of the station would be destroyed? The tiny bay they were in wasn't much wider than the secret passage they had run down, and there weren't any other ships.

Alisa groped around, looking for a button to raise the canopy. Abelardus waved his staff, and it popped up.

She started to climb in, but realized the only way into the tiny passenger area in the back was through the cockpit. "Everybody in," she ordered, waving for Mica, Yumi, Beck, and Alejandro to climb in before she did.

They scrambled in with impressive speed. Alejandro almost clunked her on the head with the staff, and she bitterly imagined them trying to find a way off the station when their only pilot was unconscious.

Abelardus threw himself into the co-pilot's seat, somehow finding a spot for his staff. Alisa clambered into the main seat. She did not delay in finding the engine switch and familiarizing herself with the control panel, but she couldn't help but look back down the passageway, hoping Leonidas would catch up to them. But if he was helping other people out, he would end up on that Alliance shuttle. Assuming the Alliance soldiers even made it out in time. They still had to spacewalk back to their craft.

"Damn you, Abelardus," she whispered, not expecting him to hear her. That keening was so loud now that nobody could have been heard over it, even bellowing.

Love you too, he responded silently, sarcastically.

Alisa waited until the very end to close the cockpit, giving the tunnel one last look.

Instead of Leonidas, she got an explosion. This one made the earlier ones seem like gum popping in comparison. Their little ship was lifted from the deck, the cockpit nearly crunching into the ceiling.

Get us out of here, Abelardus ordered. *That's just the start of it.*

Even though he was speaking into her mind, she could barely process the words with the roar of the explosion pummeling her eardrums.

She activated the ancient ship's old thrusters. They sputtered several times, and the display on the control panel winked out. If she hadn't been afraid of dying, she would have laughed. That Abelardus had planned all of this based on escaping in some decrepit ship that hadn't flown in centuries...

He thumped his fist on the top of the control panel. The dashboard lit up again. The thrusters sputtered a few more times, then ignited.

"The door?" Alisa asked, spinning the craft in the direction she assumed was the way out. The dark wall looked like all the others.

"Working on it." He closed his eyes and bowed his chin to his chest.

A circle in the wall gradually grew less solid, the stars appearing through it. Several seconds passed, and that portion of the hull disappeared altogether. The exit was tiny compared to the large doors they'd entered through in the other bay. Only this tiny ship could come and go this way. Alisa wondered if it had long ago delivered that sarcophagus.

Go, go, Abelardus ordered.

Even though they were in the air, she could see the walls vibrating as more explosions went off. A chain reaction. Or maybe each of those robots was blowing up, one after the other. Something snapped overhead, and a piece of the ceiling thumped down onto the cockpit.

Alisa flinched but took them toward the exit. She couldn't delay any longer. Still, she found a rearview mirror—this thing didn't have anything so fancy as cameras—and watched the tunnel as they flew toward the exit.

Rocks were tumbling down, pulverized particles mingling in the air with the dust. Reluctantly, she admitted that Leonidas wasn't coming, that if he made it off at all, he would be in the hands of the Alliance soldiers.

Then, as the nose of her ship eased out into space, a red figure burst through that dust. He sprinted across the tiny landing area, his legs a blur.

Alisa reached for the thrusters, intending to reverse them, to wait for him.

Abelardus caught her wrist. "Don't. The rest of the ceiling could come down at any second."

She fought against him, trying to elbow him, but he kept her from reaching the thruster controls. Their ship continued out into space.

Leonidas made it to the door as they glided away. Alisa thought he would stop, trapped, and she struggled harder, throwing a punch at Abelardus. It connected solidly against the chest of his suit, but there was no power behind it, not when he had her right hand. He did not let go.

It did not matter. Leonidas leaped away from the exit and out into space.

The ship hadn't yet picked up speed, and he sprang away at a greater velocity than they were going. He landed on the rear of the craft with a clunk, finding a place to hang on between the thrusters.

Alisa grinned so broadly that her mouth hurt.

Abelardus groaned and let go of her so he could drop his faceplate into his hand.

"What in the hells was that?" Beck asked. He and the others, squished into the rear compartment, could not see behind them.

"Our other passenger," Alisa said.

The ship did not have an autopilot, at least that she could see, so she manually turned them away from the station and in the direction of the *Nomad*. As they flew away from the hull, the shuttle came into view. Several soldiers were floating away from the station and to their craft. Some were carrying others. The dead? The unconscious? She couldn't tell, but she prayed Tomich had made it.

She flew slowly because she did not want to risk dislodging Leonidas. It wasn't as if it mattered. A hulking warship hovered over the *Nomad*, dwarfing her freighter with its imposing bulk. She realized they had nowhere safe to go.

"I don't suppose this ship has interplanetary flight capabilities," Beck said from the rear.

Alisa shook her head. "It's a short-range craft, and its fuel..." She checked the gauge. "It's only at a quarter." Not to mention that she could not take them on a days-long trip with Leonidas hanging off the back.

"Shit," Beck said, his eyes locking on that warship.

"We should be happy there were any ships to get away in at all," Alisa said.

"But it's not going to matter, is it?"

"I don't know." Alisa looked at Abelardus. He had certainly thought they could escape this way. "Want to tell us if you can do anything special with that staff?"

She didn't want to contemplate him attacking the warship—or blowing it up the way Alcyone had blown up a planet—but maybe the big stick had other powers. After all, it was called a Staff of Lore. He'd implied it had other uses and wasn't only a super powerful weapon.

"Hand it up here, Alejandro," Abelardus said. "I'll see if we have any options."

"We can't go back to the freighter, regardless," Alejandro said as he pushed the end of the staff toward Abelardus. "This ship and all of us are drenched in radioactive particles, and the *Star Nomad* has no decontamination system."

Alisa cursed. How could she have forgotten?

"Then we *have* to go back to the medical shuttle, don't we?" she asked.

"The warship may have facilities to handle us," Yumi said.

"Oh, I'm sure it does. It can give us a nice decon shower before we're shoved into the brig."

Alisa glowered at the hulking ship dwarfing her poor freighter. There was no point in flying that way. She changed direction, steering them back toward the shuttle, not that she expected to be safe there. After they had abandoned the soldiers, she wouldn't be surprised if they opened fire on her newly acquired ship. Especially if Tomich hadn't made it out.

She tapped on the comm in her spacesuit. "Leonidas? Can you hear me?"

"Of course," came the dry reply.

"How's your flight? Need me to send someone back with cocktails? Snacks?"

The sigh that whispered over the comm sounded pain-filled. She grimaced—she hadn't even thought to ask him if he had suffered any injuries.

"Are you all right?" she asked.

"Well enough for now, but I hope you're going to take us someplace slightly more comfortable soon."

"Uh, we're still trying to figure out where comfort might be found out here. Is there a chance—Abelardus said you were carrying some of the soldiers to safety. Any chance they're feeling grateful thoughts toward you?" The question seemed even more pertinent as their route took them closer to the shuttle. Even though it was a medical craft, it did have a few weapons, and Alisa had no idea where the shields were on this unfamiliar ship—or if it even had any.

"I don't know. It was chaotic, and the two men I picked up were unconscious."

"When you were running out, did you by chance see if Tomich made it out?"

A crackle of static sounded on the comm.

"I'm here, Marchenko," Tomich said.

They must have flown back into range of the rest of the soldiers. Alisa supposed that would make communication easier, but she would have preferred to continue her conversation with Leonidas in private.

"Are you coming to surrender to us?" Tomich added, his voice also a touch dry, but he sounded like he was in pain too. The outside of the station remained intact, the wheel still spinning around the axis, but Alisa could imagine the interior in shambles, men perhaps trapped under rubble for all eternity.

"Do you *want* us to surrender to you, or are you just after the staff?" Alisa looked at Abelardus. He had pulled the staff into his lap and had his hands wrapped around it, his eyes closed. She muted her helmet comm and asked, "Wasn't that glowing before?"

She distinctly remembered seeing illuminated runes and bright yellow coming from the orb on top. Now, the whole thing was dark and did not appear much more impressive than the staff they had fished out of the rubble pile.

"It gradually got dimmer as we moved farther away from the tomb," Alejandro said.

"Can't Abelardus make it light up?" Mica asked.

One of Abelardus's eyes opened, and he gave everyone a baleful look. Alisa decided that his bonding with it must not be going well. A part of her was pleased since she did not want him to have a super weapon, but another part of her acknowledged that it would have been handy if the staff had the power to help them escape.

"Admiral Moreau doesn't care about you or your freighter," Tomich said—he must have paused to contact his commanding officer. "He would like Colonel Adler. And the staff, of course."

Alisa un-muted her comm. "Colonel Adler isn't available."

"No? He looks uncomfortable hanging on the back of that relic of a ship. Are you sure he wouldn't prefer being inside somewhere?"

"Not if it means getting a private brig cell."

"I see. And is the staff available?" Tomich asked.

Alisa was surprised he didn't simply tell them they were being captured, cyborg and staff included, and that was the end of the debate. Did he think they had some power now that her team had acquired it? If so, maybe she could bluff, and maybe her bluffing would work better on Tomich than it had on that android.

"Our Starseer is rubbing it lovingly, right now," Alisa said. "You might have to discuss its availability with him. It's glowing happily and seems excited to see him."

"I have orders to keep it from falling into imperial hands," Tomich said grimly. "No matter what it takes."

"Our Starseer isn't imperial. He says he has Alliance leanings. Look, Tomich, I don't want the empire to get it, either. I didn't fight for four years so they could get a super weapon and take over the system again." She could feel Alejandro's eyes boring into the back of her head, but she did not look back.

"I'm glad to hear it," Tomich said. "I've been wondering, given your latest...antics."

"Antics? Someone clearly wants a staff shoved somewhere uncomfortable."

"So long as I can carry it to my superiors that way," Tomich said. "Why don't you board, and we'll discuss everything over a nice decon shower? I assume your freighter isn't properly outfitted to deal with your contamination."

As if they could fly over there and climb aboard the *Nomad* with that warship looming above it.

"Since you asked so nicely," Alisa said, "we will join you, but no tricks this time, Tomich. I'm sure your soldiers aren't in the mood for another battle."

"No, they're not, but Alisa? You can't escape. Please be prepared to hand over the staff."

She turned off the comm without replying. "Mica? Still got the spare staff back there?"

"Yes. Yumi and I have cleaned it off and made it look as shiny as possible."

"All right. We'll take that one with us and try to convince them it's the powerful one. Abelardus, can you make it glow interestingly?"

He flicked a dismissive hand, and silver light flared in the rear compartment. A clunk sounded as Mica dropped the staff. The runes engraved in the side now glowed with impressive light.

"How come you can turn that one on and not that one?" Alisa pointed to Alcyone's staff. It still lay dark in his lap.

"I prefer not to discuss my shortcomings at this time," Abelardus said, glaring at her.

Startled by his snapping, Alisa almost reacted by pointing out just how many shortcomings he had and how it was impossible to avoid discussing them. Instead, she lifted her hands in apology. They did not need to fight now. They needed to figure out how to keep from becoming prisoners.

"If we leave that staff here and all spacewalk over to the shuttle," she said, musing aloud, "what are the odds that they won't search this ship? That their little armada will leave the area and we can sneak in later and retrieve it?"

"The odds are zilch," Alejandro said. "Remember the piles of rubble? Tomich said it himself, that the Alliance could use those valuables. And this ship would be considered an artifact itself. They'll take it into one of their hangars, and we'll never see the staff again."

"You're probably right. Then, we'll have to take it aboard with us and hide it. Which one of you tall gentlemen thinks he can hide a six-foot staff in his trousers?"

"I do that already," Beck said. "Give it to me."

Mica groaned and elbowed him.

"What? Tell me that wasn't the appropriate answer for that line."

Alisa would have glared back at him, but they were close enough to the medical shuttle that she could see people moving around through the portholes. There wasn't time left to fritter around.

"We'll have to try to hide it in the shuttle itself," she said. "Maybe in the airlock hatch? If we can figure a way to get them to take us back to our ship after we've deconned, we'll go out that way again. Anyone have some glue? Mica?"

"You can't *glue* a centuries-old relic to the wall," Alejandro said.

"I was thinking of the ceiling. Right up in a crease where it might escape notice."

"I have some tape," Mica said. "It'll have to be thrown away anyway. Everything is contaminated."

"So long as we're not throwing away my staff," Alejandro grumbled. "That's not porous. I'm sure we can decontaminate it."

Alejandro seemed quite certain he was going to get to take this staff when and if they could escape the Alliance. Abelardus might be thinking the same thing. And the entire Alliance thought it was about to get it too. Maybe she ought to toss it out a porthole and let whoever could get to it first have it.

"Give that to Mica, please," Alisa said, leaning over to grab the staff since Abelardus was still holding it, his face locked in concentration.

He sighed but let her have it. The orb on top flared a soft yellow. It was not as bright as it had been in the tomb, but it was definitely illuminated.

"Guess it doesn't like you," Alisa said, pushing it back into the rear compartment for Mica.

Abelardus gaped at her.

The orb dimmed when Alisa let go of it. Mica accepted it without comment, and a ripping sound came as she unreeled tape.

Abelardus was still gaping at Alisa.

"What?" she asked warily.

"It responds to you," he said. "Like the door."

"So?" she asked, having a feeling she did not want an answer. "Cats like me too. It's not like I have Starseer powers and would be able to wield it."

She *hoped* that wasn't what he was implying.

"No," he agreed, rubbing his jaw thoughtfully. "But your daughter might be able to."

"Oh, sure. That's the kind of gift you should give an eight-year-old. The power to destroy planets."

"She won't be eight forever."

"The captain's scruffy daughter is *not* getting a legendary Staff of Lore," Alejandro said.

"You call my daughter scruffy again, and I'll flatten you like a cyborg on a rampage," Alisa said.

"The imperial line is related to Alcyone," Alejandro said. "The prince should be able to wield it."

Abelardus frowned back at him. "You knew all along that it was keyed to her descendants?"

"I gathered it from my research."

"A moot point now, as it's going to go into an Alliance vault somewhere unless Mica's tape works miracles." Alisa adjusted the thrusters, bringing their craft in line with the shuttle. "It's time to go for a walk."

———

Alisa watched as Beck taped a priceless and powerful artifact to the ceiling of the medical shuttle's airlock. This wasn't going to work. Tomich would take them all prisoner—he would have no other choice—and his people would notice the staff as soon as they left the shuttle.

She looked at Leonidas, who had maneuvered his way into the airlock as soon as he had seen her leaving their craft, and shook her head. He shook his right back. He also did not believe this would work. Abelardus was the fourth person in the airlock with them. He stood at the back, glowering as the staff was taped up there. He held the fake one in addition to his own weapon, which he had kept throughout the chaos. They appeared depressingly similar, neither looking like some breathtaking super powerful artifact.

Beck lowered his hands as a clunk sounded, the airlock cabin pressure equalizing to that of the shuttle. The hatch slid open. Alisa slumped as she found herself looking at the muzzles of rifles. *Many* rifles.

A dull red light glowed all around the soldiers, and the sounds of fans filled her ears. Was the entire shuttle designed for a decontamination protocol?

"Are we going to have a fight?" Alisa asked, glancing at Leonidas, surprised he hadn't immediately leaped forward to try to disarm them.

He was watching her. Waiting to see if she ordered it? Or if the men truly threatened them?

"I'd rather not," Tomich said wearily, coming into view. He had removed the helmet of his suit, and his sweaty hair stuck up in a dozen directions. "I've been talking with the admiral, trying to negotiate with him on your behalf. It's not helping things that you ran off in another direction and took another ship."

Alisa opened her mouth to say that hadn't been her idea, but he continued on.

"I did tell him that Adler saved the lives of some of our men." Tomich shrugged.

"Was he deeply impassioned and moved?" Alisa asked.

"Not noticeably so. But I think if I hand in the staff and say Adler was too much trouble to arrest, I might only be reprimanded and not lose my career." He looked over her shoulder to where Abelardus still stood in the airlock. "Is that the staff?"

Since Alisa had expected a question more along the lines of, "Is one of those the right staff?" she looked back to check.

Abelardus was working his magic. The staff from the offerings pile glowed fiercely, its runes ablaze. She almost had to shield her eyes.

"It will not work for your people," Abelardus said with a sneer and held it close to his chest, as if he would fight to keep it.

A good strategy. If they gave up too easily, Tomich would be suspicious.

"So long as we can throw it in a vault and your people can't find it." Tomich's gaze shifted to Leonidas. "Or *your* people."

"The station is due to disappear back into the rift soon, sir," one of the pilots called back. "Should we move the shuttle away?"

"Yes," Tomich said. "I don't want to go for a ride with what's left of that station."

"Especially when it might not come back," Abelardus said.

Tomich looked sharply at him. "What do you mean?"

"Did you not leave the keys in the doorway?"

"No, we grabbed them on the way out." Tomich waved toward the front of the shuttle. "We've got them in a tantalum box. My people will want to study the station further."

"You mean loot it further."

"You're the one holding a staff you stole from a woman's coffin."

Abelardus clenched his jaw.

"I suppose we'll have to find someone else who can activate the key though." Tomich looked curiously at Alisa. "Unless you'd like to reenlist while you're here today."

"If I were to reenlist, it would be so I could fly, not stand out there in a spacesuit, touching orbs."

"Perhaps the Alliance would see the value in having you fly again."

"I think that may be wishful thinking after the last couple of...incidents I've been involved in. Besides—" Alisa eyed Leonidas and thought of Jelena, "—I have other missions that are my priority."

"Your daughter?"

"My daughter." And if she could, she would like to help Leonidas find a solution to his problem. Which was also now *her* problem, unless she wanted to be "just friends" with him for the rest of her life. She almost wondered if this was the sun gods' way of punishing her, by giving her a man she couldn't have because she'd turned her back on Jonah so quickly. But if so, they were unjustly punishing Leonidas too.

"Take us out of here, Lieutenant Saul," Tomich said, waving his finger at the pilot. "Marchenko, I'll drop you all off at your airlock if you give me the staff without a fight."

"That deal sounds fine to me, but..." She lifted her open hands. "I'm not the one holding it."

"What do you say, Starseer?" Tomich asked.

Alisa expected Abelardus to feign great reluctance and then hand it over. But he stepped back as far as he could in the small airlock chamber, keeping the staff close to his chest.

"You'll have to take it from me if you want it." He sneered at the soldiers. "*If* you can."

"Ah," Alisa said, holding up a finger. "That's not—"

Leonidas surged into motion, and she stumbled back, startled. He bumped Beck as he lunged for Abelardus, and Beck tumbled to the deck, landing at the soldiers' feet. Fortunately, nobody fired. They were scooting back, gaping as Leonidas grabbed Abelardus and hurled him to the deck inside the airlock.

Abelardus fought back, pushing at Leonidas's chest with the staff. He was not strong enough to physically dislodge a cyborg, but he brought his mental powers to bear, and Leonidas flew upward. He rose so fast and far that his back struck the ceiling. Abelardus sprang to his feet. Leonidas kicked out as he fell. A boot slammed into Abelardus's chest, and he tumbled back, hitting the side of the airlock with bone-crunching force. They reached for each other, and one of the staffs flew aside, almost striking Beck. Limbs tangled, and the men thrashed, going down again.

Despite Abelardus's mental powers, Leonidas landed on top of him, straddling his torso and his hands going around Abelardus's neck in a tableau similar to the one they'd found themselves in during their sparring match in the cargo hold.

Abelardus made a strangled noise, trying to breathe. Alisa lifted a hand, not sure if she should try to intercede, or if it would be safe for her to do so. Was this some ruse that they had decided to enact between the two of them? Had Abelardus proposed it by speaking into Leonidas's mind? Or had Leonidas taken it upon himself to make this staff handoff look good?

"Leonidas," Alisa said, when it became clear that Abelardus could no longer fight back—his face was turning red as he clawed at Leonidas's armored forearms. "Let go."

She eased back into the airlock chamber and picked up the fallen staff.

Is this the right one? she asked in her mind, hoping Abelardus was monitoring her. It was so similar to the usual one he carried that she could not tell. It had stopped glowing when Leonidas attacked.

Yes. Get this troll off me.

Alisa handed the staff to Tomich. "Take it. It's nothing but trouble."

Abelardus made another wheezing noise.

"Leonidas," Alisa repeated, turning back to him as soon as Tomich accepted the staff. She dropped to one knee. "It's over. Let him go."

The fury and rage in Leonidas's eyes seemed real, not feigned, and Alisa reached out to put her hand on his armored shoulder.

"And just in case this is about that night in NavCom," she said softly, "I think the punch was enough of a punishment."

Leonidas's lip curled, but he released Abelardus and knelt back.

He looked at her as Abelardus lay on the deck, gasping for air. "I do not agree," he said.

"Then it's a good thing I'm in command and you're working for me now, isn't it?" She removed her hand and backed away so both men could stand. "Let him up."

Tomich's eyebrows lifted, but nobody else said anything. Leonidas gave Abelardus a final glower and rose to his feet. He leaned his shoulder against the side of the airlock and crossed his arms over his chest, as if to say, "What now?"

"We heading to the *Storm Fury*, sir?" the pilot called back.

Tomich eyed the staff that he now held, then looked at Alisa, and finally at Leonidas. She hoped he was weighing the likelihood that Leonidas would attack him next if he tried to turn him over to his admiral.

"To the freighter. We have some guests to drop off." Tomich lowered his voice. "And then I have to convince Admiral Moreau not to follow that freighter as it gets out of this quarantine zone and hopefully disappears from Alliance radar for a long time."

"That sounds like a good idea to me," Alisa said.

Tomich headed for the front of the shuttle.

Abelardus propped himself onto one elbow and rubbed his throat. "Don't think that your people can hide that staff where Starseers won't find it," he called after Tomich. "We'll be back for it."

Tomich did not respond. Alisa nudged Abelardus with the toe of her boot.

What? I'm adding dramatic flair.

I think the proper term is hamming it up, Alisa replied silently.

I had no idea you were a critic on acting.

I'm a critic on everything. It's part of my charm.

EPILOGUE

Alisa did not leave NavCom until they passed the warning buoy, and the Alliance ships had long since disappeared from the sensor display. She hadn't truly believed the Alliance would let them go. She had expected them to figure out the staff was a fake and for the two warships to come zooming after them, filling her rear camera and threatening to blow them all out of space.

But her cameras remained empty of anything except stars, and she hadn't heard a peep since the medical shuttle had decontaminated and cleared her team, and dropped them off at the *Nomad*. She would have known if a comm message had come in because she had not left NavCom all night, choosing to doze for a few hours in her seat instead of finding her bed. According to the *Nomad's* clock, morning had come. She had already plotted a course for Cleon Moon, so she decided she could risk slipping away for some coffee.

Judging by the squawks drifting up from the cargo hold, the chickens were already up for the day. Too bad they had been on strike and hadn't been laying eggs since the radiation incident. Alisa wouldn't have minded an omelet to go with her coffee, assuming they were safe to consume.

When she reached the intersection, she heard voices coming from one of the crew cabins. Abelardus? It sounded like him.

Her first instinct was to continue on, to avoid him whenever possible, but she still needed to find out where his brother was. More, she felt responsible for the staff since she had been a part of retrieving it. Eventually, she needed to learn what he planned, and also what Alejandro planned. Did they want to be dropped off somewhere? She hoped so, but could she in good conscience let either of them go with the staff? No. But how could she stop them? Abelardus had power she couldn't do anything to thwart, and Alejandro…He might still have Leonidas, at least in regard to the staff and fulfilling the emperor's dying wishes.

She padded down the corridor in her socks, pausing a few feet from the open hatch. It was Alejandro's cabin, but that was definitely Abelardus speaking.

"…consider working together," he was saying.

Alisa grimaced. Was that what they were considering? If Abelardus had decided to go along with Alejandro, did that mean he had accepted the idea of the emperor's young son wielding that staff? If so, Alisa might live to regret her choice to help them.

"We have different goals," Alejandro said stiffly.

"You don't know that."

"You want to involve *her.*"

"Her daughter may be able to wield the staff."

Alisa's blood chilled. They were talking about her? About her daughter?

"So?" Alejandro asked. "You want some mouthy pilot's kid to use it? *Why?* The prince has been trained from birth to make sound decisions, and he's even now being trained to use his Starseer powers."

"You don't know that. You have no idea where he is or how to find him."

"I'll figure it out. I figured out the staff, didn't I?"

Abelardus snorted. "With your cyborg's help. I understand you're losing him. To a mouthy pilot."

Alisa suspected she should back away instead of eavesdropping from the middle of the corridor where anyone could stumble across her. She would be surprised if Abelardus did not already know she was there. Still, it was hard to think of backing away when all she wanted was to run in there and kick Alejandro in the shin. Or perhaps someplace higher.

"Unless you stay on this ship with her," Abelardus added. "She might be your best bet to find the prince."

"What makes you believe that? And don't think I can't sense you trying to manipulate me."

Abelardus laughed. "With words only. I'm not that gifted at mind manipulation. I might be able to temporarily convince you of something, but it wouldn't stick. As for the rest, my brother apparently kidnapped her daughter."

"What does that have to do with the prince?"

"Durant is thoughtful and academic. If he took the girl, he had a reason. He may have figured out long before I did that she's descended from powerful Starseers. Alcyone, very possibly. I don't know enough about the Staffs of Lore to be certain that they're keyed to certain dynasties, but it does seem possible, especially now that I've watched Alisa touch it and bring it to life."

"If you think I want some Alliance-loving rebel's kid to have access to that staff, you're spaced."

He had all manner of adjectives for her, didn't he? Alisa glowered at the wall to his cabin.

You can come in and join the conversation if you wish, Abelardus said dryly into her thoughts.

I might kick Alejandro if I did.

I wouldn't object. It would be nice to see you unleash your temper on someone else.

I only unleash my temper on people who deserve it, she growled in her mind.

I do apologize for that. Sometimes…sometimes when you want something badly enough, you don't realize you're influencing those around you to get it.

"Are you listening to me, Abelardus?" Alejandro asked.

"Yes, Doctor. My point is that my brother may know more about where the prince is than you do. Didn't you say that he's with Starseers?"

"I didn't, no, but I suppose you know everything that's in my head."

"I learn what I wish to learn."

"Leonidas is the one who said he's with the Starseers, some that were friendly to the empire. That's all he knows. The Alliance is offering two hundred thousand tindarks for that information."

"They might be wiser to put out a bounty on my brother. He always sided with the empire." Abelardus grunted. "He may even be with the prince now. Alisa's daughter could be too. He could have been the one to collect both of them. Perhaps others too. Other children who might become powerful enough to change the course of history."

Alisa rested her palm on the cool metal wall, hardly able to process his words. Powerful? Jelena? A girl who could barely get a volleyball over a net?

"You said you don't know where your brother is," Alejandro said slowly, "that he hasn't responded to your messages."

"This is true, but I know where he was last seen. And we're already heading in that direction."

"Cleon Moon?"

"Cleon Moon."

A touch on Alisa's shoulder made her jump. She spun, putting her finger to her lips before she caught herself.

Leonidas stood in the corridor, wearing his loose exercise togs and holding two mugs. He tilted his head back toward the intersection. She blushed at having been caught listening, but was glad he did not say anything and give her away. Abelardus hadn't mentioned her presence, judging by Alejandro's comments. Not that the good doctor held back that much when she was actually in the room.

Alisa followed Leonidas to the mess hall, where he handed her one of the steaming mugs of coffee.

Though her mind was reeling from listening in on that conversation, she took a moment to smile at him and say, "Thank you."

"Was your eavesdropping fruitful?" he asked.

"More like disturbing. And don't pretend you and your enhanced cyborg ears have never eavesdropped."

"Hm." He eyed a few chicken feathers scattered on the deck and sat at one end of the table.

The ancient, powerful, and mysterious Staff of Lore lay atop it like a toy someone had forgotten to put away. It wasn't as if anyone on the ship didn't know about it, so Alisa supposed there wasn't much point in squirreling it away.

"The problem with eavesdropping," Leonidas said, "is that you sometimes hear unpleasantries that you might have been happier not hearing."

"Is that the only problem?" Alisa wondered how long he had been behind *her*, also hearing that conversation.

"One might also list the questionable morality as a problem."

"But only if one was particularly sanctimonious, right?" Alisa started to sit across the table from him but decided to be cozier since they had the mess hall to themselves. She slung her legs over the bench and sat beside him.

"Probably."

She leaned her shoulder against his and sipped from her mug. "Ah, good. Strong. Coffee and chocolate shouldn't be diluted."

"I agree." He sipped from his own mug.

She wouldn't have minded if he had slipped an arm around her waist, but maybe it was better to keep touching to a minimum, since nothing could come of it.

"The ship is heading to Cleon Moon," she said. "Have you looked to see if there are any cybernetics facilities there? I know it's not an overly modern and industrialized world, but there are some research outposts, if memory serves."

"There aren't any facilities."

"Ah."

"I have been contemplating finding a fast ship and kidnapping Admiral Tiang."

Alisa almost choked on her coffee. "Truly?"

"Would you object? Because he's an Alliance officer now?"

"I...don't know. He used to be an imperial officer, right? If he flip-flopped that easily, he's probably not that loyal to anyone."

Of course, if *she* went along on his kidnapping mission, she could get herself in trouble with the Alliance. Again. She strongly believed Tomich's involvement was the only reason she had been allowed to fly away from Alcyone Station. If she ever ran into any of the officers who had been involved in the attack on the Starseer temple, they would likely shoot her on sight.

"He's loyal to his research," Leonidas said. "Some people don't care who's in charge, so long as they can pursue their passions."

"Then when they realize they *can't* pursue those passions, it's too late to do anything," she grumbled.

She reached out and laid a finger on the staff. Once again, the orb lit with a soft glow. She sneered at it. Had it been a fluke when it lit up at her touch before, she would have been happier. She wouldn't need to be wondering about her heritage now or worrying that Jelena would become a pawn in some power struggle. She just wanted to find her little girl. Was that too much to ask? She already felt like a horrible mother for traipsing around the system when she had no idea where her daughter was or even if she was all right. It frustrated her that she barely knew where to start looking. Would Cleon Moon lead to anything? Or was it simply a place that her daughter's kidnapper may have visited months ago?

Growing aware of Leonidas gazing at her, Alisa pulled her finger back. The orb on the top of the staff went dark again. All of her concerns about him condemning her for having Starseer genes came back to her, and she cursed her thoughtless gesture.

"Apparently, this mighty artifact's main use is as a nightlight." She waved dismissively, hoping he would forget what he had seen—and also that she had been the one to open that door.

"For you."

"So it seems."

"How long have you known you have Starseer genes?" he asked, his tone neutral.

She shrank into herself, now wishing she had chosen to sit on the opposite side of the table. Then she could more easily climb under it and hide from his sight.

"Not long," she said. "A few days. When you brought that blood back for Alejandro to analyze, his DNA sequencer was already set up, so I stuck a drop of my own blood in there. Something Abelardus said had made me wonder."

"Abelardus," Leonidas said, growling into his coffee mug.

"Yeah. Did you attack him spontaneously back in that airlock?" she asked, pleased to change the subject. "Or was it his idea?"

"He told me to. For veracity. I didn't mind going along."

"I imagine not."

Alisa clasped her hands around the warm mug. She could understand why he disliked Abelardus, and he had little reason to like any of the Starseers he had met in their temple, but would he consider her...tainted?

"Does it matter?" she asked softly.

"What?"

"That my father might have worn some of those black robes."

Leonidas tilted his head. "Did you know him?"

"Not in the least. Whatever role he played in my mother's life, he was gone before I was born."

"He may have simply carried the genes without having any talents. That's how it is for most people with the mutations."

"Yes, that's true." She eyed him sidelong. "But if he did have those kinds of talents...would it matter?"

"To whom?" He frowned slightly, truly seeming puzzled.

"You."

"Why would it?"

"You've made it clear that Starseers and cyborgs are mortal enemies."

"The empire and the Alliance are mortal enemies too," he said dryly.

And he was still sipping coffee with her. Right. She supposed that had been a foolish concern. She might have laughed that she had worried about it, but she found her thoughts distracted. He was smiling slightly, his eyes drooped to half-mast as he regarded her.

"If I didn't know you better," she said, "I would consider that a come-hither look."

"A what?"

"You know, a silent way of telling me that you want to relocate to your cabin for hot sex."

His eyes flew open in surprise.

"How young did you say you were when you signed up for the military?" Alisa asked, suddenly wondering if she was having coffee with a forty-year-old virgin cyborg.

"Not *that* young," he said, catching her drift. "I was actually a precocious youth, if you must know, but it's been so long since I've even..." He lifted one hand, groping in the air for a word or a way to explain. "It's just hard to remember what it was even like. Noticing innuendos. Or caring about sex." He lowered his gaze to the table, and she thought she caught a hint of shame in his eyes.

Alisa winced. She hadn't wanted to embarrass him or hurt his feelings.

"Then it's settled," she said, hoping to distract him from the discomfort she had caused.

"What is?" He regarded her warily.

"The kidnapping scheme. First, we find my daughter, and then we go and kidnap your admiral."

"Technically, I believe he's *your* admiral now."

"Something I'll appreciate you not pointing out to him while you're doing the kidnapping. But I'll hold the rifle on him while he performs whatever surgery you need. To make sure he doesn't do anything shifty while you're unconscious."

"I would appreciate that," he said.

He slid his arm around her waist. She smiled and leaned closer to him. That was nice. It would do for now.

As he took another sip from his mug, Beck and Mica walked into the mess hall from the direction of the cargo hold. Judging by their clothing and the sheens of sweat on their foreheads, they had been exercising.

Alisa thought about leaning away from Leonidas and striving for a modicum of professionalism, but he did not lower his arm. She supposed a freighter captain could fraternize with her crew. This wasn't a military ship.

Beck stumbled a little when he noticed them sitting together. Mica didn't bat an eyelash as she veered toward the coffee dispenser.

"I think he's getting his thigh touched again," Beck whispered, grabbing two dented mugs from a cabinet.

"Are you still bitter that nobody touched yours?" Mica asked.

"It was more the implication that my thigh wasn't useful that embittered me."

"Not every limb can be as versatile as an oscillating multitool."

"I can oscillate."

"You really know how to woo the women, Beck," Mica said, taking her mug and sitting across the table from Alisa and Leonidas. "Are we still heading to Cleon Moon, Captain?"

"We are."

"Good. There are a ton of moons orbiting Aldrin, some with substantial populations. Someone's sure to have challenging and rewarding work for an engineer. I have my résumé ready."

"You're leaving us?" Beck asked, bringing his coffee to the table to join her. "Isn't the pay good enough?"

"There's pay?"

"Uhm." Beck looked at Alisa.

"We never did discuss your payment rate for security officers," Leonidas said.

Alisa poked a finger into her coffee. "I've heard of this before, that uncomfortable moment when your employees compare salaries. Did you know that some of the people on this ship *pay* for the honor to ride on such a fine craft as the *Star Nomad*?"

"I wonder if there are any culinary angel investors on those moons," Beck said, his expression turning wistful.

"You better wonder if there are any White Dragon operatives," Leonidas said.

Beck groaned. "Can't the captain wave her new staff and magic them away? It glows for her."

Alisa eyed the staff distastefully. "I don't believe it works that way. And it's not mine. You'll have better luck asking your new colleague for help."

"My new what?"

"Your fellow security officer." Alisa laid a hand on Leonidas's biceps. "Were you not there when we made it official?"

"I—what?"

"I outrank him, right?" Leonidas asked.

"*What?*" Beck set his coffee mug down with a clunk.

"We'll figure it out along the way to Cleon Moon." Alisa's gaze fell to the staff again. "We have a lot to figure out."

THE END

CPSIA information can be obtained
at www.ICGtesting.com
Printed in the USA
LVOW08s1247190117

521521LV00002B/190/P

Love, Betty

LAURA KEMP

ORION

An Orion paperback

First published in Great Britain in 2022
by Orion Fiction,
an imprint of The Orion Publishing Group Ltd,
Carmelite House, 50 Victoria Embankment
London EC4Y 0DZ

An Hachette UK Company

1 3 5 7 9 10 8 6 4 2

A CIP catalogue record for this book
is available from the British Library.

ISBN (Mass Market Paperback) 978 1 4091 8921 3
ISBN (eBook) 978 1 4091 8922 0

Typeset by Deltatype Ltd, Birkenhead, Merseyside